SEAL TEAM BRAVO
ASSAULT ON
AL SHABAAB

ERIC MEYER

SEAL TEAM BRAVO
ASSAULT ON
AL SHABAAB

ERIC MEYER

FOREWORD

A knifelike pain seared through her body as realization came to her. Her worst nightmare had just come true. She hung up the call from her lawyer and slumped in a chair, trying to recall the conversation. Analyzing every word, in case there was some mistake.

"I'm real sorry, Ma'am." His voice had been sympathetic, but how could he know what she was going through? "We've tried everything, but they won't budge."

"But he's my son. His place is with his mother."

"We know that, Ma'am. We explained it all, but they're not interested. Most Muslim countries aren't big on the rights of women."

"What about the rights of children? I'm his mother. Surely I can at least go over there and visit him?"

"No. They won't even issue a visa for you to get into the country. Not in cases like this, where the custody is in dispute."

"You're telling me he'll never know me."

A pause. "Maybe when he's an adult, he'll visit you. I

believe their age for adulthood is twenty-one. Yeah, it's possible."

They both knew he was lying, trying to soften the blow.

Luke is only a year old. In twenty years time, they'll indoctrinate him. I doubt he'll even speak English.

"Is there any appeal, anything I can do?"

"Nothing, we've explored everything."

"I see."

I've lost my son.

She ended the call and sat unmoving as she considered the future. There was no future. How could she be a mother, when she had no son? Damn her Arab ex-husband, who'd taken him on vacation in Saudi Arabia and refused to allow him to return home. Even though the US courts had given her custody, he's over there now, with Luke, if that was still his name. The documents from the court stated he'd applied to register a name change, an Islamic name. So if she went looking for him, she wouldn't even know his name.

She sat for hour after hour in a trance. Finally, she came to her senses. There was only one way out of this. If she wasn't a mother, she was nothing. Dead. She walked up the stairs to the bathroom and found a new blade for the razor in the medicine cabinet, Sharp, surgical steel, pristine, and perfect. She regarded the blade for long minutes, thinking her last thoughts of Luke.

Goodbye, baby. I'll love you for eternity, but not in this life. They won't allow me to.

She climbed into the bathtub and lay back. It wouldn't do to make a mess on the clean tiles. She was always proud of her clean house. Then she ran the blade along one wrist and then the other. Bright red blood oozed out, pooling beneath her. She cut again, and the flow increased. She started to feel weak and knew it wouldn't be long. Her last thought was how useless and insignificant her life had been. Her death would also go unremarked. She was wrong.

In chaos theory, it was known as the butterfly effect. Theoretically, a butterfly could flap its wings, and years later a hurricane could form.

The butterfly had just flapped its wings.

CHAPTER ONE

"Hey, Ed, would you take a look at this one."

The White House mail supervisor, Ed Levins, glanced across at Betty Dukakis. She wasn't an alarmist, wasn't given to constant false alarms. He heaved himself from behind his desk and walked over to look for himself.

"Where did it originate?"

"Africa. The franking is a bit smeared. It says Som, something or other on the customs declaration. Sporting goods, baseball equipment. The President is a keen baseball fan, so I guess it may be okay."

It seemed innocent enough. However, he still felt a tremor of alarm.

Somalia, Jesus!

"How the hell did it get in here? USPS is supposed to intercept uncertain packages before they get this far."

She shrugged. "No idea, Ed. Maybe they were having a bad day."

She wasn't smiling. Neither was he.

"Let's run it through the explosives scanner before we

look inside. Just in case."

He was tempted to press the big button, the alarm system that would cause all hell to break loose, but not yet. He wasn't given to unnecessary panic either. But the results were unequivocal. Nothing. She looked at him uncertainly.

"Whose gonna open it?"

A sigh. "I guess that's what I get paid for. I'll probe it first."

He made a tiny hole in the cardboard carton about two feet square and inserted a tiny probe. He used the joystick to control the camera as is peered at the contents of the packaging. Five objects, wrapped in paper. Could be baseballs, but could also be anything. He directed the probe inside the paper and sent its tiny nose deep inside, searching for the hidden object inside the packaging - brown, leathery baseballs. He switched off the probe.

"It looks okay. Let's get it open and take a look."

Between them they ripped open the carton and looked inside. The five innocent brown paper wrapped items lay at the bottom. Levins picked up the first and carefully peeled back the wrapping, smiling at Betty.

"Sure looks okay. Wait, they're not...holy shit!"

It was instinct that made him race for the big red button. A split second later, the White House was a chaos of alarm sirens, and Special Agents racing along corridors shouting orders. Doors slamming shut, security shutters lowering to lock in place. An agent raced into the mailroom, earpiece connected to his walkie-talkie, and automatic pistol in his hand.

"What kind of a threat do we have?" he shouted.

Levins waved him toward the box. "In there."

The man approached cautiously and looked inside from a distance.

"Holy shit!"

* * *

"I want those sons of bitches," President of the United States Maxwell Taylor shouted. His normally smooth, pale face was blotched red with anger.

His Chief of Staff, Joe Phoenix, nodded. "Sir, you need to..."

"Don't tell me what I need, Joe!"

Phoenix had rarely seen him so shaken up, so angry.

I thought it was we Latinos who were supposed to be temperamental.

"Of course not, Sir."

"I want someone to chase this one down. Starting right now. We're gonna nail those mothers."

"And, what about raising the alert level?"

"Yeah, do it. That package got through, who knows what else is on the way. We're under attack, and when I served in the military, they always taught us the best defense was to hit back hard."

"Chairman Mao."

"What?"

"The Chinese leader, Sir."

"I know who the fuck he was, what's he got to do with it? Don't tell me he didn't die?"

"No, Sir. I mean, yes, Sir, he did die. It was his saying. 'The only real defense is active defense'. Or maybe it was Confucius."

Taylor fixed him with a savage glare. "I don't care if it was the White House switchboard operator. Find out who sent it, and fast."

"And when we have that information, Mr. President?"

"Put them out of business. Permanently."

"I understand, Sir. First, I'll put your order in place to raise the alert level."

Taylor nodded, but his mind was already elsewhere.

America has long been the world's policeman, defending peace and freedom across the globe. Now it's personal. They sent 'that' into the home of the President of the United States. The message is clear. They issued a declaration of war. Did they think I'd stand by and do nothing? They're wrong.

* * *

He paused outside the imposing building, waiting. His nostrils filled with the familiar odors, the smell of the sea, or to be more accurate the smell of the land. Rotting seaweed, with the distinct tang of iodine, combined with the underlying freshness of salt air blowing from offshore. The faint breeze came from the east, although sometimes it varied, at times sucking in the sour smell of the land. A mixture of deserts and swamps out in the countryside, intermingled with the omnipresent city odors, sewage running raw in the streets. Garbage was strewn everywhere, as well as rotting carcasses. Not all were dead animals, for this area until recently had been a battle zone. No one bothered to clear the bloated corpses that lay where they fell. No one cared.

The man was waiting to enter the mansion that had once belonged to the governor of the Somali port city of Kismayo. The previous owner wouldn't need it now. They'd killed him after their successful attack to retake the city. Nabil Barre remained motionless for a moment more and then walked forward. A man rushed to open the door for him. It was important to make a grand entrance. He'd learned that in the past, along with other skills, like persuading other men to do his killing.

He was a strange figure, often underestimated by his enemies. His figure was spare, his body almost wasted after a lifetime of denial, poor diet, and sporadic health care. His head was hairless, and inside his sunken cheeks, his mouth was empty of teeth. He wore round glasses over his eyes, and his trademark robe, shabby and patched. Because of the broken glass still not cleared, he wore simple peasant sandals on his feet. Most of the time he went barefoot. As a result, people often compared him to Mahatma Gandhi, the revered architect of Indian independence. It was a comparison he was careful to encourage. Not that he believed any of Gandhi's nonsense about non-violent confrontation. Nabil Barre was a devout Muslim, and Allah required him to put enemies of the faith to death. It was a command he followed with the greatest of enthusiasm.

The men stood up and clapped as he walked into the big room, his sandals crunching on the broken glass. He went forward to the vacant seat at the head of the bloodstained table and gestured for them to be seated. He remained standing, surveying them with a gaze that people said was his most powerful weapon. His eyes were jet black, glowing with the inner belief of an absolute fanatic. Not one man present doubted his commitment, or his ferocity. The table at which they sat was still covered and bore the marks of its most recent use. The dried blood belonged to one of Barre's lieutenants, a man accused of treachery.

He'd made them hold the man down on the table while

he disemboweled him with his dagger. The screams had echoed around the city, and every man present vowed never to give the Sheikh any reason to doubt their loyalty. This was his objective. After they removed the body, he'd stopped one of the women who came to clean the surface of the table.

"Let it be a reminder of our cause. Blood is what binds us together, and blood is what we shall spill when we finally defeat the Western infidels. Anyone who considers treachery will see his own blood spill out on this table, to mingle with the blood of the other traitor.

No one argued. None dared.

He sat down and indicated they could begin. The windows were bare of any glass, and the stench he'd noticed from outside wafted into the room. It was familiar and comforting, the smell of Africa, his Africa.

"First, tell me of our operation to aid our friends in Al Qaeda. Was it successful?"

His second-in-command, Hasan Anglana hastened to reply. He was taller than Barre, with the lean, hard body of a fighter. His features were heavily scarred, after an American UAV launched a missile that wiped out his unit. At the time, he'd been returning from a local village where he had a woman. He was fifty meters away when the missile hit, a jet of flame and shards of hot metal did the damage to his face. Nevertheless, he lived. Soon, he'd replace the men; there was no shortage of volunteers to join the struggle, when it meant the priceless gift of food and an automatic weapon.

"Our reports tell us they boarded the ship without problem. They changed course toward the African coast, and if all goes well, our Northern brothers will assist them when they dock. As for the demands, we have no knowledge. I doubt they have made any, not yet. Let the infidels sweat over the fate of the unbelievers. My Sheikh, do you wish me to contact them for an update?"

Barre waved irritably. "We will know everything in due course, if Allah wishes it. Praise be to his holy name."

They enthusiastically echoed the salutation. Then Barre nodded them to silence.

"The success or failure of that mission is of little importance to us. The Al Qaeda attacks on the West are very worthy, but we have our own agenda; a far more important operation than killing a few white people on a floating toy. What is important is for them to return the aid we have given them, to help us carry out our own operation. Are the young shaheeds here?"

Hassan Anglana nodded. "They are waiting outside, my Sheikh. Shall I bring them in?"

"Of course. Let us greet them, and give them words of praise for the holy mission for which they have committed their deaths."

Anglana stood up and left the room. Seconds later, he returned leading a group of men, although they were hardly men. The group was comprised of eight teenagers, some of them looked no older than fifteen years. They made the correct Islamic greetings to Barre and then to the other men. Barre raked them with his laser gaze.

"You are ready? You have dedicated your lives to Allah?"

"Yes, Sheikh Barre!" they replied as one.

"I am not a Sheikh," he admonished them, in an attempt to appear modest. He smiled to himself.

It is a worthy title; one that I've earned many times over. One day, all men will call me Sheikh.

"Have you also dedicated your deaths to Allah?"

"Yes, Sheikh Barre!" they replied again in unison. They ignored his admonition not to use the honorific 'Sheikh'. With Nabil Barre, it was best to err on the side of caution.

"That is good." He climbed to his feet, "Your mission will represent the ultimate expression of the power of our movement. I promise you, the world will tremble when they know what you have achieved. Afterward, you will take your places in Paradise, surrounded by the rewards the Prophet has promised. Musse Daud, has any member of your group expressed any doubts?"

The young man almost leapt to attention. "No, Sheikh. We are as one, and we look forward to our glorious martyrdom."

Inside, he quaked. He'd overheard two of the boys talking, terrified by what lay ahead. Yet more terrified to step back. He should have admonished them, but he'd had the exact same thoughts. He glanced at the bloodstained table.

Yes, I need to be careful in this place. True, my fate is to die, but not now. That will come later, as a martyr.

"You have done well, Musse. You young men carry a heavy responsibility on your shoulders. Nothing less than the future of our Caliphate lies at stake, and history will remember your sacrifice. Your names will never be forgotten."

The teenager swallowed his misgivings and beamed at the praise. He was slim, tall for a Somali, at about six feet. Like the rest of his teenage companions, he was beardless, with short hair cut in a Western style. In that moment, he knew he'd go through with it even though it meant his death. Martyrdom was a glorious path to Paradise. He knew that for certain, hadn't their Imam told them that exact same thing?

Barre rested his gaze on each of them for a couple of seconds and finally waved for them to leave. Musse lagged behind to speak to Barre.

"My Sheikh, might I be permitted to say goodbye to my mother? This will be the last time."

He thought for a few moments and then nodded. "Go, but be quick."

He gave him a slight bow and trooped out. Barre slumped back in his chair, exhausted after the labors of the past few days. As well as preparing for the operation, and giving aid to Al Qaeda, it had been necessary to comb the city for anyone not sympathetic to their cause. They'd found plenty, and he now realized he was getting too old for the business of mass executions.

He glanced at his number two. "I am satisfied with the progress so far. Continue to make the arrangements, and let me know if you hit any problems. I trust we have no difficulties with finance?"

"Al Qaeda has been generous, my Sheikh. We have sufficient money, more than enough."

"The package, the one we sent to the American President. Did it arrive?"

Anglana looked puzzled. "Yes, we understand it arrived on time, and our reports suggest there was a massive security lockdown in the White House at the same time. But I don't understand, why did you send it? Surely it will alert them we are planning an attack?"

"Exactly. An attack, but that is impossible for them to prevent. Do you know the object of terrorism, Anglana?"

The man shook his head, still mystified. "To kill, my Sheikh?"

Barre smiled, the man was a skilled fighter but no great thinker. "The object of terrorism is to terrorize. And that is what I plan to do. Already, the United States will have raised their threat level, at great cost and inconvenience to themselves. And what did it cost us? One simple cardboard carton. The next attack, as you know, will be different; a devastating strike at the heart of the infidels. But every attack, large or small, hurts them. It is like shooting bullets at an elephant. A single shot will sting but not inflict mortal damage. But hit that same elephant with scores of bullets and missiles, and it will fall. So shall it be with America."

He waited for a response.

"My Sheikh, that is inspired. I cannot wait to see the American elephant fall."

Privately, he thought Barre had acted like an idiot. If the man wanted to recite maxims, he had one he could offer. 'Forewarned is forearmed.' But wisely, he kept it to himself.

"Excellent," Barre smiled, "I will go to my quarters and leave you to continue. I am very tired." He glared around the room. "Make sure I am undisturbed."

"Yes, my Sheikh," every single man replied.

They all knew how Barre lived in his private rooms, how he spent his time, and with whom he spent it. The last man who had interrupted was now only a distant memory, his body rotting in an unmarked shallow grave.

He climbed to his feet, and they all followed suit. He walked out of the room slowly, despite his rising excitement. Everything was going well, perhaps too well. Yet there was nothing wrong with that, why shouldn't they have some successes? A guard stood outside the door to his apartments, and the man quickly opened it to allow him to pass.

He walked inside and immediately the scent of his private living space entered his nostrils, a musky scent, and a mixture of perfumes, spices, and women. They were all waiting to greet him, his wives, five of them and all young. The youngest was his favorite, and he beckoned her forward.

"Saba, my flower. Prepare my bath, and I require your sisters to prepare food. You may serve my meal in my bedroom. Afterward, I require you to pleasure me."

She bowed low. "Yes, my master. It shall be as you say."

"How is my son?"

"He is well, my master. Sleeping in the crèche."

"Excellent. Attend to my bath, at once."

She hurried off to obey his wishes. Her real name wasn't Saba. Neither was she a Somali. She'd been christened Emily Carillo, of American parents. Her home had been New Jersey until four years ago. Somali pirates captured her family's round the world yacht and executed her parents in front of her young eyes. Barre hadn't wanted ransom. He wanted her. She was white, with blonde hair, a healthy smile, and even perfect teeth. Everything about her excited him, especially her youth. Twelve years was the perfect age to take a wife, as every sensible Muslim knew. Breaking her to his wishes hadn't been too difficult. Western girls had such a low tolerance to pain. And she had even blessed him with a son, Mukhtar, born last year just before her fifteenth birthday.

He looked up as she came back into the room.

"Your bath is ready, my master."

He smiled at her. "Good. Follow me. You may undress me."

Life is good, very good.

She bowed low, servile and cowed as he walked past her. It was time for this American to submit to Nabil Barre. Soon, the entire nation of infidels would know his name, and it would become a byword for the horror he planned to inflict on them. The Islamic world would take its revenge for the humiliations heaped on it by the Americans.

* * *

The drone of the four huge Pratt & Whitney F117 turbofans blended with the shriek of the turbulence outside. They were flying at ten thousand meters in the Boeing C17, breathing oxygen as they waited to jump. The loadmaster had just lowered the ramp. Chief Petty Officer Kyle Nolan watched as his platoon commander, Lieutenant William Boswell carried out his tasks, checking each man's rig and equipment to make sure there were no screw-ups. He grinned to himself. As usual, the officer's camos were that bit smarter than the rest of the unit, his webbing and equipment new, yet carefully 'aged'. Boswell made sure he had the best of everything, provided it had the patina of authenticity. He should have looked every inch the tough, experienced vet, but he didn't.

He looked every inch the smooth-faced Ivy League professional. He couldn't help it; it was in his genes. Under the helmet, his blonde hair was neatly trimmed, and the officer always sported a small blonde mustache. Even his camos looked tailor made. He was slight in build, like many

Special Forces operators who were of less than average height. Their trade required subtlety and stealth, not six foot six inch muscle-bound apes. But it was his smooth and easy confidence that marked him out as a WASP. At least, it had. Lately, he'd changed, and he reminded Nolan of a petulant kid.

Since he'd joined the unit, Boswell had struggled to make the grade. Not as a Seal, he always managed to score highly in exercises. As a commander, he lacked that certain something that made for a platoon leader in the shadow world of Special Ops. Even with Lucas Grant, a decorated Seal vet to back him up, he waxed and waned. Right now, he was on the wane.

He'd made it clear a few weeks back that he wanted Nolan transferred out to another platoon. The reason was obvious; he and Grant were as thick as thieves. Probably he'd offered the experienced Seal a position in his father's brokerage house after he left the US Navy. In the meantime, he wanted his buddy to be his second-in-command, which would mean promoting him to Chief Petty Officer. And there was only room for one second-stringer in Bravo.

So far, he'd managed to sidestep Boswell's efforts and had stayed put. But it was getting difficult, reaching the time when the infighting could become a danger to the men when they were operating behind the lines. When it reached that stage, Nolan would have to make a decision. He didn't want to transfer out, and with the exception of Boswell and Grant, not a single man in Bravo wanted it either. He grinned again. It was not unlike those old Western movies.

'There's only room for one of us in this town.'

And the Lieutenant, as senior man, called the

shots. Nolan snapped out of it, this was no time for woolgathering. There wouldn't be any screw-ups, Boswell or no Boswell. They were Bravo, a unit of Navy Seals. Men selected by United States Naval Special Warfare Command, NAVSOC, because they were the best in the world at what they did; clandestine insertion and target elimination, as well as hostage rescue.

Lieutenant Boswell generally did his best to make a good impression, especially with his superiors. Backed up by Seal veteran Lucas Grant, a member of the DEVGRU outfit that took down Osama bin Laden, he was said to be a coming man. In the Navy, as well as the beckoning arms of Washington, where his family had staked out a political future for their war-hero son.

Nolan kept a careful eye on him. Despite occasional flashes of enthusiasm when he was capable of earning his pay, they knew the wealthy and ambitious officer was going through the motions. Not that there should be any problems, not on this trip. They were almost six miles over Luneberg Heath, the vast region in Lower Saxony, Northern Germany, and for decades NATO's preferred training ground. Even though the Cold War was over, little had changed. For infantry and armored maneuvers, it had no parallel in Europe. It was also perfect for Special Forces, where they could operate in a variety of simulated scenarios with total anonymity.

Luneberg Heath was famous for another reason. Or perhaps infamous would be more accurate. On May 4th, 1945, Field Marshal Bernard Montgomery accepted the unconditional surrender of German forces at the end of World War II in Europe. It was also the area where the body of Heinrich Himmler, head of the Nazi SS legions, was secretly buried in an unmarked grave, following his suicide. Not that anyone cared to look.

"Three minutes."

The jumpmaster held up three fingers, in case anyone wasn't listening to their commo. They were already standing in the center of the vast cabin, and they moved toward the open ramp, gripping the handholds to avoid being sucked out by the howling slipstream whistling around them.

"You all set?" Boswell asked him.

"Roger that," he replied automatically. The question was pointless. Recently, much of what Boswell said came into that category.

"Two minutes."

Two fingers held up, to the point. They were all ready, every man in that relaxed and alert posture, waiting to jump out into the night and free fall almost to the ground before they opened their 'chutes. Called a HALO jump, high altitude, low opening, they developed the technique to allow parachutists to jump far from a target zone that could be under fire. It was perfect for Special Forces. The nature of their work invariably meant they wanted their arrival to be a big surprise.

It was also dangerous, very dangerous, and the Seals were no strangers to fatalities, especially in night HALO drops; hence the constant training.

"One minute."

One finger. Nolan smiled; it was almost an insulting gesture. He led his fireteam forward to the ramp. As well as him, there were Dan Moseley, Zeke Murray, and Brad Rose. They were almost shoulder-to-shoulder, waiting to make the giant leap as one. The jumpmaster started to count down with the fingers of both beloved hands. At the same time, they heard him call the count.

"Nine, eight, seven, six, five, four..."

It was a sudden movement, as the huge aircraft abruptly banked hard to starboard. They hung on grimly, not sure if it was an in-flight emergency, whether to jump or stay.

"Abort, abort, abort!"

The jumpmaster waved them back, and they shuffled away from the open ramp. He pressed the button, and the motors whined as it began to close.

Brad looked at him and put his mouth next to Nolan's ear.

"What the fuck! What's going on, Chief?"

He shrugged, as if to say 'my guess is as good as yours'.

They saw Boswell racing forward to the cockpit. They waited a couple of minutes for him to return, and it was obvious from his expression that someone, somewhere, was in trouble. Even behind his goggles, they could see his eyes were dilated, and his pale skin was flushed with excitement. He waved them around him in a bunch.

"Change of plan. A bunch of camel jockeys hijacked a cruise liner somewhere in the Mediterranean, with more than eight hundred passengers held hostage. Most of them elderly and many of them Americans."

"How many crew?" Nolan asked.

He turned to stare at his second-in-command. "Crew? I don't know, Chief, three, four hundred maybe. Anyway, we're the nearest, and we've been tasked to fly down there, release the hostages, and deal with these people."

"Al Qaeda?" Lucas Grant asked him, his face grim.

Something was bugging Lucas. He'd been angry about something for a couple of weeks. He'd even snapped at Boswell. He resolved to find out and try to help. It was his mob, even though Grant was Boswell's poodle.

His crutch, more like; brought in to 'put some backbone' into his leadership. He'd sure needed it. When he first joined Bravo, he had as much idea about what made a Seal as the average Girl Guide.

He smiled at Grant. "No question. Our old friends are up to their tricks. Good news is we're flying direct to the ship and infil with a HALO drop, so we'll rack up some jump hours."

Lucas gave him a cold glance and turned away.

Whatever's bugging him, it's something bad. Real bad.

Nolan forgot about Grant, his mind was buzzing with a thousand questions. There were advantages and disadvantages in rushing straight in. The terrorists wouldn't expect a fast reaction, and there was a chance to catch them with their pants down. On the other hand, lack of preparation was one of the prime reasons for mission failure. He got Boswell's attention.

"Lt, what's the current position of this cruise liner? Do we know if it's stationary, or underway?"

"Currently, she's about fifty klicks from the Spanish Mediterranean port of Cartagena and steaming at maximum speed, heading for the coast of North Africa. They reckon it'll be Libya. That place is a nest of vipers since Gaddafi went, and some of the militia are tied to Al Qaeda, so they'd be able to get help from their friends."

He pulled his tactical tablet out of the case and switched on. Immediately, the screen filled with map data. The northwest Mediterranean, so the mission controllers had up linked it ready for him to brief the unit. His fingers raced across the screen, and images appeared and disappeared.

"The latest position of the ship is here, off the coast of Southern Spain."

His fingers moved the map away, and an image of the ship appeared and then disappeared, to be replaced by a schematic.

Intel has moved fast, very fast. Impressive.

More images flashed on and off-screen, but he didn't leave them any time to study them. Finally, he returned to the schematic.

"This is the way I see it. She's one hundred and eighty meters long; that's almost six hundred feet." As if his men didn't have the math to make the conversion, "I'll split us up into three teams. Nolan, you and three men to take the bridge."

"You mean the bit at the front?"

Boswell gave him a sour look, and Grant sniggered. "Right. My team with Grant, Weissman and Eisner will land on the Lido deck. Bryce and Merano will land aft, and find a good defensive position close to the stack, to the rear of the sundeck. As soon as we're in position, we'll move in and take down these gomers. Any questions?"

It had all happened fast, much too fast for Nolan to connect the dots.

"The name of the ship?"

"She's the Arosa Star, a Greek flagged vessel."

He felt a lurch in his guts. Back home, Kyle Nolan had a couple of kids looked after by their grandparents, the Robsons, since their mother was killed in drug-related drive-by shooting. They had a nice place up near Sacramento, and based in San Diego, he was able to make the trip every weekend when he was home. Several weeks ago, they told him they wanted a vacation. It was during school time, so he fixed up for his ex-girlfriend, Carol Summers, to move in with the kids while they were away.

It was a good arrangement. Carol had almost become a surrogate mother to Daniel and Mary, which meant the Robsons were free to leave, for a Mediterranean cruise on the Arosa Star. His mind wandered over the possible outcomes. They were good folks and had become an important part of his children's lives. The kids were recovering well from the death of their mother, but it had been a long, dark, and hard road. It was a shame things had not worked out between him and Carol, but they had remained friends.

"Do we know how many terrorists are on board, and what kind of weapons they're carrying?"

It was Will Bryce who'd spoken, the tough, hard PO1. He was immensely strong, always dependable, the unit rock, and one of the most respected men in the entire Navy. Will was one of the finest soldiers Nolan had served with. The African American was huge, his body clad with slabs of hard muscle, a Seal operative at the very peak of physical fitness and skill. Behind his goggles, he had gray, watchful eyes, undoubtedly a throwback to some long forgotten mixed ancestry. If ever there was a perfect soldier, a man you'd trust more than any other with your life, it was Will.

"Good question," Boswell acknowledged, "The answer is no. They seized the ship and shut down all communication. At a guess, I'd say at least twenty, with a maximum of about forty. Weapons?" He chuckled. "We all know what these people carry. AK-47s, and they'll likely have RPG7 rocket launchers, as well a good quantity of explosives. The only message they sent out was that the ship is wired to explode. Any attempt at a rescue will result in immediate detonation and the deaths of all on board.

Including the rescuers."

"Best not screw up then," Lucas Grant murmured. Again, he had that faraway look.

"No. Remember, the ship is ablaze with lights. It's a cruise ship, after all. It means we'll lose the advantage of night the moment we land. So we'll have to be extra careful. Don't give these fuckers a chance. Anyone makes a move; kill them. It shouldn't be too hard to make out the passengers; most will be white. The terrorists, all black, that goes without saying."

"And the crew?" Bryce asked.

"A mixture, I guess," the Lieutenant answered after a moment.

Bryce stared at him and said nothing, but the meaning was clear. Shooting black men indiscriminately could kill plenty of the good guys.

"Er, right, we'll need to be careful. We should be over the target in a couple of hours, so I suggest we take it easy for a bit. The rest of the night is likely to be busy."

The briefing broke up, and Nolan settled down on the aluminum floor of the aircraft. He found a bunch of spare parachutes to rest against, and after a few moments, Will Bryce joined him.

"Chief, something wrong?"

Nolan was about to deny it, but this was Will, his best friend in the unit. He explained that his kids' grandparents were on board the vessel.

"They can't afford to lose them, Will. Not after everything they've been through."

At first, Bryce said nothing. They'd been through too much for him to serve up a few false platitudes. Besides, they knew what kind of odds they were facing. At worst, the terrorists would destroy the ship and everyone aboard. At best, Bravo would kill all the hostiles. But ten men against as many as forty meant there'd be some shooting, and when the bullets started to fly, civilians got hurt.

"Give me a minute," Bryce said.

He climbed to his feet and went away. A few moments later, he returned carrying Boswell's tactical tablet. He switched on and scrolled through the menu options. Then he grinned.

"I thought so. They uploaded a full passenger manifest. You can find the cabin where your family is staying. Maybe it'll help when the shooting starts."

Nolan stared at the display. The names, Mr. and Mrs. P Robson, were prominent, listed in Cabin 5064 on the Main Deck. Bryce glanced over his shoulder.

"They're next door to a staircase. It'll make it easier to locate the cabin. You know what'll happen when we go in. The shit will hit the fan, and it'll be chaos on there."

He took the tablet and looked closer. "Looks like they're in my sector, Chief. I'll keep an eye out for that cabin. First chance I have, I'll go find them."

"If they're in there."

His gray eyes darkened for an instant, and he nodded slowly. "Yeah, if they're in there."

He tried to rest, but his mind was racked with turmoil. Because of his work and his wife's murder, the Robsons offered the stability his kids so desperately needed.

If they're killed...Christ, it doesn't bear thinking about.

But he had to look to the future. His kids needed someone at home, someone to welcome them when they returned from school, to make sure they could do the things normal kids did. Carol, his ex-girlfriend was an angel, but she had a career of her own, a plainclothes cop in San Diego.

If anything happens, I'll have to...

"We need to get ready, Chief. You okay?"

He looked up startled. Three men stood next to him. They'd been split into fireteams, and these were the men he'd fight with, Moseley, Murray, and Rose. Brad Rose stared at him, his handsome surfer's face split in a wide grin. He was the unit dandy, slightly below medium height, powerfully built, and no matter what clothes he wore, he always managed to look good; like a playboy or a California beach boy. His long, blonde hair was hidden beneath his Gallet half-helmet, although some stray strands peaked out underneath.

Nolan checked his watch. "I'm fine. I make it thirty minutes until we jump. Anything changed?"

"Twenty six minutes, according to Boswell. We've picked up a tailwind. We'll pick up speed on the descent. With any luck, we'll hit the bastards before they see us coming."

"We need more than luck, Brad."

"In that case, I'll talk nicely to them."

"That should do it."

* * *

Ten minutes before they reached the target, they started to go through the rituals before the jump. They stood up, checked the harness of the man in front, and bunched near to the ramp. It started to open with a whine of electric motors, and the jumpmaster hooked on his harness and stood ready. Nolan grinned; it always reminded him of a hotel doorman waiting to escort his guests out to a waiting limousine. Except it was unlikely any plush Manhattan establishment would send people on a six-mile plunge into the night. Besides, the guy didn't wear a top hat. He held up his fingers and continued with the ritual.

"Five minutes."

He held up five gloved fingers. Nolan continued the last minute checks, tagging on the webbing strap of his rifle as he always did. He was one of two unit snipers, and carried the tool of his trade, an SWS Mk 11. The precision semiautomatic Sniper Weapon System could deliver a lethal 7.62mm round to a range of almost a mile. The Leupold Vari-X Mil-dot riflescope mounted on top meant he rarely missed.

He moved his hand to his 9mm handgun in the holster strapped to his leg, a Sig Sauer P226, the choice of many Special Forces operatives, and a final check on his helmet. They had no night vision equipment; the cruise liner would be lit up like Times Square, making it useless. Last of all, he checked his harness. Again. It was unnecessary, other men around him had already checked.

But what the hell, it's my neck. And I have nothing better to do, not for the next few minutes. No, make that, two minutes.

The jumpmaster was holding up two fingers. His fireteam moved into a bunch nearest to the open ramp, as they were slated to be first out. Despite their thick clothing and equipment, the wind cut through an icy blast that felt like tiny razorblades hacking at the skin.

"One minute."

They moved almost to the edge of the ramp, holding onto the safety lines.

"Ten seconds, nine, eight…"

Time to go to work.

"Green light, go, go!"

They stepped out into the chill dark, the icy blast of the slipstream as cold as the Devil's breath. He adjusted his arms and legs into the classic skydiving position, checked his wrist mounted combined GPS and altimeter, and settled into the descent. At first, they were in cloud, and it was like swimming in a bowl of soup. But after the first few minutes, he was underneath the cloud. There was no sign of their target, although it was possible to make out the lights of small vessels making their way across the Mediterranean.

Carrying cargoes from North Africa to Spain, perhaps. Some would be smugglers, for the strip of ocean was one of the most popular in the world for drug traffickers, people traffickers, and in the opposite direction even electrical goods. The Spanish enclave of Melilla was situated on the coast of Morocco. It was a source of amusement to Spanish officials that Moroccans would purchase a large appliance in the town, like an icebox, and then float it on a raft to circumvent the steep customs tariffs Morocco charged to its citizens.

He stared ahead. It had to be near, unless something had changed, like the terrorists detonated the charges and sent the Arosa Star to the bottom.

Dear God, no! Not that. Over there! A ship lit up like a Californian town.

He checked his position and shifted his weight to make a slight adjustment to his course. It had to be it; there was nothing else near. He looked around, and twenty meters to his right and slightly behind, he could see one of the team, Will Bryce. It could only be him. No one else was that big. He gave him a wave, and Will sketched a mock salute. He chuckled. It was a good omen, the PO1 looked relaxed. They were nearing the ship, and he made another adjustment. Will did the same, and they separated. He aimed at the bridge while the other man pointed aft.

He checked his altimeter again. The ship was coming up fast. It was time. He pulled the cord, and the dark night camouflage 'chute snapped open with the familiar and comforting jerk. This was the critical moment. He had to land on the Bridge Deck, Deck 8, unseen by the enemy, but on top of the bridge was Deck 9, the Observatory; a perfect place to land, but also a perfect defensive position. Instead, his fireteam headed for Deck 7 where there was a tiny platform, which should be large enough for them to land. From there, it would be easy to climb up to the bridge. Provided they got down safely on a space barely big enough to accommodate a family car.

It was closer now, and he could pick out the LZ. Up above, on the Observatory deck, there were four men to each side keeping watch. As expected, they were armed with Kalashnikov AK-47s. The iconic banana shaped clips marked them out immediately. Below, he could make out two heads staring out of the bridge window. Both were black, and he knew from the briefing, the bridge crew was mainly Greek. Below, the platform was empty, and he breathed a sigh of relief. Another adjustment, and he was drifting toward it, making an allowance for the speed of the ship and the wind shear.

The LZ hurtled toward him, and he was about to touch when he saw a figure standing at the side. It happened in a split second and a blur of movement. A short, thin black man; he was dressed in jeans and a ragged T-shirt. His AK was slung over his shoulder while he smoked a cigarette. Nolan gave a gentle tug on the line, and the other man never stood a chance.

Instead of a neat landing, he angled his body so that his boots smashed into the terrorist. The man looked up, his eyes wide and terrified at the dark specter that had appeared from nowhere. If he was superstitious, and he probably was, he would have assumed it was an evil spirit summoned from hell. The moment lasted less than a second. Nolan used him to cushion the landing, and as they rolled over, he slammed the edge of his hand into his target's neck. It was a killer blow, and he ignored the man to correct his landing.

Instead of standing on the platform, he was tumbling over. The need for the attack meant he wasn't able to stow his parachute in the normal way. The lines entangled his legs, and as he tried to free himself, the ship fell victim to wind and sea and plunged over. He began to slide off the edge, as he banged on his harness release and kept working to free himself. One leg went over the edge, but he hooked the other on the extension of a flimsy post.

He'd almost made it, and was pulling himself back onto the platform, when the post began to bend. He looked around frantically for another handhold, but there was nothing. He tried to use the bent post as support, but it only bent even more. He was going, sliding over, and there was nothing left to stop him, when the shape of a dark angel glided inches over his head. In a fluid movement, Zeke Murray snapped his harness and clamped a hand on Nolan's webbing. He started pulling him away from the edge.

"Going for a swim, Chief?" he murmured.

"Thanks, Zeke. Any sign of…"

Two more black angels skimmed overhead and dropped to a perfect landing, so close their 'chutes were almost entangled. Dan Moseley with his M249 slung on his back, and Brad Rose, who was already stepping out of his harness and preparing his HK 410. They'd all made it. Just. He wondered about the other two teams, Boswell and Bryce, but it was too early to make contact. He looked at the men.

"Communications check."

"Read you, strength five." They all came back the same. It was time to go.

"We'll take the bridge. You noticed the gomers on top, on the Observatory deck?"

They all nodded. "Couldn't miss 'em," Brad grimaced, "They could cause trouble if they come down to the bridge."

"Yeah. We'll hit the bridge, and the second it's secure, you and Zeke can go up there and put them out of their misery. Let's move out, and remember, there'll be friendlies on that bridge. We just have to hope that one of them can give us the heads up on the location of the explosives."

"Unless it's bullshit," Dan murmured.

"You ever know a time when people like this missed a chance to blow something up?"

"Point taken. Maybe we can persuade one of the hostiles to let us in on the secret."

"These guys are fanatics. It'll take powerful persuasion to get them to talk."

"Powerful is what I had in mind."

They checked their loads. Brad shouldered his HK410, the same weapon carried by Zeke. Dan Moseley was a machine gunner, and in addition to his SAW, the M249, he elected to carry a lightweight SCAR, Special operations Combat Assault Rifle.

The Belgian designed weapon had a folding stock and a ten-inch barrel. Even with the suppressor fitted, it was tiny enough to carry under his coat, and he'd fitted a couple of extras, like the EGLM, a 40mm grenade launching module, as well as a laser sighting mechanism. He carried the M249 on his back and the SCAR in his hands. For close quarter battle, it had few equals.

Nolan gazed around a final time, shouldered his sniper rifle, took out his handgun, and gave them the nod. It was time to earn their pay.

"Let's go."

They crept forward, hugging the shadows, and stopped when the distinctive chatter of a 7.62mm AK-47 ripped through the night.

They know we're here! Fuck.

CHAPTER TWO

"Let's move! Straight up to the bridge, and anything gets in the way, kill it."

The only thing that would help them now was speed. They had no idea why the shooting had started, but it didn't matter. The show had begun.

They raced up the ladder to the bridge deck and stopped. In front of them was a small open space with the elevator doors. As they arrived, the doors opened and a man stepped out. He was black and wearing bright Bermuda shorts and a ragged T-shirt. He also carried a pistol in his hand, which sealed his fate. Nolan shot him, and the round tore through his head and splattered part of his brain onto the wall behind him. Even before his body slammed into the soft, luxurious pile of the carpet, they had started to run.

The door to the bridge was only three meters away, and it was closed. They surrounded it and knelt down, waiting, while he gently tried the handle. Locked. He gave the signal to Brad to prepare a stun grenade. Then he took out a small magnetic demolition charge, set it for five seconds, and signaled them to step back. A last check around, he hit the detonator and dived for cover.

The explosive roared, completely blasting the bridge door from its hinges, and while the shock waves were still roiling around them, Brad leapt forward and tossed the grenade inside. They flattened against the wall outside the bridge structure as it exploded. A second later, Nolan was through the door, his Sig Sauer leading the way.

The bridge space was a scene of devastation, with men sprawled on the floor, many clutching their heads to ease the pain of burst eardrums. It was very different from a US Navy warship. The rear area was wood paneled, and the watchmen had comfortable padded chairs on pedestals. The rest was immaculate pristine, smart paintwork and gleaming wood and brass trims. When the passengers did the tour, they'd expect to see nothing less.

He counted a total of ten men on the bridge, of which eight were hostiles, garish in their ragged, brightly hued clothing, and the other two displayed the uniform of the Merchant Marine.

One of the hostiles was trying to pull himself to his feet, and he helped him back to the floor with two 9mm rounds. Behind him they were finishing off the others, and within five seconds of the breaching charge detonating, the bridge was theirs. Zeke was helping a man in the uniform of a senior officer to his feet. Nolan went over to speak to him.

"We're US Navy, Sir, and we need your help. Who are you?"

He shook his head. "I, er… what happened?"

Nolan grabbed him by the shoulders. There'd be plenty

of time to recover his wits later. "Never mind, we need to know who you are, and how many hostiles came aboard the ship?"

He seemed to straighten. "I'm the Captain of the Arosa Star, Costas Constantinides. Yes, the numbers. I made a note. I thought it'd be important, but…"

His voice tailed off, and Nolan did the only thing possible. He slapped his face.

"Captain, there's no time. How many hostiles?"

He saw the man's eyes flare in anger, but it brought him to his senses.

"Hostiles. Forty of them, I'm sure of it." He looked at the eight bodies on the floor. "I'd guess that means thirty-two left. Your work?"

"Yeah." He swung around to Dan Moseley. "We have to work through the ship. I'll leave you here to take care of the bridge with your M249. Anything happens; you know what to do. The rest of you, follow me."

"What do you want me to do?" the Captain asked, "I don't know if it's possible to stop the ship."

Nolan looked around. The ship was still underway, heading south. "No need. Spin her around one hundred and eighty degrees and head north."

"North? Which port?"

"You were headed for Cartagena, in Southern Spain. No need to change your itinerary."

The man looked mystified for a moment, then nodded. He bent down to help his crewman, as Nolan led his men back out to the interior of the cruise liner. Over thirty hostiles left to take down. They stopped at the head of the staircase that led down to Deck Seven, the Lido Deck, where they expected the main attacking force to be concentrated. It was close enough to the bridge, and yet central enough to control the entire vessel, passengers, and crew. It's what he would have done. And where they'd agreed to meet up with Boswell's fireteam.

They raced down the stairs and along the wide promenade. They reached an open area that spanned the entire width of the boat, where they'd arranged to rendezvous with Boswell's group. It was empty. He keyed his mic.

"Bravo One, this is Two. Bridge is secure. We just reached the Lido Deck. Where are you?"

Boswell came back a couple of seconds later. "This is Bravo One, we're below you on the Lounge Deck Six."

Shit, they were supposed to clear the Lido Deck and report in. Has something gone wrong?

"Copy that. Did you clear the Lido Deck?"

"Negative, negative. We ran into a bunch of hostiles, and Lucas thought it would be best to leapfrog them to secure the engine room. Stop the boat heading any further south."

He worked hard to control his anger. There were times when Boswell came through, but this wasn't one of them.

"Copy that, where are the hostiles?"

He got his answer sooner than expected. A hail of gunfire swept past them, the distinctive chatter of AK-47s fired on full auto. They were already diving to the deck as another barrage of shots whistled overhead.

"We're not sure…"

Nolan ignored Boswell's reply and concentrated on facing the new threat. He emptied the clip in the direction of the enemy, who were hiding behind some of the ship's lifeboats. As he rammed in a new clip, and unslung his rifle, he turned to the nearest man, PO3 Brad Rose.

"How many?"

Rose squirted off half a dozen shots and was rewarded with a scream from up ahead.

"There's a whole bunch of them back there. I'd guess about ten."

"Roger that. Work around to their right flank, Zeke, and take the other end. I'll try and pick them off from here."

They scrambled away, and he lay prone on the deck, focusing his Leupold Vari-X Mil-dot riflescope on the targets up ahead. A ragged T-shirt briefly presented itself a couple of inches beneath the lifeboat, and he squeezed the trigger twice. Two rounds spat out the suppressed barrel, two 175-gram chunks of lead, flying at a speed of 2,580 feet per second. The kinetic energy of his burst punched the gaudy T-shirt backward, and the scream of shock and agony echoed around the luxurious Lido Deck. Immediately, two more men leapt up and aimed their weapons at him. It was a gift. He hit them with a single shot apiece, each time he aimed for the head, and each time he hit. Their days of annoying innocent passengers on cruise liners were over. Three down, seven to go. And then he barely heard the 'thunk' of a suppressed shot, as one of the other men began to get on the scoreboard.

A couple more bursts sounded from the AK-47s as they turned to face the new threat, and he heard more 'thunks' from the Seals' weapons. Three men jumped to their feet, forgetting the sniper that watched them and tried to run down Brad's position. They were firing on full auto, and he ignored the bullets that whistled and ricocheted around the deck to concentrate on taking them down.

He hit two of them, and the third dived for cover as he realized his danger. He keyed his mic. "Brad, report your status."

"Took a couple of hits on the vest, and one punched a dent in my helmet, but I'm not hurt. Only my pride."

"Copy that. You saw that guy dive for cover under the lifeboat?"

"Roger that. As soon as he pops up, I'll take him down."

Nolan swept the area around the boats with his scope. No target presented itself, not yet. He heard shooting from upstairs, and it seemed Will Bryce and Vince Merano had come under fire. A second later Will's voice came into his earpiece.

"Bravo Two, this is Three. We have ten; repeat ten hostiles, pinned down up here. Wait one." A pause for a couple of seconds, "Make that seven. With any luck, we'll finish them off. Whoever trained these guys didn't know his business. Every time a man pops up, Vince knocks him down. How's it going down there?"

He explained about their firefight with the enemy on the Lido Deck.

"What about Boswell? He with you?"

"Negative. He went down to the engine room."

A pause, and then Will replied, "Understood."

It was one word spoken in a flat tone, and with no intonation. He couldn't have better underlined his disgust. Nolan heard another burst of gunfire from up top.

"We're busy up here, Chief. Call you back."

"Yeah, keep your heads down."

He was still scanning the lifeboats, moving his rifle barrel in an arc, side to side. As he did so, he caught sight of movement. His finger instinctively tightened on the trigger and loosened; a flash of camouflage, Zeke.

Eight men on the bridge, ten on the top deck engaged in a fight with Will and Vince. Ten down here, their numbers being whittled away. That made possibly twelve unaccounted for. He keyed his mic.

"Bravo One, this is Two. Have you sighted any hostiles?"

"This is Bravo One. We ran into six, and two of them are still giving us trouble. I'll call you when we're done, Chief."

The Lieutenant sounded irritated, as if the work they were doing was the most important part of the operation. Nolan ignored him and adjusted the count. With Boswell's six hostiles, that left six, assuming the Captain's assessment was correct. Where were they, about to detonate the explosives? It was no time to linger.

We need to finish these guys, and fast. I estimate one or two left in there. There isn't time to do this the easy way.

"Zeke, Brad, listen up, my guess is one or two men left behind cover. I'm going to show them a target. The minute they try for the shot, hit them." They both argued, but he ignored them, "On my count, three, two, one…"

He climbed to his feet, bracing his body for the shot. Two men jumped up, their teeth like a vivid scar against their black faces as their lips spread in a leer of triumph. One got off a shot, which thumped into Nolan's ballistic vest, hurling him backward to the deck. But the two Seals were ready, and they went down under a barrage of almost noiseless shooting.

He felt himself almost passing out with agony, and he knew one of his ribs was badly bruised, maybe even cracked.

Too bad, I've had worse.

He looked up into the eyes of Brad Rose.

"You okay? That was a crazy thing to do."

"I'll survive."

"If he'd taken a headshot, we'd be burying you at sea. How'd you know he'd go for the body?"

"These people are crappy shots. It was obvious."

Zeke ran across to join them. "I've checked around. That was the last of them."

"Roger that. I make it six of them still on the loose. And remember, they say they have charges set to explode."

Brad looked around. "Christ, this ship is big. Where the hell do we…?"

The screams echoed up a nearby stairwell. Lounge Deck Six. He catapulted to his feet and ran for the stairs.

"That answers your question. It sounds like they've got a bunch of passengers down there."

Dear God, not the Robsons. My kids have lost enough. They can't afford to lose their grandparents. They were on Deck Five. Maybe they were lucky.

They reached the foot of the staircase, just as Will reported in.

"We're clear up top, Chief. You want us down there?"

"Right away. Hostiles on Deck Six, so watch your step and hold somewhere at the base of the center stairwell. With any luck, you'll be right behind them."

"Copy that, give us a few minutes."

They held a couple of steps above Deck Six, and he peered around the corner. Every light on the ship was switched on, but it only meant the enemy would see them coming, an enemy somewhere behind a huge bunch of passengers. There must have been hundreds of them bunched in the restaurant area. They all had their hands on their heads, those that were still alive. The carpet was covered in bodies, shattered, bloody bodies of the victims of the attackers. He was about to turn to Brad and Zeke to spell it out when a voice shouted.

"Mister! You want these people to die, you go right ahead. You want them to live, you come out here and talk."

A man stepped forward, black, Somali, yet he carried himself differently to the others, more erect, more sure. Instead of the artificial swagger, there was the confidence of someone who knew what they were doing. This was the man in charge, the commander. Nolan turned to the two men behind him.

"It looks like he wants to parlay. There's nothing we can do. Right now, they hold all the cards." He keyed his mic. "Will, what's your status?"

"We're in position, but there's a couple of guys covering their six. If we start shooting, there'll be a bloodbath."

"Copy that. Sit tight. I'll see if I can talk him down. All of you be ready to take the shot the second it looks doable, without losing any of the passengers."

He handed his sniper rifle to Zeke, made sure his Sig Sauer had a full clip, loosened it in his leg holster, and walked forward. He kept his hands spread wide, palms up, to show he was unarmed.

"We can settle this. There's no need for anyone to die. Who am I talking to?"

The man's response was just a slight smile. "If you wish to know to know who you are addressing, I am Mohammed Ibrahim. But you haven't heard my terms yet. Maybe you won't like them, Mister. Condition number one, I want you and your friends off this ship. Condition number two…"

45

"That isn't going to happen. If I leave you aboard, I'll be risking the lives of the passengers."

"And if you don't get off, they'll die anyway."

"What's condition number two?" he asked, to gain time.

Another smile. "That's easy. Condition number two is the government of the United States will pay ten million dollars into a bank account. As soon as you comply, we'll let them all go."

"And the ship?"

He chuckled. "Oh, no, no. The ship is ours. You're not getting that back."

It was then he saw John Robson clutching his wife in the center of the frightened passengers. One of the terrorists had a gun to Violet's head, in case the husband decided to be brave.

If this goes wrong, they're dead.

He heard a voice in his earpiece, a whisper. Will. "We've got a bead on five of them, two at the back near to us, and three hiding in the middle of the passengers. If you can take out the guy in front of you, we're in business. I can see you're busy, so give me one click to acknowledge. The second we see you move, we'll take 'em.

He touched the transmit button. One click. The guy in front of them didn't appear to have noticed. He waited calmly for a reply.

How the hell can he be calm? He must know Special Forces have infiltrated the ship and killed most of his men. That we'll be waiting to send the rest of his little band to Paradise. Why so calm, when he knows he's about to die?

The answer came to him in a flash. That's why he was calm. They didn't board the liner to come out alive; the intention was to die. He studied the man opposite carefully and noticed the device held in his hand. It was the shape and size of a mobile phone.

That's the detonator, for sure.

The man understood and smiled even wider.

"Yeah, you're right. This is your one-way ticket to hell, Mister. Now get off my fucking boat, and take the rest of your men with you. I'm giving you sixty seconds to start moving."

Another murmur in his earpiece, "Chief, this is Brad. I've got a bead on that remote. I reckon I can destroy it the moment the shooting starts."

He gave him two clicks, negative.

It's one hell of a chance. It could stop the detonation, or it could trigger it, a fifty-fifty chance. Except if we leave the transmitter in one piece, he will detonate. Which changes the odds. I don't have a choice. God help me, with one click of a button, my kids may lose their entire family, and every man, woman, and child on this boat could die.

The enemy commander was watching him intently. There was no smile on his face, and he was holding out the remote trigger, to underline the threat. If Brad would ever have a shot, this was it. He keyed his mic.

"Shoot."

A microsecond later, his men opened fire. First to go was the remote trigger. Brad's bullet smashed through the plastic case, shredded the internal components and went on to pierce the hand that held it, and exit the other side. The man shrieked, his face a mix of agony and rage. Then Zeke's shot hit him in the chest, and he fell. The muffled 'thunks' of the Seals' weapons sounded above the frightened murmurs of the passengers. The six Somalis went down, their fall cushioned by the thick carpet. It made no difference. They were all dead before their bodies hit the deck, except one.

Nolan rushed forward, jerked the man's pistol out of his belt, and tossed it away.

"The explosives, is there any other way for them to detonate? You've lost. There's no need to kill all these people."

The Somali stared back at him, and his mouth moved. Nolan bent down to listen to his words, but to his astonishment someone pulled him aside, and he fell, sprawling on the carpet. As he watched, a black girl took his place next to the Somali and began speaking to him in a language he assumed was native Somali or Arabic. Her skin was the same color as the fallen terrorist, but that was the only connection. When she spoke, she was all African-American.

"What the fuck..."

She turned her head aside for a moment to look at him. "FBI, undercover agent Amelia Stowe. Leave this to me. This man has information we need to know."

She turned back to him and continued talking, and he replied in a few words. The conversation only lasted a few seconds, and then the man twisted his head to look at Nolan. He said a few more words, and then his head lolled back as the last breath whooshed out of his body.

The girl stood up, shaking her head in frustration. "Shit, I'm sure he was about to tell me something. "

"What did he say, right there at the end? When he looked at me?"

She seemed to be working something out, but finally she returned his gaze. She wore the uniform of one of the officers. It fitted her curves to perfection even though it was stained and torn.

"He said this was only the start. That America is next, and this time, the bleeding won't stop."

"Any ideas what he meant?"

She nodded slowly. "Some. Listen, whoever you are, we need to get this ship back on course."

"Already done. We took the bridge, and the Captain turned her around."

"Good. If the ship is clear, I'll go to the radio room. I need to contact Washington. By the way, who are you? Delta, Force Recon, Seals? I know you're not FBI HRT."

"Seals, I'm Chief Petty Officer Nolan." He was irritated by the way she seemed to have taken charge, "You can show me some ID?"

"And you?" she flared, by way of a reply.

He held up his Sig Sauer. "I reckon this is all the ID I need."

She nodded and reached under her skirt to pull out a small credentials case. She passed it to him, and he felt a tremor of arousal. The case was warm, and it smelt of her, musk with a hit of her fragrance. He squashed the feeling and glanced at it. FBI Special Agent Amelia Stowe, Office of the Director, Washington. She was on the level. He handed it back to her.

"I need to check to make sure they're all dead." He keyed his mic. "Bravo One, this is Two. We've cleared the Lounge Deck. What's your status?"

"This is Bravo One. We're clear down here, Chief. Lucas is searching the bodies in case there's anything interesting for our intel guys. Any news on the explosives?"

He confirmed the hostiles were all down, and they'd removed the risk of detonation.

"We have an undercover friendly up here, Boss. FBI, I checked her credentials."

"FBI? A woman? I don't know what the fuck she's doing, but until this operation is over, keep her with the rest of the passengers. We'll deal with this. We'll join you in a few minutes. Bravo One out."

He looked back at Amelia Stowe. He had a suspicion the feisty young FBI undercover agent would not take well to Boswell's order to keep her with the passengers. She was already walking toward the stairs on her way to the radio room. He called to her.

"Agent Stowe."

She turned back to him, and he caught himself thinking of that credential wallet he'd held in his hand, now back under her skirt. She was short, but held herself with that confident but relaxed pose of someone who knew they could overcome any problem the world threw at them.

No doubt the child of a successful and wealthy family.

She was also very pretty, with short-cut dark hair to match her flashing, almost luminous eyes. Everything about her was in proportion. Everything about her was gorgeous. Her rich, bow-shaped lips parted in a slight grin, as if she knew he was weighing her up, and she arched one perfectly sculptured eyebrow.

"Chief?"

"Uh, be careful. We think we got them all, but you never know."

She gave him a taut nod. "Thanks, but I took this off one of the bodies."

She showed him the weapon, a small, Tokarev 7.62mm automatic pistol; flat, black, compact and lethal. Russian made, the preferred weapon of Soviet Commissars for killing suspected traitors, to save the cost and bother of a trial.

She turned and ran lightly up the staircase, and he went in to find John and Violet. At first they were puzzled until he ripped off his helmet.

"Kyle!" Violet Robson rushed into his arms, "My god, I thought they were going to kill us."

"You'll be fine," he comforted her. Robson shook his hand, held on tight, as if he wouldn't let it go. "I have to go, but you're safe now. I'll be in touch soon as I get home."

"That was some rescue, Jesus Christ. We'll never forget what you did here."

"It wasn't just me, John. It was..."

"The US Navy Seals, at your service, folks. You're just lucky we happened to be in the right place at the right time."

Boswell with Lucas Grant at his shoulder; the Lieutenant carried a half-amused grin.

Real hero style.

But he also noticed Grant's wince of embarrassment.

"Lt, yeah, I have to get topsides. I'll get moving."

He ran up the staircase. Brad and Zeke followed right behind. For some reason, Boswell seemed like a politician on the stump. If there'd been a handy baby, he for sure would have kissed it.

They relieved Dan Moseley on the bridge. Captain Constantinides was busy on the ship's communications system, making an inventory of the fallen. Nolan looked at Dan.

"How bad does it look?"

"About twenty of the crew are dead, another half dozen

wounded. He's not sure yet. It's bad, real bad. Although it could have been worse."

"Yeah."

He looked around the bridge at the bloodstains and the bodies.

Bastards.

Amelia Stowe bustled through the door and gave him a wave.

"Chief Nolan, I made my report to Washington. They're sending choppers out to pick us up. They'll be here inside of thirty minutes."

"Us? We take care of our own transport, Agent Stowe."

He hadn't meant to snap at her, but that's the way it came out, too late to pull back.

"I'm sure you do, normally. Come through to the radio room. It's at the back of the bridge. There's someone you need to speak to."

She put her hand on his arm to pull him along, but he shook her off.

"I don't need to speak to anyone. We have business here to finish up."

"You need to speak to this guy. He's your boss."

What the hell does Rear Admiral Drew Jacks want?

If anyone knew the importance of tidying the loose ends when an operation was over, double-checking for any hostiles unaccounted for and dealing with casualties, it was Jacks. He followed her in silence up to the radio room, wondering what the connection was between an FBI agent and the Navy Seals based at Coronado. She left him outside the door, saying she had to locate Boswell.

He walked through the door into a world of electronic equipment, communications consoles, and satellite receivers. A young seaman sitting in front of the main console gave him a nervous glance.

"Chief Petty Officer Nolan? It's all set up ready for you, Sir. The call is on a satellite frequency, which means it's encrypted, although not to military standards."

"Understood."

He took the offered telephone handset and grimaced. It still bore the traces of the attack, a long smear of blood down the black plastic. "This is Nolan, Admiral. We're looking good here, just a few things to finish up before I'm ready to report in."

"I'm pleased to hear it, but this isn't Admiral Jacks. You're speaking to your Commander-in-Chief."

Jesus Christ, the President of the United States. There's no doubt. The voice is familiar worldwide.

"Mr. President, yessir. What can I do for you, Sir?"

"First of all, congratulations on a job well done. I take it there were no casualties?"

"Our unit is intact, Sir, but the passengers and crew were hit hard. A lot of them were killed, some hurt bad."

"I'm sorry to hear that. We'll have medics standing by as soon as the ship docks in Cartagena. And I've ordered a couple of SAR helicopters on standby to take off any of the wounded who're critical."

"That's good news. Some of them need urgent treatment."

"They'll get it. Listen, Chief, Special Agent Stowe has gone to fetch your unit commander, Lieutenant Boswell. In the meantime, I wanted to speak to you. Admiral Jacks tells me you're the man who makes things happen in that platoon."

He stayed silent and waited. The President continued.

"I have something of a problem, Chief. Agent Stowe was working undercover because of intelligence chatter we've been picking up for several weeks now. I understand the terrorists who hijacked the Arosa Star were our old friends, Al Qaeda. No surprises there."

"No, Sir."

"NSA has analyzed a bunch of recent intercepts, and it's clear they didn't operate on their own. They had help. Al Qaeda's plan was to take the ship to a friendly port in North Africa, and release the surviving passengers in return for a hefty ransom. It would have given them a huge boost for their international profile."

Where do these people get their information?

"Mr. President, I'm not sure your information is correct. The guy I spoke to, Mohammed Ibrahim, gave the impression they intended to go for maximum publicity from this stunt. They'd have demanded a huge ransom to be paid into their funds. But afterward, they planned to destroy the ship with everyone on it."

A silence. "Destroy it?" His voice was shocked, "You mean…"

"I mean a suicide mission."

"You're sure?"

"I'd say there's no doubt. It was a one-way trip for those guys."

"Jesus Christ. Give me a minute, Chief."

He muted the sound, and Nolan stood waiting for him to come back. He turned as someone entered the communications room, Boswell with Agent Stowe behind him. The Lieutenant came up to him, his face angry.

"What's going down, Chief? Is that our boss on the line?"

"Yeah, Lt. He put me on hold."

"Next time, remember who's running this platoon. Anyone needs to know anything, it goes through me, clear?"

Behind him, Amelia Stowe was grinning broadly, and Nolan worked to keep his face neutral.

"Clear, Lt."

"Right. Gimme the handset."

He snatched it out of Nolan's hand and put it to his ear.

"Admiral? This is Lieutenant Boswell. I just explained to the Chief he should have passed your call to me, as the officer in command. I assume you want a status report?"

They watched him wait for a reply. The expression on his face was comical, as it moved from shocked incredulity to embarrassment in a couple of seconds.

"Yessir. Nossir. Understood, Sir. Yes, I get it, Mr. President. He's right here. I'll put him back on."

He passed the handset back. "He wants you."

Nolan took it and spoke, "Mr. President, Sir."

"Chief, I ran that past my National Security Adviser, and it changes everything. Especially in the light of what happened in Kenya. These people have begun a new campaign to attack America."

"Al Qaeda? I wasn't aware they'd ever stopped. We've just managed to hold them off until now."

"No, no, not Al Qaeda. You're right. We've uncovered the worst of their plots, and so far I guess we've been lucky to head them off. But this is something different. They've already hit us, just a threat, but it sure kicked sand in our faces and caused a heap of trouble. It looks like a major attack on the US may be on the cards, another 911. Their intention would be to undermine our economy and destroy a hefty chunk of our infrastructure. It's much more serious than we realized."

He was mystified. If it wasn't Al Qaeda, who was it? He was about to put that question, when the President brought the conversation to an end.

"I want your team to work with Agent Stowe. You can pass that on to your Lieutenant. It's an order. They caught us with our pants down this time, and a lot of people lost their lives. Chief, your platoon is on the spot. Talk to Amelia Stowe and put something together. I want you to locate and hit these bastards before they hit us. Nice talking to you, Chief Nolan, and you can pass my congratulations on to the men."

The call ended, he passed the handset to the radio operator, and glanced at Boswell.

"He says we're to work with Agent Stowe, Lt, and conjure up a plan to hit these terrorists before they hit the Continental US."

It was obvious she was working hard to keep a straight face. Lieutenant William Boswell almost went ballistic.

"First you go behind my back and talk to the President of the United States, and now you're telling me to work with this broad. You can forget it. We're the US Navy Seals, not the Fucked-up Bunch of Idiots."

He glared at her, but Amelia Stowe didn't rise to the bait. She just stood with that relaxed and confident half-smile on her face. He switched his gaze to Nolan.

"You'd better tell me the rest of it."

He recited the gist of the conversation. "Just one thing, Lt, the President gave a direct order for us to work with Special Agent Stowe. I mean, if you want to play it differently, I guess you'd need to get back to him. It's way above my pay grade."

He turned on his heel and without a word stalked out of the room. Nolan looked at the girl.

"I guess that means we'll be working together. There are a million things I don't know, but the most important is those guys we just killed. Do I understand they weren't Al Qaeda?"

She shook her head. "It was an Al Qaeda operation. They put the money into it and supplied the weapons and explosives. At least, that's my take on it. But no, I believe that the leader and most of the fighters were a different group."

"Somalis, I guess."

"For sure. You know the terrorist attack on the Westgate Shopping Centre in Kenya?" He nodded, "Same group."

He stared at her. "You're not serious?"

"There's no doubt. This was a broadside from Al Shabaab. And the next one will hit the US of A."

CHAPTER THREE

He lounged in his quarters, listening to the sobbing of the American girl. She was cradling her baby who was crying loudly, upset by his mother's sadness. Should he beat her to make her stop? Perhaps later, when Mukhtar, his baby son, was asleep. In the meantime, he thought about his plans for the Americans, the real enemy, not this weakling girl who he'd taken for a wife. He decided to spare her the beating, enjoying the knowledge of what was to come.

Revenge was a dish best tasted cold, he was well aware of that maxim. He'd already served the aperitif, a slap in the face for their baseball-loving President. Before the main course was served, he would show them the entree. During the war between Russia and Georgia in 2008, he'd come into possession of a pair of Polish-built Grom shoulder-launched missile systems. It was time to send a message to the Americans, time to introduce them to the hard edge of his wrath. The missile was deployed ready, close to one of their major Middle Eastern air bases. It was just a question of waiting for the right target and deciding whom to give the mission to. It could be a suicide mission. The second the missile launched, all hell would break loose, and it was almost certain the shooter would achieve martyrdom.

He thought about his number two, Hasan Anglana. Was he becoming a threat to his leadership? It was possible. Something about the man irritated him lately. His commitment didn't seem so genuine. Yes, it was the perfect solution. He'd brief him later today and send him on his way, for good.

* * *

He had a lot of questions for the pretty young FBI Agent, but they had to wait. His first job was to enlist the aid of the crew and conduct a thorough search of the ship. It was possible one of the passengers or crew could be lying injured in some hidden space. It was equally possible one of the terrorists had hidden themself, waiting to pop out and inflict more hurt and pain.

While the ship was steaming steadily northward, heading for the port of Cartagena in Southern Spain, they took two hours to scour the vessel from deck to bilges, stem to stern. They came up with nothing, and he was able to get Boswell together with Amelia Stowe to pick up where they left off. The Lieutenant sat sullenly in the first officer's cabin that they'd borrowed. The first officer wouldn't need it any more. His corpse was lying in the ship's freezer, along with the other victims of the attack. Nolan sat one end of the berth, and Amelia Stowe the other end. She was still relaxed, still with that same half smile on her face.

"Okay, first of all, you may be asking why I'm involved in this. That's an easy one. My parents came to the US from Somalia, and I'm fluent in Somali and Arabic. As I said earlier, we picked up intelligence on a possible attack on the Arosa Star, and they sent me to join the crew undercover. When I…"

"Look, forget the life history," Boswell snapped, "The President ordered us to cooperate, and I'll make damn sure my men do just that. Just tell me what it is you want."

She stared at him in surprise.

The first thing would be to replace you with someone professional.

She took a breath. "Okay, I'll cut to the chase. The big player behind Al Shabaab in Somalia is a man called Nabil Barre. Since the Westgate Shopping Mall, we've been working with Homeland Security and CIA to project their likely moves, and we figure they're planning a major attack on the US. Do you know anything about Al Shabaab?"

"Bunch of savages," Boswell muttered.

Nolan saw her eyes widened fractionally. It could have been a racial slur on her ancestry, or maybe not. Either way, it was about as unhelpful a remark as he could have made. She rolled with it and took a breath.

"That's something of an understatement, Lieutenant. Savages sums them up quite neatly, but they're much more. As you know, they're a primarily Somali organization. Al Shabaab means 'the youth' or 'the boys'. They got their start as an Al-Qaeda cell, back in 2012. They control large parts of the southern areas of Somalia, and have even imposed Sharia law. We estimate their numbers to be in excess of twenty thousand, and growing rapidly. You can imagine their appeal to impoverished Somali youth. They offer them support, a home, and a cause."

"And a fucking AK-47."

She winced, but once again let it ride. "Sure, that too. They've had their bust-ups with Al Qaeda, but their Kenya operation put them back in the driving seat, and they're all buddy-buddies once more."

"How come the President is so closely involved?" Nolan asked.

She grimaced. "That's a recent development. The White House received a cardboard carton. When they opened it, they found the shrunken heads of five American soldiers, men who'd gone missing in the region. It was a declaration of war, no question. President Taylor took it seriously, and he wants to hit them before they reach American soil."

"Do we know where to find these guys?"

"One guy, Nabil Barre, he's the driving force behind the group, the man with the contacts and the means to make it all happen. Remove him from the equation, and the rest of them could collapse like a pack of cards. And no, we don't know where to find him. That's what President Taylor requires, to locate Barre and take him out."

There was silence in the cabin for almost half a minute. Boswell looked aghast.

"Let's get this straight. There are more than twenty thousand of these Al Shabaab terrorists running around the leafy lanes of Somalia. He wants Bravo to drop in and look him up, then put a bullet in his head. It's lucky Osama bin Laden is dead. Otherwise, he'd want us to deal with him at the same time."

Nolan had had enough. "Take it easy, Lt. It's not Agent Stowe's fault if our bosses want us to do this thing." He looked at her, "Although I have to say, it sounds pretty far-fetched. I mean, what's the population? About five million?"

"Ten million," she corrected him, "and the country occupies an area of a quarter of a million square miles. It's a big place. Fortunately, we won't be going in without help."

It took both men a second or two before they realized what she'd said.

"We?"

"You're joking?" Boswell added.

"I assure you, Lieutenant, I'm deadly serious. I have the background for this operation, the language skills, and a number of contacts in country. The most valuable is likely to be the UN coordinator for Famine Relief, Ashe Ahmed. He is a distant relation of mine. Ashe will be able to sound out the local UN fieldworkers, and with any luck, we'll get a line on Barre. As soon as we have a location, we can go in and finish the job." She saw Boswell's skeptical glance. "If you think this is just a job for macho Navy Seals, think again. I scored in the top three on my marksmanship course at Quantico, and if necessary, I can take the shot."

Nolan said nothing, just watched her.

I wonder has she ever killed a man. Probably not, but she sure is some woman.

She finished up by giving them a detailed insight into the politics and culture of the target country, and finally Boswell declared he needed some fresh air, so he'd go and see how things were going with the men. He walked out the door, and they both breathed a sigh of relief. She turned to face him.

"How the hell did an asshole like that ever get to command a platoon of Navy Seals?"

He shrugged. "He's not so bad, usually. You just learn

to roll with it."

"He doesn't like you," she observed, "Doesn't that make things difficult? I mean, you're in a tough business, and the last thing you need is that kind of internal conflict."

"It's a tough business," he agreed, "I get paid to deal with the difficult. The impossible too."

"You said it. Listen, Chief, I need to get cleaned up. I haven't told you the rest of it. They're picking us up from Cartagena in a Spanish Search and Rescue helicopter. Our destination is Torrejon Air Base, near Madrid. The US Air Force has a flight waiting for us to take us onward to Kuwait, Ali Al Salem Air Base. Your boss will be waiting for you when we get there. He'll deliver the briefing, and we'll kit out ready to go into Somalia."

"My boss? Not the President of the United States again?"

She chuckled. "No chance. This time it's a more familiar face. Rear Admiral Drew Jacks."

"He's coming all the way out to the Middle East just to brief us?"

"No, he's coming to direct the operation in the field. I don't know the details, but he'll probably be based on board a ship in the Indian Ocean, just off the coast of Somalia."

He stared at her. "Are there any more surprises?"

Like the ID wallet she pulled from under her skirt.

She returned his gaze, and there was something in her eyes, a glint perhaps. As if she knew exactly what he was thinking. Which, he considered, was fair. After all, how could a woman as pretty as this one, who would have been the target of advances all her adult life, not know what was in a man's mind?

"We'll see."

* * *

The Spanish Air Force had a helo waiting on the wharf at Cartagena as the ship nosed into harbor. Boswell had vanished, and Lucas Grant made excuses for him. Apparently, the Lieutenant was 'in signals' with the Pentagon. Probably brown-nosing the brass, to make sure credit went where it was due, to him.

Nolan explained the outline of the mission to the men of Bravo. Agent Stowe watched on, and he was thankful for her. At least she diverted them from asking too many awkward questions. Questions he couldn't answer. But the consensus came down to one word.

"Somalia! Fuck it. Begging your pardon, Ma'am."

She took it all well, even smiled at them. It lit up the room. "I've heard worse, a lot worse. You go right ahead and pretend I'm not here."

As if that is possible.

"Admiral Jacks is waiting for us in Kuwait, so he'll be able to fill us in on the details. I can tell you this operation is the result of months of intelligence work, and the threat is very real. They've already sent their calling card to the White House."

She explained about the package of heads, and the room was quiet for a few moments.

"You should be aware they are rumored to have shoulder launched missile systems. They could be planning on shooting down an American airliner. We need to keep an eye out for those."

"What's new about that?" Will Bryce rumbled in his

deep baritone, "The Somali RPG7s hit us hard during Gothic Serpent."

"There aren't RPG7s. I'm talking Polish GROM 2s."

They all stared at her in shock. "GROM 2s. Now that is new," Nolan acknowledged.

She nodded. "Yes, it is."

"Chief, what about infil and exfil?" Brad broke the silence, "What do we know?"

"Haven't a clue. Ask Jacks when we reach Kuwait. My guess would be a night HALO jump, so we'll at least catch up on our training. Then again, if the target is on the coast, we could approach underwater."

"Did the FBI teach you to swim?" Vince Merano asked Agent Stowe.

"Yep, I even got the lifeguard gold medal."

That earned a laugh. They were starting to relax when Lucas Grant growled, "Did they teach you anything about Operation Gothic Serpent, Ma'am?"

The room went quiet. Gothic Serpent was a 1993 operation conducted by United States Special Operations forces. Their primary mission was to capture Mohamed Farrah Aidid, a vicious warlord. Supervised by the Joint Special Operations Command, JSOC, the operation was a disaster.

She stared at his grim face for a moment. "They didn't need to. I lost a member of my family during the Battle of Mogadishu. I doubt I'll ever forget. It's not easy to see a relative come home in a coffin."

Grant nodded, and his gaze softened a little. "No, it is not."

* * *

They docked in the crowded port of Cartagena. As ports go, it had little to distinguish it from similar docks the world over, except for its history. Cartagena translated as New Carthage. The North African warlord Hannibal, who almost overturned the mighty Roman Empire, made it his European headquarters. The city was filled with history dating back to the Punic Wars, with an excavated amphitheater, and even a section of the original defensive wall.

The helicopter waiting on the concrete pad close to the wharf was a Spanish Air Force Sikorski S76, fitted for Search and Rescue. A crewman was waiting for them at the foot of the gangplank. He greeted them briefly and led them across to the aircraft. The rotors were already turning, and as the last man climbed into the cabin, the big helo lifted off into the clear blue sky of Southern Spain.

The flight was hot and noisy, and it reminded each man of how long it had been since they'd eaten or slept. Nolan glanced across at Boswell, who was sitting with Grant, as usual. They were talking to each other, their heads close together, so they could hear over the roar of the engine and rotor blades.

Talking about what?

He knew for sure that Boswell wanted his pal Lucas Grant to replace him. He'd almost said as much on more than one occasion. Sly hints, like 'Isn't it time you thought about a move, Chief? I could maybe get your promotion to Master Chief. I'd like to think the senior men in Bravo rotated, so keep it in mind'. It was more than hints. The man's attitude had changed, a one hundred and eighty degree turn. When he first joined the unit, he had only one priority. Lieutenant William Boswell.

After a couple of missions, he'd settled down and seemed to have the makings of a good officer. Everything changed about the time he brought Grant into the platoon. It wasn't hard to figure. His wealthy family connections mapped out his future for him, and they'd have been concerned to make certain he pointed his feet in the right direction. A stint in the Navy Seals, and then he'd retire a hero. Aided by Lucas Grant, who'd already found celebrity, at least within military and government after the bin Laden raid. And Boswell now had an even greater incentive to push him to the top. His older brother was due to inherit the family fortune. However, he was recently diagnosed as terminally ill, which meant Lieutenant Boswell was in line to take the lot.

Then it was a sure step into politics, probably Congress, followed by the Senate and maybe even a run at the top job. He shuddered.

President William Boswell, God help us all.

The Lieutenant would see Nolan as an obstacle to his immediate success. He wanted the glow of the hero of the bin Laden raid at his side when he claimed credit for successful operations. Not an anonymous Navy man like Nolan.

It wasn't that simple. What Boswell did in his own time and on his own dollar was up to him. When it involved the safety and security of the men of Seal Team Bravo, it was something different. His push for glory was a problem, no question. The men were worried, and worried men were at less than a hundred percent efficiency. They got killed. Lately they'd hit more than their fair share of trouble because of the Lieutenant's poor decision-making. Men had been wounded. Men had been killed.

Fuck him! I'm staying, no matter how Boswell tries to sideline me.

He'd have to be careful. The man was ruthless, but he was no fool. Thankfully, Lucas Grant was a straight shooter. He'd have little choice but to support his platoon commander, especially if he intended to hang on to the man's coattails after he left the Service, so he'd back up the Lt, but not if it risked the security of the unit. Boswell, on the other hand, had no such scruples.

He made an effort to shove it out of his mind and drifted into a light doze.

"Chief Nolan."

A woman's voice, it was Special Agent Amelia Stowe. He checked the time. He'd had all of twelve minutes.

"Yeah?"

"You weren't trying to sleep or anything?"

"Nope. What is it?"

"I, uh, well, I guess… I wanted to say thanks." She saw his puzzlement, "For supporting me. That Lieutenant of yours, I get the impression he would have done anything to make things difficult for me."

He shrugged. "I wouldn't know about him. But whatever, you're welcome."

"He doesn't like women."

Nolan had already drifted away into his thoughts. It was this girl; something about her seemed to distract him. Not the ideal person to take on an operation. Except the problem was his problem. He'd have to deal with it himself.

Her words jolted him.

Boswell doesn't like women? Is it possible the officer is gay? Moreover, if he is, how does it change things? It shouldn't change anything, but...

There was always the but. Not every gay man was comfortable with others knowing his secret, even though things had changed, in and out of the military. Then again, Amelia Stowe could be wrong. And there was another possibility. Boswell was one of those vile sons of bitches who didn't like anyone, male of female. It was something else to watch for.

She let him drift back into a doze until the flight crew alerted them they were approaching Torrejon. He looked out the window with interest. Torrejon was a major Spanish Air Force base, as well as a secondary civilian airport for Madrid. Situated twenty kilometers outside Spain's capital city, the strip had been home to the United States Strategic Air Command, SAC, during the Cold War. Now, the nuclear-armed B-52s were long gone, and the stands were littered with fighter and support planes. The helo touched down close to a squadron of familiar aircraft, McDonnell Douglas F/A 18 Hornets, capable of flying supersonic at speeds of Mach 1.8. These guys had good taste in their chosen fighter jets.

As he watched, a pair of the Hornets began taxiing toward the strip, and as they were disembarking from the Sikorski, they took off with a roar. He noted that two pairs of General Electric F404-GE-402 turbofans could make one hell of a racket. The warm Spanish air was heavy with the stink of kerosene, as the fighters leapt into the sky and climbed almost vertically.

A couple of hotshot pilots, no doubt. Then again, what fighter pilot isn't?

They had a gleaming white bus waiting for them close to the helipad. A Spanish Air Force officer approached

Boswell.

"Sir, I am Capitano Luis Moreno. If you care to board the bus, your transport is waiting."

Boswell fixed him with a sour look. "I thought we'd have a chance for some chow. What's the hurry?"

The Spaniard stared at him in surprise. "I was told to transfer you for the onward journey as quickly as possible. As for the need to hurry, I have no idea. Those were my orders. Do you wish me to ask if it is possible to change the arrangement?"

He gave a loud theatrical sigh. "Okay, no need to sweat." He turned to Nolan. "Get 'em aboard, Chief."

"Roger that."

They were already drifting toward the white bus. It was the same as used in civilian airports when the aircraft stand was some distance from the terminal; room for eighty people, with seating for ten. The doors closed, and the driver stamped on the gas to make the vehicle lurch forward.

Yep, exactly like the way they do it in civilian airports.

They threaded between rows of parked aircraft, even a big Airbus, just like the civilian passenger jet, but this one was painted in the livery of the Spanish Air Force. The bus halted as a generator truck passed in front of them, another jerk and they were on the move again. They approached their destination, a familiar sight.

"Déjà vu," Brad grinned.

"That it is," Nolan acknowledged.

They slowed next to a big Boeing C 17, and a glance at the tail number showed it was the same aircraft they'd used for training over Luneberg Heath in Germany. The driver stamped on the brake pedal, another lurch, and the bus stopped right next to the ramp. They filed out of the bus, up the ramp, and once again they were inside the vast aluminum cavern of the Globemaster. The crewman who greeted them did a double take.

"Christ, you again. Doesn't the US Navy have any other Seals they can use?"

"It sure feels that way," Will replied.

"There is another explanation, PO Bryce," Boswell interjected, "When they want the best, we're the ones they call."

Lucas Grant was right behind him. The Seal Team 6 DEVGRU vet grimaced but kept quiet.

They pulled down the jump seats and made themselves as comfortable as possible for the journey. The engines were already spooling up, and the interior began to darken as the ramp closed. Once again, they were treated to the ear-shattering roar of the four mighty Pratt and Whitney turboprops as they warmed up for takeoff. It was the start of a journey of four thousand kilometers, all the way down the Mediterranean and across Iraq to the Persian Gulf state of Kuwait.

And then what? A journey into Somalia to kill warlord planning an attack on the United States mainland.

Nolan knew it would be more difficult than that, a lot more difficult. Their boss, Rear Admiral Drew Jacks, would be waiting for them at Ali Al Salem Air Base, Kuwait, and doubtless they'd get answers to many questions. If the attack were in an advanced stage, killing Barre wouldn't put a stop to it. It meant a vital part of the mission would be intelligence gathering. And then he thought about Amelia Stowe.

It explained a lot. Without doubt, she was one of the

Fed's Somali specialists, given her ancestry. The Somali community in the US was a source of recruitment for Islamic extremists. It was no surprise they'd want someone who was comfortable with the language and culture to monitor them. Her presence on the cruise liner as an undercover agent to investigate an Al Qaeda attack suggested she'd done her homework. If they uncovered intel during the coming operation, there'd be no one better able to assess its value than she would.

Once again, he tried to doze and take up on some rest. The operation was gathering momentum, and he had little doubt when they reached the Middle East, there'd be few opportunities for shuteye. He managed to shut out the din of the vibrating, echoing aluminum cavern they were flying in, and the excruciating discomfort of the hard jump seat. Within minutes, he was asleep.

His subconscious was lit up by scenes of battle, missiles, automatic fire, and helicopter gunships racing across the sky in support of ground troops. But it wasn't anything he'd experienced first-hand. He was recalling the movie, Black Hawk Down. The epic depiction of Operation Gothic Serpent, when US forces, including Rangers and Delta Force, went into Somalia to capture the infamous warlord Aidid.

* * *

In his nightmare he was part of the battle, looking down at the devastation from the vantage point of a Hughes Defender MH-6 'Little Bird'. Maybe it was the talk of Al Shabaab having ground-to-air missiles, but they were passing an apartment block, and a kid stood on the roof with an RPG7 missile pointed straight at them. They were so close, he could see the holes in the kid's jeans and the white trainers he wore on his feet. If he fired, the chances were the Little Bird would go down.

He angled his long rifle, the Mk 11 SWS, and aimed. The boy was in his sights, and Nolan hesitated, his finger already taking up pressure on the trigger. The target couldn't have been more than ten years old. Was this what war had become, killing children to save yourself? Yet he had no choice. It wasn't just him. There was a pilot, a crewman, and four Seals on board the helo. He took up the final pressure, and the heavy slug left the barrel to travel the short distance to its target.

He saw the boy fall one way, and his missile tube rolled away from him. He kept watching through the Leupold Vari-X riflescope, and he could see where his bullet had entered. The range had been so short, he'd been able to go for the headshot, and now the ruined face filled the optics. Strangely, although his heavy bullet had taken out the nose and mouth, the boy's eyes still stared back at him, filled with condemnation. And then another man stood next to the boy's body, and in his hands he held a second RPG7 launcher. Nolan reeled back in shock. It wasn't a Somali. The man had a white face, blonde hair, and a small, blonde mustache. Boswell. No, no...!

* * *

"Chief."

He struggled for a moment. Someone had hold of his arms. Then he opened his eyes, and he was looking at the face of Will Bryce. Amelia Stowe was standing next to him, her face anxious.

"You okay?" she asked, her voice pitched just loud enough to be heard above the cacophony of the C-17 interior.

"I'm fine."

She looked relieved. "Do you normally talk in your sleep? Shout in your sleep would be more like it. I could hear you even over this racket."

"It's nothing."

She raised her eyebrows. "We're coming up on Kuwait. We should be landing in about fifteen minutes."

"Thanks."

She gave him a tight smile. They both knew she understood he was thanking her for easing him down from the tumult of a vicious nightmare. It was already hot inside the cabin, which told him they were flying low above the desert sands of Kuwait. He got to his feet and began to get the circulation moving.

"I'll take stroll up to the flight deck. I need to loosen up."

"Sounds like a good idea."

He left her, walked through the cargo hold, up the steps, and through the narrow door into the cockpit. The pilot, a USAF Captain, was swigging a can of Coke, ice cold, with beads of condensation formed around the tin. He looked at Nolan.

"You want one?"

"Like you wouldn't believe."

The man reached down to an insulated box and fished him one out. Nolan pulled the tab, glugged it down, and looked at the Captain.

"Thanks, it tasted like champagne."

"No sweat, you fly around these parts and you learn keep a few in stock."

He glanced ahead at the instruments and dials, and made a couple of adjustments.

"Autopilot is off, I have the controls."

The co-pilot looked around. "You have the controls," he confirmed, "We should be over the field in nine minutes."

"Copy that."

The pilot chatted to Nolan while he kept staring ahead, steering the giant aircraft as if he had his own human autopilot switched on.

"I take it you boys are headed to some hairy corner of the Middle East?"

"Something like that."

He smiled. "It's okay. We're used to flying guys like you around the world. We never know where you are headed, but it doesn't stop us speculating." He glanced aside at his co-pilot. "Larry, what's your best guess for this bunch of US government licensed assassins?"

The man chuckled. "Now let me think. Yemen, that's my guess. Plenty of nasties running around that place, am I right?"

"Spot-on," Nolan confirmed.

The pilot let out a belly laugh. "Spot-on my ass. Larry, if this guy says they're going to Yemen, they're going nowhere near the place."

The other man grimaced. "Spooks, same the world over, but I have to hand it to you guys, you took down Osama. That was one helluva job. Any of your guys take part in that one?"

"Not one."

"Yeah, right."

They flew on, and Nolan sipped the last of his Coke. Even in a few minutes, it was lukewarm. Something about this part of the world, fly at ten thousand meters, and it's cold enough to freeze off your balls. Or come down to a few hundred meters above the ground, and it's hot enough to fry your ass. He could see the airfield a couple of clicks ahead.

Not long now. With any luck, we'll have time for some chow and a long cold shower.

He was looking forward to meeting up with Jacks. No matter what his troubles with Boswell, he'd be able to have a serious talk with the Admiral about the coming operation. He knew Jacks wouldn't like what he had to say. They were stepping into a hornets' nest, and although he hadn't seen the mission brief, it had the stink of something dreamed up by the President. He recalled Taylor's anger when he'd spoken to him. It was the wrong emotion entirely when you were planning a military operation. Especially when you're going to kick sand in the face of the Somalis. They had a reputation of kicking back. Hard.

He turned as someone came through to the flight deck. Lucas Grant.

"Chief, there's something…"

"Missile launch ahead of us! Evasive action! Hard to starboard! Firing flares, now. "

The pilot reacted in a split second and threw the control column over. The huge aircraft banked steeply to the right and plunged nearer to the ground. Nolan could see the missile a kilometer in front of them, trailing smoke as it blazed straight at them. The aircraft was alive with warning sirens and shouted orders from the crew, but he couldn't take his eyes off that weapon closing on them.

He had no way of knowing what kind of missile they were facing, but he was already registering that it was tracking them with an infrared aiming sensor. He'd seen plenty of RPG7s in his time, but this was something different. Faster, and it responded much quicker to the frantic efforts of the pilot to decoy it from its inexorable course. Either side of the aircraft was lit up with flares deployed from the Globemaster, but the missile ignored them and bored straight to the port side engine.

At the last second, they veered again, in a maneuver that almost tore off the wings. Instead of slamming into the engine and exploding close to the fuselage, which would have torn off the entire wing, the abrupt change of course caused it to impact low on the front of the aircraft, right on the nose and several meters below the windshield. He was thrown to the deck with the last maneuver, and so he didn't see the explosion and jet of flame that spurted up in front of them. The windows in the nose shattered instantly, turning the flight deck into a maelstrom of flying glass fragments.

"I can't see, I can't see!" the pilot screamed, "Larry, take over!"

The co-pilot didn't reply, and Nolan crawled over the glass-strewn deck to find him unconscious, jammed into the gap between the seats.

He shouted at the pilot, "The co-pilot is down. What do you want me to do?"

The man seemed to freeze in that moment. He shook his head, a ghastly sight, covered in blood from a thousand cuts.

"There's nothing you can do. We're going down. Tell your buddies the aircraft is about to crash."

CHAPTER FOUR

The wind screamed through the empty gaps in the windshield, and the big aircraft was still losing height. Nolan climbed to his feet, and he could see the ground only three hundred meters below, sitting at a crazy angle as the aircraft yawed more and more to starboard.

He reacted immediately and jumped over the body of the co-pilot and into his seat. He put his hands on the control column but met with resistance, and he saw Larry's leg jammed against the stick. Even as he reached down to move him aside, Lucas Grant was there, pulling the body away to free the controls. Nolan nodded his thanks and set to recovering the aircraft's course. His first move was to push the throttle levers forward. He knew they'd need plenty of power to regain control, and he recalled what was needed was to slowly ease their descent until he could put the nose up and gain height.

The problem was vision. The slipstream knifed in through the broken windshield and almost blinded him. He reached up to pull down the goggles from his helmet, but in the emergency they'd slid off and disappeared. He couldn't search for them. He was trying to control the aircraft and knew if he took his hands off the column, they could flip over.

Grant pulled a pair of goggles down over Nolan's eyes. At last, he could see, yet they were not out of trouble. The controls were sluggish; obviously the missile had damaged the control systems. Probably he was flying on some second or third set of backup system. Still, he managed to slow their rate of descent. Only slow it, they were still going down. He glanced aside. Grant had helped the pilot out of his seat and took his place.

"Chief, you want me to lower the gear?"

"Not yet," he shouted over the scream of the wind, "We need to gain height to level off. The landing gear will make it more difficult. Contact the tower, and tell them we have an emergency."

"I think they know that."

Nolan risked a quick glance, and sure enough, the field below was alive with racing emergency vehicles, fire trucks, and ambulances.

"In that case, I need a hand with the controls. You flown one of these things?"

"Couple of hours in a T44 Pegasus, the Navy's Beechcraft King Air. Nothing this size."

Great.

He'd checked out on the Navy's T44 Pegasus turboprop, and once he'd sat in the right-hand seat of a C-130, which was another turboprop, although it did have four engines; useful experience, but not ideal preparation for flying a crippled giant Boeing C-17 Globemaster. Let alone making an emergency landing.

"Roger that. Contact the tower. We need a clear runway. The moment we have control, we're landing, and it could be hairy. I guess the guys in the back know that, too."

"For sure."

"Okay, ease back on the throttles. We're almost level. We need to make a gentle turn and come back in."

Grant talked to Ali Al Salem Air Base, and they assured him the runway was already cleared for their emergency landing.

"What about the missile shooters?" He heard him ask them.

"We sent people to look for them. We'll get them."

"Amen to that."

Nolan managed to bring up the nose a little more and climbed to a thousand meters. Then he began the long, slow process of bringing the aircraft around ready for a second approach to the strip. He heard Grant calling for a medic to come forward and attend to the crew. Seconds later, Zeke Murray appeared on the flight deck. Amelia Stowe was right behind him, and they began pulling the injured men away from the front of the cockpit to make them more comfortable at the rear. Then they began dressing their wounds. Both men had suffered badly from the influx of glass and debris, and their faces were red with blood, their skin crisscrossed with scores of gashes.

The eyes were something different. Rudimentary first aid would not be sufficient to remove glass fragments from them, and their chances of flying again were remote. Even if they weren't permanently blinded, they'd be unlikely to recover the near-perfect vision required of a military pilot.

Nolan struggled to bring the aircraft in a wide circle to make the final approach for a landing. Everything was wrong; the controls sluggish, the aerodynamics thrown off-balance after the explosion, and there'd be no way to assess the damage until they were on the ground. It was ten minutes before they were in position to try for a landing. The airfield was three kilometers in front of them, and they were flying low, at three hundred meters. He'd no idea of the landing speed for the huge cargo jet, and besides, even if he did do it by the book, the damage from the missile strike meant everything had changed.

He told Grant to bring the air speed down and gave him the word.

"Increase flaps and drop the gear. We're going in."

Literally. There'd be no second chance. The aircraft was flying as much by willpower as the power of its engines and the aerodynamics. The flaps rumbled out, and the aircraft slowed. The big motors under the wings were loud as the hatches opened and the big wheels lowered. But no noise came from beneath their feet, the nose wheel.

"It's stuck," Grant shouted over the roar of the slipstream, "The explosion damaged the gear."

"Bring the wheels back up. We'll go belly down." He shouted to Zeke, who was at the rear of the cockpit, tending to the casualties with Amelia. "Go aft, and warn them we're making a belly landing. I guess thirty seconds, no more."

"Roger that."

He rushed out to the cargo hold, and Nolan made final preparations for the landing. He knew there were a hundred things he should have done, like jettisoning unnecessary fuel, and securing some of the electrical systems to guard against fire. But he didn't have time to read several thousand pages of aircraft manual. It would have to be a 'seat of the pants' landing.

Nearer, nearer, they brushed over the lighting tower at the head of the runway, and then they were over the tarmac. Either side of them, emergency vehicles were racing along to catch up with them. There was little he could do except lower the big aircraft as gently as possible, which wouldn't be very gentle, and no way of knowing how far off the ground they were, as he was sitting so high up in the cockpit. He looked ahead and was astonished that already he was halfway along the runway, and still they hadn't touched down. It was now or never. He pushed the column forward and shouted.

"Hold on!"

The aircraft smashed into the ground and sent a bone-jarring shock through everyone aboard. Incredibly, the aircraft weighing in excess of two hundred thousand pounds bounced. Maybe a couple of feet, but it bounced before it settled back on the tarmac and skidded along, sending up showers of sparks in its wake. Speed slowed, and Nolan watched the ground speed indicator carefully. Seventy, sixty, forty; it was still going too fast. They were close to the end of the runway, and already the fire trucks either side were firing jets of foam over them to contain any chance of fire. They finally stopped when the nose of the wrecked Globemaster hit the lighting tower at the far end of the runway, and it tilted over at an acute angle.

He snapped open his harness. Grant did the same, and they hurtled back to help drag the two wounded pilots to the door. Someone in the cargo hold had the sense to get the doors open, and men were wading out through the sickening foam. They helped pull out the casualties. Nolan gave Amelia Stowe a hand down where men waited to help them to the ground, and then he exited the aircraft with Grant. They didn't stop running until they were outside the extinguishing foam and had their feet firmly on hard tarmac. He turned to Grant.

"You did a good job back there, thanks."

The Seal vet nodded. "That landing was down to you."

He stared at him for several seconds, and Nolan had the impression he wanted to tell him something. But he seemed to change his mind, and he grinned. "I hope they're well insured."

They joined the men who'd climbed out of the cargo hold. Vehicles were approaching from the terminal, half a dozen Humvees. Will Bryce was talking to Boswell. He seemed angry about something, and the Lieutenant whirled as they approached.

"Chief, I've given PO Bryce an order. He seems to think he can please himself in this unit."

A new voice intruded. A voice they all knew well. "That's because he can."

Admiral Jacks had just stepped out of a Humvee bearing the markings of the Kuwait Air Force.

"Good job, men, getting that bus down. Who was flying it?"

Grant pointed at Nolan. "Him."

Nolan pointed at Grant. "Him too. It was a joint effort."

He nodded. "You did damn well. Lieutenant Boswell, you're lucky to have men like these serving in Bravo. You should be proud of them."

"Yes, Sir, I am."

Nolan smiled at the Lieutenant's attempt to cover his look of dislike. He didn't fool anyone. Least of all Jacks.

"Let's get you men over to the terminal and checked

over by the medics."

* * *

They were enjoying a meal in one of the base canteens. In view of the attack, the Kuwaiti Air Force had surrounded the building with troops. The base commander had also assured them they were conducting a thorough search for the missile shooters.

"We are a desert nation," he said grimly, "It will be difficult for them to hide in this area. I promise you we will have them soon. As soon as we do, our intelligence people will question them and find out where this attack came from."

He left them to their chow. Jacks stayed and apologized for the need to brief them right there and then.

"The clock's ticking, guys. The enemy is close to mounting an attack on the US, and after that missile launch, I don't think any of us are in any doubt they mean serious business."

He went through the details of the coming operation. Some they knew, like the destination, Somalia. Some they didn't, like infil and exfil, and the big question. Nolan halted the Admiral when the name came up.

"Sir, this Somali warlord, Nabil Barre, what are our orders? I know the US wants him, sure, but dead or alive?"

Jacks' face was as bleak as an Alaskan winter. "You bring that guy back alive, and there'll be a trial that will make world headlines. In addition, his buddies are sure to take hostages to try and do a deal. Alive isn't an option."

"Roger that."

Jacks continued. "We'll fly you down the Gulf, out into

the Indian Ocean. You'll parachute into the sea where a sub is waiting to pick you up and carry your party to a point ten kilometers off the coast of Somalia. We can't take you any nearer. The Somalis have patrol boats that are pretty active in that area. "

"It's a long swim," Grant observed.

"Not this time. You'll be traveling first class, courtesy of our Seal Delivery Vehicles. The sub has a Dry Dock Shelter on the deck, with two Mk 8 SDVs inside. You'll approach the shore underwater, and you shouldn't have any problem reaching the outskirts of the town undetected. You'll be met by Ashe Ahmed, the local UN Commissioner."

"The UN? It's not like them to get involved in a kill mission," Will Bryce observed.

Jacks nodded. "Yeah, you're right. Ashe is sick of burying his people every time Barre's men hijack their food convoys, so he's offered to help out. He's made it clear he will do anything to remove Barre from the equation. And you're going to need his help. Kismayo is Barre's town, and it needs a local with good connections to help you find a way through it. We don't want another Gothic Serpent. When the operation is complete, the Navy will send in a couple of fast RIBs to bring you out to one of our missile cruisers we're diverting from the Gulf. Any questions so far?"

"You mentioned Gothic Serpent," Nolan said, "Sir, are you sure this isn't just a repeat?"

The mention of the ill-fated 1993 operation to arrest two aides of the Somali warlord Mohamed Aidid, codenamed Gothic Serpent, caused more than a few shudders. At the end of the fierce firefight in and around Mogadishu, eighteen US troops from the combined Ranger and Delta

Force contingent were dead. Two Black Hawk helicopters were destroyed, another seriously damaged. It was a blow to American prestige, and a boost for the Somalis, even though more than a thousand of their people were killed. The politicians had decreed 'never again'.

There was a further footnote to the operation. Osama bin Laden, who was living in Sudan at the time, cited this operation as an example of American weakness and vulnerability to an attack. Some suggested it might have inspired him to plan the attacks on 911. True or false, the so-called 'Battle of Mogadishu' triple underlined the strength of Somali response when they were under attack.

Boswell was the first to react, cutting across Admiral Jacks.

"What's up, Chief? You nervous about taking on those black Somali savages?"

Before he could answer, Jacks cleared his throat. "Uh, Lieutenant, Special Agent Amelia Stowe is of Somali extraction. She is also black."

Boswell glowed red. "Right, yeah. Sorry, I just meant..."

"You been to Somalia, Lieutenant?"

"No, Sir."

"I thought not. Chief Petty Officer Nolan was part of a kill mission inside that country before you joined the unit, a successful kill mission. So I'd be careful about upsetting these people. Without Nolan and Agent Stowe, I doubt you'd have a ghost of a chance at succeeding with this."

"No, Sir." He shut up.

"Good. You were saying, Chief?"

Nolan nodded. "Gothic Serpent. They failed because they underestimated the enemy, and when things went wrong, they had no armor to support their withdrawal, as

I recall. If we hit similar problems, it would be a field day for our enemies. The US can't take another bloody noise in that region, Sir."

"You're right, but this mission is different. I'm hoping you're in and out before they even know you're there. However," he held up his hand to forestall the obvious argument, "If things do go wrong, point taken. You need something to fight them with. I've arranged for some heavy firepower to help out if things go awry.

First, I have two UAVs, Predators, lined up to give you cover all the time the mission is ongoing. Even if they need to refuel, it means one can be overhead at all times. Second, the Somali RPGs, they are the principal problem if a firefight develops. I realize the missile that hit your C-17 was something different, and we'll analyze what they used as soon as possible. However, if you run into any of their RPG7s on this mission, I want you to have the means to hit back hard. You'll be carrying two of our M3 MAAWS. They'll be fitted with an image intensifier system, so you'll be able to acquire targets at night. Which is a luxury your enemies will not have."

The men broke into smiles. Known as 'Carl Gustavs', the missile systems had the range and the stopping power to deal with anything the Somalis threw at them.

They can even destroy armor, at ranges of up to a thousand meters, Nolan thought to himself. Then it struck him.

"He has armor, Sir? This warlord, Barre?"

Jacks hesitated a fraction of a second. "Not as such, Chief. But he does have a line into the HQ of the local Somali National Army, and they do have a couple of old Soviet era T54s."

The room went quiet.

"T54s," Vince repeated, "They're big bastards, Admiral."

"It's doubtful you'll even smell one, let alone see it. But if you do, you'll have the Hellfires overhead, and the M3s on the ground, so you can deal with anything you come up against." He checked his wristwatch. "I need to break this up. They're flying in a replacement Globemaster to take you out to the drop point. Your gear is already here, in another part of the building. Weapons, underwater gear, and commo, it's all ready for you. Take a few hours. I'll send someone to come and find you in good time, and get you kitted up ready for when your C-17 lands and refuels. That's all."

They sat in silence for several minutes after he left. Boswell was first to speak. He got to his feet, as if he was about to make a speech, which he was.

"Men, just a few words. This is an operation as vital as killing bin Laden. I know Somalia is a tough country, but remember, this guy Barre is part of the same group, Al Shabaab who slaughtered those people in the Kenya shopping mall. Now they plan to take the war to the US. No matter how it goes, when you get back home, you can roll up your sleeves and show your scars, and tell them these wounds I picked up in Somalia. We're a small unit, a band of brothers, going up against an enemy that has proved their strength. I'll tell you, just like after the raid on bin Laden's compound, every single US Navy Seal will regret they weren't a part of this fight. Let's give 'em hell!"

He sat down as if he'd run out of words. Nolan was thoughtful.

Something about those words, they sound familiar.

The room was silent after his exhortation. It was as

if he was talking to a bunch of green recruits. Someone clapped and all eyes turned. Amelia Stowe.

"You've read Shakespeare, Lieutenant," she exclaimed in mock astonishment.

His brow furrowed, but underneath his face had reddened.

Shakespeare has nothing to do with it," he replied.

It was obvious to everyone in the room he was fighting to keep his voice level. The FBI Agent was having none of it.

"Henry V. You paraphrased the famous speech. 'And hold their manhoods cheap while any speaks, that fought with us upon Saint Crispin's day.' Something like that, nice job though," she concluded with more than a trace of irony.

Nolan was close to Boswell, and he heard him mutter under his breath, "Fuck you."

* * *

Hasan Anglana ran. His loader, Ali Feiruz, stumbled along behind him. After the successful launch of the Grom missile, they'd watched as it tracked the big American aircraft and then impacted on the nose. They both cheered as they waited for the massive plane to crash into the ground. Yet incredibly, they'd managed to regain control, and even brought it in for a belly landing.

He cursed as he ran. Sheikh Barre would be unimpressed. In order to acquire the two missiles he'd paid a large sum, and bringing them into the country had involved even more money for bribes. Perhaps he could persuade him to allow him a chance at using the second missile. Next time, he'd launch at a lower level and make doubly sure of a hit.

He heard the sound of vehicles in the distance, and more serious, the clatter of a helicopter climbing from the base. They were both running as fast as possible, and yet he knew it wasn't fast enough. The problem was the launcher. It was slowing his loader down. He was about to instruct Ali to ditch it when he had a better idea.

"We have to split up. You have west, and I'll go in east. Make sure you look after the Grom launcher. The Sheikh insisted we bring it back." Ali started to protest, but he overrode him. "It's the only way. Listen, I'll try and distract them to give you a chance to get away. As soon as you're out of sight, I'll wait for them and shoot the first man to appear. They'll come after me, and you'll have a chance to escape."

The man stared at him. "You could sacrifice your life, Hasan. You would do this for me?"

"Fool, I do it for the launcher. You must return with it. Our lives are as nothing. Now go!"

The young man stumbled away, but he was slow, burdened by the heavy weapon. He also carried an AK-47 slung on his back, together with ten clips of ammunition. It would be enough. The slow-moving man would attract the attention of the pursuers, giving him a chance to disappear. He briefly considered ditching his own AK-47 but decided against it. He had one spare clip of ammunition, hardly enough to slow him down. He ran.

A few minutes later, he heard the sound of gunfire in the distance. He dived beneath a clump of bushes and looked up into the sky. The helicopter was hovering over a stretch of ground five hundred meters away, and the gunner was pouring a stream of bullets at a target on the ground. He smiled to himself; his plan had worked. With any luck, when they inspected the body of Ali, they would assume he'd work on his own and not look for another man.

He examined his hide and decided to stay there. Any movement would attract the Kuwaitis, whereas if he'd stayed where he was, he could wait until they'd gone and then slip away. He decided to abandon the assault rifle and ammunition. If he was caught, he could claim to be a foreign worker. Provided he was unarmed. He started to scrabble on the ground to dig a hole to bury it. He was so absorbed in his task that he failed to hear the trackers approach.

"Come out with your hands up!"

He jerked, as if someone had given him an electric shock. Slowly, he looked around to see a face staring in at him through the bushes.

Have they seen the weapon?

"Leave the gun. You won't be needing it where you're going."

Sadly, he felt the crushing weight of defeat. He hadn't completely destroyed the aircraft, and Ali was dead. He would be dead too, unless he could come up with a convincing story.

I found the gun? Yes, that might work.

He crawled out and stood with his hands held high. In front of him, a Kuwaiti officer stared at him. Then the man stepped forward and clubbed him with a huge automatic pistol, and everything went dark as he fell to the sand.

"Tell us your name! Who do you work for?"

The voice seemed to be coming from inside his head.

His eyelids were heavy, but he managed to open them and found he was staring into a bright light. When he tried to move his hands, they were stuck. He looked down. He was strapped to a steel chair. He glanced around the room, and in the wash from the light, he could see the tools and instruments of torture racked around the walls. His heart thumped, for he knew now what he faced. The Kuwaitis had a certain reputation with torture.

He tried to stall them at first, but it was a feeble effort. When they started pulling out his fingernails, he gave them the name of his organization, Al Shabaab. At first, he refused to tell them who'd sent him to destroy an American aircraft. They went to work on his teeth, and when they'd ripped out two of them, he gave them Barre. He knew if he ever got back to Kismayo, he was a dead man for giving up the information. Except few prisoners escaped the Kuwaiti torture chambers, so getting back wasn't likely. No, his best option right now was to give them everything they wanted, and pray for a quick death.

"Have you told us everything?"

"I have, I have," he screamed.

His interrogator was the officer who'd hit him with the pistol when they took him. The man was big, with the hard, cruel face common to men in his profession. He stepped forward, and in his hands he held a shining steel instrument with a hooked claw at its tip.

"You know what this is? It's something I devised. When spies enter the State of Kuwait, they see things they are not supposed to see. My job is to discourage them. I find that removing their eyes serves a dual purpose. They tend to tell me everything, and afterward, they will be unable to spy on my country again."

"No, no," he shook his head violently, "I told you everything I know."

The man smiled. "In that case, I'll make sure you learn nothing more."

The Kuwaiti felt excited. In truth, intruders to his country were few. What was the point after the Iraqi invasion in 1990, which demonstrated to the world how seriously America took threats to its oil-producing ally? It had been some time since a specimen such as this one had fallen into his hands. And he was sure the man still had more to tell. He pushed the hooked instrument forward. As it went into the eye, the man let out a piercing scream, as expected.

"Why did you target that aircraft?"

"I don't know. I don't know! I was ordered to do it. He didn't tell me why."

"This Sheikh Barre?"

"Yes, yes, aargh..."

* * *

They were grouped inside the terminal, waiting for their ride out to the C17 that was on the tarmac, ready to take them down to the Indian Ocean for their rendezvous with the submarine. They saw the bus motoring toward them, and then Jacks stepped into the room, wearing camos and full jump gear. Boswell turned to him in surprise.

"Admiral! What gives?"

"Didn't you know? I'm coming with you, and I'll make my base on the submarine. I want to be on hand in case you need anything. I'm sure you realize our nuclear boats have one of the finest communication systems in the world, and I'd sooner run things from a little piece of America, rather than…" He gestured around at the dusty air base. Kuwaitis were walking around, most of them wearing Arab headdress over their more conventional military uniforms. They were allies sure, up to a point.

"That's good news, Sir," he responded with enthusiasm.

The other men smiled to themselves. One thing was the sure, when he reached Washington, he'd already be expert in the arcane art of kissing political ass.

"I'm happy you're pleased. Before we board the bus, I can tell you they caught the guys who launched the missile that hit your plane. One of them died, the other was brought back and survived long enough to pass across some useful info. The attack was Al Shabaab, which may or may not be a coincidence."

All eyes were on the Admiral now. He grimaced.

"Yeah, I know coincidence is stretching it a bit far. However, there's no indication they knew there was any connection between the men on that aircraft and Al Shabaab. That's all we know, I'm afraid."

"Admiral, there must be more he can tell us," Lucas Grant called to him, "Jesus Christ, the guy's a direct link to our target. He must be a goldmine of data. Names, places, unit strengths, it's an opportunity we can't miss."

Jack's gave him a bleak smile. "I'm afraid we have to miss it. He died."

The room went quiet. In those two words, 'he died', there was a world of meaning. The Kuwaitis were no strangers to torture, and their military had a record of accomplishment of prisoners dying in their dungeons. The arrival of the bus broke the silence. They climbed aboard, and the driver headed in the direction of the stand.

He went to the rear of the aircraft where the ramp was already down. They climbed aboard into the cavernous but crowded cargo space. Once again, they pulled down jump seats and started to make themselves comfortable. The center of the aircraft was filled with vehicles and spare parts. A man walked forward to greet them; he had to be the pilot, wearing an A2 brown horsehide flight jacket over his military shirt. The name on the jacket said, Jordan. He sported a battered baseball cap on his head, and black Ray-Bans over his eyes.

"Major Arthur Jordan," he announced, coming forward with his hand outstretched, "You must be Admiral Jacks."

They shook. "That's me," he replied. He introduced the Lieutenant, "This is William Boswell; he's in command of the platoon. And his number two, Chief Nolan."

They shook hands.

"Nolan is the guy who belly landed the Globemaster after the missile hit, " Jacks explained.

The man took off his Ray-Bans and looked more closely. "That was you? We were en route to Bagram Air Base from the States with a pile of gear for the Army. They diverted us here and told us about your little adventure with the missile. That was quite something, bringing her down in one piece."

"It wasn't just me. I had a lot of help."

Jordan glanced at Boswell. "You helped land her?"

"Uh, no. I was in back, taking care of my men. It was Grant."

He pointed to Lucas, who was rearranging packs and gear to make him comfortable.

"Right." He looked back to Nolan. "When we're airborne, if you have a minute, come forward. I'd like to know the story."

"No sweat."

They settled down for the journey of almost three thousand kilometers that would take them to their meeting with the submarine in the Arabian Sea. The Globemaster cruised at five hundred miles an hour, and the trip would take them somewhere in the region of four hours. It was timed for nightfall in the region. It wouldn't do for them to be seen dropping into the sea by some local fishermen; even worse, one of the pirates still infesting those waters.

As soon as they reached their cruising height of ten thousand meters, the pilot began to give them updates on their position and heading. If they hadn't been forced to sit in excruciating discomfort, it may have felt more like a regular airliner, although there was no pretty cabin crew to bring round coffee and muffins. With their knees pressed against the vehicle parts and wheels, the vibration seemed to drill right into them.

Nolan went up to the cockpit and sat in a jump seat close to Major Jordan. He gave him a quick account of the landing.

"We were lucky. If the missile had struck the nearside engine, we'd have lost the wing. Instead of a Seal platoon, you'd be carrying a cargo of coffins."

Jordan nodded. "Even so, landing a bird this size with the windshield missing and no landing gear was quite something. And you haven't been cleared on a C-17?"

"Nope. Neither do I want to be. It frightened me to death."

"Yeah, they are overpowering, especially when you're not used to them."

They shared some coffee, and then he returned to the

cargo hold. Jacks called him over, together with Boswell, while he went over some of the mission brief.

"You may be wondering about the M3 missiles I promised you. Everything is waiting for us on board the submarine. She's a nuclear boat, the Southampton, a 688 Los Angeles class attack sub. Her skipper is Commander Blake Regan. No relation", he smiled, "the name is spelled differently to the former President. Blake was patrolling the Indian Ocean when we asked for the nearest boat that had a Dry Dock Shelter aboard. Fortunately, he'd just come off a training mission with another bunch of Seals, so he was good to go. The SDVs were already on board, so all we had to do was give him new orders, and ship out the equipment. You'll find a Raven you can take with you, the hand launched drone. There's plenty of other stuff they were carrying back after the exercise. A real stroke of luck."

Boswell nodded enthusiastically. Nolan was still.

So why don't I feel lucky?

An hour before they were due to jump, Major Jordan called Jacks to the cockpit. He returned a few minutes later, with an expression he was trying to conceal. Trying and failing.

"What's the problem, Admiral?" Nolan asked him.

They brought up armor, those T54s we mentioned. Two of them, and they're parked in the town square. It's almost as if they know we're coming."

Boswell joined them. "I thought they were obsolete."

Jacks grimaced. "On a modern battlefield, sure, they'd be completely outclassed by our M1 Abrams and the Brit Challengers. But they are being used for something different, to beef up their security."

He pulled his tablet from his pack and punched in a few numbers. Then he looked up, and he wasn't smiling.

"The T54 carries thick armor and mounts a 100mm main gun, as well as a heap of secondary armament. They weigh over thirty tons and carry a crew of four. Top speed is thirty miles an hour, which is quite a lick for a museum piece."

"How do we deal with it, if we come across one?" Boswell asked, his expression anxious.

"In a word, you run for cover," Jacks told him, "You'll have the Carl Gustavs, the M3 MAAWS. You ever faced down thirty-six tons of Soviet armor, Lieutenant?"

"No, Sir."

"No. Sure, the M3 will knock out a T54, assuming you hit it in the right place. But when one of those monsters is hammering toward you, spitting fire out of the main gun and the secondary machine guns, it tends to spoil your aim. Just hope you don't run into them." He looked at Nolan. "Anything to add, Chief?"

"Sir, I'm sorry, but turning your back on the enemy is the way to get killed. If we see a tank in the vicinity, we need to deal with it. Kill it, before it kills us."

Jacks smiled. "You're right, of course. You men will be out there in the field. I guess I was seeing it from the perspective of a backroom boy." He turned Boswell. "You hear the Chief? You see something big running on tracks, make it a priority target and destroy it with an M3."

"Roger that," he replied.

The meeting broke up, and they went to break the news to the rest of the men. After that, a grim silence descended. The shadow of the 1993 debacle hung over them. It had failed for lack of American armor, and the news they could be facing Somali tanks was about as bad as it could be.

Thirty minutes before the drop point, they began to gear up. They packed their weapons into waterproof bags and changed into wetsuits for the plunge into the sea. On top of the wetsuits, they hung their parachutes, then checked and double-checked the webbing harness. Agent Amelia Stowe for the first time looked uncertain. Brad glanced at her and smiled.

"Anything you need a hand with?"

"Uh, this is my first time."

"You're a virgin?" he asked her.

She glared back at him. "What the hell?"

"A virgin. Your first jump."

She was confused for a moment. As double entendres go, it sure was confusing. Finally, she decided he'd meant first parachute jump.

"No, I've jumped from a light aircraft. But nothing like this."

"No problem, the jumpmaster can fix you up with a static line. That means…"

"I know what a static line is, thank you."

Brad went to speak to the jumpmaster, and he fought his way past the chaos of men putting on their equipment to reach her. He had a quiet word, and then went to arrange for her jump. They made the final checks; then began to bunch up close to the ramp. The crewman listened to his headset and then announced, "Ten minutes to jump. Switch to oxygen."

They pulled on their masks, and when they were fixed, gave the thumbs up. Nolan helped Amelia with her own mask, and she allowed him to double-check the fit on her face.

"Depressurizing now, nine minutes to target."

The air inside the fuselage changed, and the pressurized chill of ten thousand meters of altitude became a mind-numbing freeze of forty degrees below zero as the air leaked out, and the pressure equalized with the outside.

"Lowering ramp. Seven minutes."

"I'll jump last," Jacks informed them. "Amelia, you can jump right before me."

She nodded, and Nolan could see her eyes dilated with fear. No problem, anyone who wasn't frightened at his first jump from ten thousand meters was a fool.

"Five minutes."

They bunched up close to the end of the ramp and waited as the time counted down.

"One minute."

On an impulse, Nolan took Amelia's gloved hand and gave it a squeeze, together with a reassuring glance. She nodded her appreciation.

"I've got you," Jacks added, "Back in the US, people pay money to do this."

She turned to him. "In my opinion, they should lock them up."

The Admiral chuckled. "You could be right."

"Thirty seconds."

They moved a step closer to the ramp. He counted off the final seconds, and then Boswell stepped off first, followed by the rest of the men. Nolan was toward the back, in front of Amelia. After he jumped, he twisted to look back up and saw the shape of the FBI Agent hurtle off the ramp. She was connected to the aircraft with a thin umbilical. A slight jerk, the line parted company with her pack, and her 'chute opened.

Thank Christ. It's a long dive into the Arabian Sea.

The descent was pleasant enough. As they got lower, the air warmed, and off to the west it was possible to see the dark gloom of the African continent. Not so dark in places, the lights of a few towns were visible, although it being Somalia, the lighting was no competition for Times Square.

Poor bastards. All they want is a decent life, food, electricity for light and heat. Education, jobs. What do they get? Islamic terrorism.

Somalia's only growth industry, since the pirates had started to dwindle in the face of military action to stop their activities.

Several times he looked up, but he couldn't see her. She had a wrist mounted GPS, and guiding the parachute to the target parameters would be simplicity, especially for someone like her who had at least a few previous jumps. Even so, when he hit the water, he disconnected his 'chute and started looking around for her.

The sub found him first.

"Ahoy there, you looking for a ride?"

He looked up as the black bulk of the conning tower of a nuclear submarine loomed over him only thirty meters away, and yet he hadn't heard it.

Well, they said those boats were quiet. I guess it's true.

A few minutes later, they pulled him aboard. Four men were there already, including Will Bryce, Lucas Grant, Admiral Jacks and Lieutenant Boswell. The dock for the SDVs was a dark bulge on the deck, a reminder of where they were going, and how they'd get there.

"Any sign of Amelia?" he asked straightaway.

They all shook their heads.

"They're looking now. She won't be far away," Will told him.

Up on top of the sail, four sailors were scanning the sea with night vision binoculars. It was as much as they could do. There was no question of using a searchlight that may alert the Somali patrol boats.

The rest of the platoon scrambled aboard, and still no Amelia Stowe.

She has to have made it. Has to. Unless her 'chute tangled somehow, and she candled.

"Body in the water, fine on the port bow!"

They jerked around at the shout from one of the lookouts. Fifty meters away, it was possible to make out the irregular shape bobbing on the choppy surface of the sea. He jumped in and started to swim. Grant was with him, and Will. The three of them reached her at the same time. She was unconscious but face up. Nolan put his fingers inside the neck of her wetsuit and waited to feel a pulse.

Yes!

"She's alive. Let's get her back."

Between them, they towed her to the sub, and a dozen hands plucked her from the sea. The medics were already waiting, and seconds later the FBI Agent was bundled through the hatch in the side of the sail to be taken to the sick room. He went to follow, but the medic stopped him.

"We got it, Chief. She'll be fine, but we need some space to work on her. Come and visit when we've got her comfortable, say half an hour."

"Yeah, thanks."

He stood on the deck for a few minutes, watching as they secured the last of the 'chutes to stow them away from Somali eyes. Then the bridge speaker sounded.

"All hands, prepare to dive."

They filed into the open hatch, down the ladder into the bowels of the vessel. A walk through passageways lined with control valves, electrical conduits, and they reached the door to the control room. And stopped, as the overhead speaker blared, and a voice announced, "Dive, dive."

They watched and waited as the deck tilted and the giant nuclear vessel slid under the waves, away from prying eyes. Somali eyes.

An officer order, "Set course due west. Go to flank speed."

"Due west flank speed, aye."

They felt the slight vibration under the deck as the screws bit into the water and pushed them forward, but it was still very quiet.

Nuclear quiet, Nolan reminded himself.

As is SOP on American boats, junior crewmen manned the helm. In this case, neither of the sailors looked to be older than nineteen years.

The skipper, Blake Regan, came to greet them.

"Welcome aboard the Southampton. I had a report on your casualty. They say she just suffered minor concussion. She's conscious, and they'll release her from sick bay soon."

Jacks nodded his thanks as they shook hands.

"Good news, Commander. How're things looking?"

"As you heard, we're on the way. We're hitting thirty knots, so we'll have you in position inside of an hour. The SDVs are checked out and ready, and the weaponry is locked away in the ship's gym. Maybe you'd like to check it all out?"

"Sure."

Jacks, Boswell, and Nolan followed him through crowded passages, past men quietly moving from station to station, to the ship's small gymnasium, now doing duty as the temporary Seal armory. Regan unlocked the door, and they went in. Wooden crates littered the deck. Two were marked 'MAAWS M3, Carl Gustavs. There were further crates containing more tools of the Seal trade. Explosive charges, grenades, a dozen commo headsets, and a backpack labeled 'Raven'. The RQ-11 Raven was a small remote-controlled unmanned aerial vehicle and widely used by Special Forces. The craft was hand launched and powered by an electric motor. With a range of ten kilometers, it could fly at almost five thousand meters above sea level, at speeds of up to sixty mph. The real benefit was the superb 'look down' optics that gave the operator a live bird's eye view of the battlefield.

"Your tanks are stored with the SDVs, in the dock," Regan informed them, "So unless we've missed something, you should have everything you need to go in and kick some Somali ass."

"I'm of Somali descent," a voice intruded, a female voice.

They whirled. Amelia Stowe. Nolan felt a twinge of relief.

"It's good to see you up and about. You up to this?"

She gave him a wan smile. "Semper Fi, buster."

"That's the Marines," he corrected her.

"Oh, right. Whatever. We always get our man," she finished, with a somewhat sardonic expression.

Boswell adopted a slight sneer. "Wrong again, Agent Stowe. That's the motto of the Canadian Mounties."

She shrugged. "Got it. Thank you, Lieutenant. I just knew you Harvard boys were good for something. Shame about the humor."

He gave her a hard stare, murmuring 'fuck you, lady' under his breath, and then looked away."

Jacks and Regan didn't hear the insult, but he did, loud and clear. Maybe that was his intention. It was a frozen, awkward moment, and in a split second, Nolan knew it was all going to go wrong. Their only chance to succeed was to go in as a tight, well-coordinated unit, thinking, moving, and fighting as one. First Boswell was doing his best to push Nolan out of Team Bravo, and now he was going out of his way to upset the FBI Agent who was to be their eyes and ears on the ground. In this case, the most dangerous ground in the world. Somalia, graveyard of plenty of US lives during Gothic Serpent.

Should I talk to Jacks about the problem? No, this close to the jump-off, what can he do? Nothing. Moreover, he may think I've got some kind of a grudge against Boswell. There's nothing I can do, except work even harder to pull off the impossible. And pray he doesn't foul up, at least, not so bad we can't put things right.

CHAPTER FIVE

They glided through the dark waters of the Arabian Sea; carried along by the powerful electric motors of the SDVs. Dressed in their camo wetsuits; they were almost invisible. When they went ashore, the dark, random pattern would blend with the natural surroundings of the target area. The plan was to abandon the SDVs at a predetermined set of GPS coordinates where they could be retrieved later. Yet they would be ready if they were needed in an emergency.

Agent Stowe was sitting in the seat immediately in front of him, and so far, there was no sign the concussion had caused her any problems. If it was a deeper dive, things could change. However, this journey was conducted at a depth of less than ten meters. They reached their destination and unhooked the waterproof equipment bags. Nolan flooded the buoyancy tanks, and the SDV settled slowly on the bottom. He looked across and could see Grant doing the same. Provided they had their wrist mounted GPS devices, they could find them again. They were only thirty meters from the shore, and they continued to the beach, walking up to the start of the jungle, which grew to the very edge of the sand. Grant and Bryce collected the tanks, fins, and masks, stowed them in the now empty equipment bags, and took them back out to the vehicles where they would be stored. All being well, the Southampton would send a couple of divers to retrieve the gear when the mission was successfully concluded. And that meant they were all back. Alive.

A sudden noise in the bushes made them swing around fast, their weapons ready to fire, but a tall, distinguished looking black man stepped out. He wore cream chinos over desert boots, a linen safari style jacket over a crisp, white shirt, and a blue and white baseball cap inscribed with the legendry, 'UN' in bold letters. His hands were held out, palm upward, empty.

"Hold your fire," Will snapped at them.

The new arrival glanced at him. "I'm Commissioner Ahmed, Ashe Ahmed. I was told to meet you here. Are you the man in charge?"

Will pointed at Boswell, and he bustled forward.

"Lieutenant William Boswell, Sir. Thank you for meeting us here."

The man nodded. "It seems the militia in Kismayo know something is happening. There are more of them on the streets. I suggest we hurry to our destination. Nabil Barre has a compound on the west side of the town, and according to my information, he is there now."

"That's no problem. We'll be ready to move in minutes."

"That would be a good idea. Lieutenant, one more thing, you know how dangerous Somalia can be for invading troops." He paused for a moment, and every man there was reminded of the disastrous invasion, "If anything goes wrong, and you need somewhere to hide out, my uncle has a house on Avenue of the Prophet, number 14. His name is Dr. Ayub Ahmed, and he is totally reliable."

"Doctor? He's a medic?"

The Commissioner shook his head. "He is a Doctor of Cultural Anthropology at the University in Mogadishu, but he is at home right now, during vacation time. He hates the militia, and Al Shabaab in particular, so you may trust him."

"Yeah, good." He brushed off the offer, as if it was of no consequence and turned to Bryce. "I'm separating the unit into two fireteams. You'd better start distributing the gear."

"Not a good idea," Bryce mumbled, "We're stretched thin as it is. We should just stay with this UN guy and push on to the target."

"That's not your decision to make, Petty Officer Bryce. Besides, it doesn't affect you. We need to cover our six, just in case anything forces us to abort. I want you and Chief Nolan to stay and hold this position. If we hit serious problems, we'll fall back here."

He stared at Bryce and then looked at Nolan. "Any questions?"

"It's a bad plan, Lt. We're not going up against the local Boy Scout Troop. We need every man on deck for this operation, and I mean at the sharp end. Not sat on our fannies back here."

He knew why Boswell was doing it, every man in the unit knew. He wanted Nolan sidelined, so his sidekick Lucas Grant would have a chance to act as his second-in-command and hopefully make such a good job of it, he'd be able to push Grant forward to replace Nolan.

Bryce was the next man in the chain of command and could have made things difficult for Boswell. By leaving both men on the beach, he was effectively cutting out any opposition to his plan.

He was also chopping out the two most experienced men in the unit.

Doesn't he know he's almost condemning Bravo to a bloody defeat? Maybe he doesn't care. His outlook has become almost death or glory, like some 19th century US cavalryman. Perhaps that's how he sees himself. Battling Boswell, a great introduction to politics in the US, maybe even to the top job. Alternatively, it'll make a slick epitaph on the headstone.

Amelia Stowe turned and gave Nolan a searching glance as they prepared to move out. The men were overloaded with weapons and equipment, as they were now two men short. As well as their personal weapons, they had two M3 missile launchers and an M249 machine gun. Will held the second SAW, together with plenty of spare ammunition. In Nolan's opinion, they were going to need it. The two fireteams finished distributing packs laden with ammunition and explosives, carried out a final check on their commo and night vision systems, and moved out silently into the darkness. Boswell led his small team to the north, and Grant let the other team to the south. Seconds later, they'd disappeared into the night.

Bryce looked at Nolan. "This is a crock of shit, Chief." He shrugged, "Being as we're here, I guess I'll prepare the SAW."

"Negative. We are not waiting here for the shit to hit the fan. Will, you know he's going to screw up?"

Bryce nodded. "I know, but he's the boss."

"He's an ass, and he's going to get everyone killed.

Even Grant won't be able to save him this time. And I don't intend to sit by and wait for my friends to be killed."

Including Amelia Stowe, who I haven't even had time to get acquainted with.

Will picked up his machine gun and shouldered his pack. "What are we waiting for?"

They left the beach and sprinted along the jungle path toward the town of Kismayo. They neared the outskirts and started to encounter small huts and half-derelict houses dotted between the palm trees and dense jungle. They had no choice but to keep running, and both men searched ahead through their NV goggles for signs of people. It only needed one person to make a call on their cellphone, just as they had in 1993, to alert the militia. He almost missed them. Several slight shadows, a faint movement in his green tinged vision.

"Cover!" he murmured, just loud enough for Will to hear.

They dropped into the scrub shoulder-to-shoulder at the side of the path and prepared for the oncoming hostiles. There was no question of making any sound, so Will unholstered his Sig Sauer P226, an ungainly looking weapon with the attached suppressor. Nolan prepared his rifle, the SWS Mk11. In the distance, they could see four militia fifty meters away and heading straight for the beach.

"We have to take them," he murmured, "We can't risk leaving them in our rear."

"Roger that. How do you want to do it?"

He measured angles and distances. No matter how he worked it out, the rifle was the wrong weapon. He laid it gently on the ground and unholstered his own suppressed P226.

"We'll hit them when they're right in front of us. I'll take the two in front, the two in the rear are yours."

"Copy that."

They waited as the men neared them, some were laughing and chatting. Others' lips were moving rapidly, but it wasn't from talking.

"Khat," Will murmured.

"Yeah, it's common in these parts. It means they'll be wide awake."

Khat was a flowering plant grown in the Horn of Africa. The leaves contained an amphetamine-like stimulant, which caused excitement and euphoria. The effects were haphazard. It could make the men more alert, or they could be in the grip of psychotic delusions.

Nearer, only ten meters ahead, and now they could smell them, their body odors carried to them on the breeze; an unhygienic stench of unwashed bodies. Five meters, and Nolan took up the pressure on the trigger. A faint 'thunk' as the first bullet left the chamber, then another and another. Each man fired four rounds, two for each of the militia. Less than a second after they'd opened fire, there were four bodies strewn on the ground, and with hardly a sound made.

"That's it. We'll clear the bodies and…"

"Ismail, I can't see you. What was that noise?"

They froze as a fifth Somali came into view, a young man, maybe fourteen years old. He'd been dawdling in the rear, and he was about to see the bodies in front of him. He clutched a rocket launcher over his shoulder, the ubiquitous RPG7. Both Seals knew he'd catch sight of the bodies on the path any second. And when that happened, he'd sound the alarm. At forty meters he was still too far away for an accurate shot, and there wasn't time to use the sniper rifle. But he had to go down.

"Another ten meters, and we'll both open fire. One of us is sure to score a hit."

Will didn't get the chance to reply. At that instant the clouds parted, and the rays of the moon illuminated the night that had been so dark. The boy stopped, and his lips parted in horror when he saw the bodies of his comrades. Nolan and Bryce opened fire in the same moment, and at least two of their shots smacked into him, but they weren't killing shots. The Somali gasped and dropped to one knee. His face was contorted in agony, but he managed to climb back to his feet, and although they kept firing, he began to run toward Kismayo to alert the militia.

Nolan scooped up his rifle and catapulted to his feet. Bryce joined him, and they took off after the boy. In the distance, they saw him reach a single story house and start beating on the door. It was his mistake. If he'd kept running, he may have made it into the town and lost them. By the time the door opened, they were almost up with him. The man who stepped out wore camo trousers and was bare-chested. He'd probably just climbed out of bed. At first he appeared to be unarmed, and Bryce took down the kid with a pair of well-aimed shots. Nolan hesitated with the man at the door, until the moonlight cast the familiar shadow of an assault rifle with a banana shaped clip against the whitewashed wall of the house. He took him on the run, one shot in the chest and the other in the head as he came up to him.

"Let's get 'em inside. We'll have to speed it up if we're going to close with the fireteams. We've been lucky so far, but it can't last. Any minute, someone will pull a trigger, and this place will be hotter than hell."

It took less than two minutes to drag the bodies out of sight. Will ran back to toss the first four victims into the scrub at the side of the path, while Nolan dragged the other two bodies inside the house. He picked up the weapons they dropped, the RPG7 and the AK-47, and closed the door. Will joined him, and they pressed on toward the town until they reached the checkpoint.

A group of militia, about ten in all, had slewed a four-wheel-drive vehicle across the point where the path widened and became a junction. It was obvious they'd just arrived, for the commander was shouting orders and sending his men to concealed positions.

"Shit!" Will breathed, "They know something's up. The patrol could have been coincidence, but not this. It means they'll be waiting in ambush when our guys come back."

Nolan nodded as he surveyed the ground ahead of them. Where the path widened, three tracks converged. One skirted the town to the north, another to the south, and then the wider track that ran into the town itself. Less than a hundred meters from the roadblock, the houses became more numerous. Houses meant people, and when the shooting started, the Somalis would come pouring out. And another debacle would be on the cards. Will pointed to the north.

"I can work my way around there without them seeing me, Chief."

"Go for it. I'll take the other side, and good luck. "

The big PO3 nodded and went off at a crouching run. Despite his size and strength, he had the ability to move through hostile territory in almost total silence, and within seconds he'd disappeared into the night. Nolan waited for a chance to head south, but the path was blocked when the militia suddenly bunched up across the route he needed to take. It was then he heard the first shots coming from somewhere inside the town.

The men in front of him were alerted but not unduly worried. This was Somalia, after all, and gunfire was more common than the sounds of children playing. Still, it lessened his chances of following in Lucas Grant's footsteps. Ahead of him, the entrance to the town beckoned. A town full of Somalis, any one of whom would be more than happy to see him dead with his guts spilled out over the ground. He was still agonizing over which route to take when one of the militia shouted, and they bunched around the track that skirted south. Leaving the direct route into the town unguarded.

He didn't hesitate, just got to his feet, and ran as silently as possible. All the time, he was watching the hostiles; the closest was only forty meters from him. He thanked the night vision goggles that made it possible. He was staring at them, as if it was broad daylight. And yet, because the moon was once again hidden, they couldn't see him. He looked up and saw the clouds scudding across the sky. Any second, there'd be a window and beams of light would shine through to eliminate the area, and he'd be lit up like a Christmas tree. He kept running and made into the street, just as the clouds cleared and the area around the checkpoint briefly lit up.

He hurried through the deserted streets, going due west. A few more shots split the night, and then a long burst of machine gunfire. Unless there was more than one kill team operating inside Kismayo, it meant one of fireteams had hit trouble. The shots were coming from the south, which meant Lucas Grant's group. They needed help, and he found a narrow lane that led in what he hoped was the right direction.

A shape materialized in front of him, and he almost open fire when he realized the person was wearing the camo wetsuit of the Navy Seals. They were limping, and this person was too small to be one of the Bravo operators. It was Special Agent Amelia Stowe, and she almost fell into his arms.

"Nolan, thank God," she exclaimed, "We walked right into a trap."

He pulled her into a darkened doorway.

"Tell me what happened."

"It was that stupid bastard Boswell. He radioed the order to speed it up. Lucas called back and told him it would make too much noise, but he overrode him and insisted. We were running, when we hit a couple of fighters who were sheltering behind a ruined well. We didn't see them, but they saw us, and they got off a few shots before our guys ran them down and killed them. But the damage was done."

"You were hurt?"

"It's nothing. A bullet went through the outer layer of skin at the top of my leg. It hurts like hell, but it's not dangerous."

"We'll get a dressing on that as soon as possible. Where are Lucas and the other three men who were with him?"

"I don't know. They told me to get into cover, but after the shooting stopped, they'd disappeared."

"Shit. The town is starting to come alive. If we don't kill Barre pretty soon, they'll come gunning for us, and we'll be lucky to get out of here alive. Where exactly is his compound?"

"On the west side of town. But surely we have to get out of here. You just said the town is waking up to the fact they're under attack."

"It doesn't make any difference. We came here to do a job, and I'm not pulling out until it's done. You have to lead me to Barre's place."

He heard her mutter, "Stupid macho bastard," under her breath. She nodded.

"Yes, I can do that. But Nolan, we really are running out of time."

"In that case, we'd better start moving now. Lead the way."

They changed direction, and she led the way, running lightly through dark and noisome alleys and lanes. The stench was fearful, and he assumed the locals tossed out their sewage at night, so the rats and vermin could feast on them before dawn. The problem was, the locals were so hungry as a result of decades of warfare they'd eaten the vast majority of the rats. The result was the night soil lay where they'd thrown it. How they managed without frequent epidemics of disease was a puzzle, but Nolan reminded himself they didn't manage. Diseases such as typhus and cholera cut down large swathes of Somalia at regular intervals.

"Stop!" she hissed.

He halted. "What?"

"I heard something."

"Wait there. I'll take a look."

He peeked around the end of the alley into a small square. Two meters away, a Somali militiaman was standing, watching. Looking in the opposite direction, but it couldn't last. Across the square, more fighters were on guard, and he counted eight men in all. It was an obvious junction, a choke point. He retreated back to Amelia. They needed another route, but as he joined her, he could hear more men behind them.

"They're sweeping through the alleys, Chief. We can't go back."

"We can't go forward."

She was looking around for some way out, but there was none, only forward or backward. Both ways would deliver them into the guns of the militia. Except...

"Chief, the staircase," she whispered, pointing to a narrow doorway.

It wasn't the entrance to a house. It was a flight of stairs leading up to the open roof. He gestured for her to go ahead and then followed her, just as the first of the militia rounded the corner behind them. The staircase was narrow, so it brushed his shoulders, as it was built of rough concrete. They ran out onto the flat roof and waited. Nothing. He looked over the top and could see the Somalis advancing along the alley, calling to each other in low tones.

"They're searching the whole town," he told her, "From here on in, we need to be even more careful."

The question uppermost in his mind was how to join up with Lucas Grant's fireteam. They'd run into a hornets' nest, but there was still a chance to save the operation.

So far, the only a hostiles who saw us are dead, so they'll likely put it down to a skirmish between warring factions.

He turned to the FBI Agent.

"We need to find Grant, push on to Barre's house, and kill him. Except the alleys and lanes are alive with the enemy."

She looked around for a few moments. "We can go across the roofs. Most of them are flat, and the gaps between the houses are generally no more than a meter."

He nodded. "Excellent. Let's see where they are."

He keyed his mic. "Bravo Three, this is Two. Say location."

He waited a few seconds, praying Grant's team hadn't hit trouble. The reply came.

"This is Bravo Three. Coordinates as follows." He read off a list of numbers, "What's your status, Two?"

Nolan explained he'd found Agent Stowe. "The whole town is alive with militia. We need to join you."

Grant was silent for a moment; obviously surprised he'd disobeyed orders to remain at the beach. But when he spoke, it was with some relief.

"Thank Christ for that. I thought we'd lost her. We're holed up in a derelict house. It's only a few hundred meters from Barre's place, but we can't move, not yet, not without being seen."

"What about Boswell? Any word from him?"

"Nothing. I think he's in an area where he can't receive our signals."

"What about the satcom? You could put a call through to Admiral Jacks. He'd patch you through."

Grant chuckled. "The Lieutenant has the satcom."

"Roger that. We're coming across the rooftops. With any luck we should be able to reach it."

"Yeah, we thought about that to get to Barre, but the area around his house is an open space. No rooftops."

"Understood. We'll get you as quick as we can. Bravo Two out."

He nodded to Amelia. "Let's go."

The going was easy at first, and they jumped from rooftop to rooftop. They were within a block of Grant's position when they were halted. There was a wide gap between houses, about five meters. The only way was to descend to ground level and cross to the next building. Unfortunately, a half-dozen armed Somalis were on the ground, milling around a parked truck. The nearest man came close, and only three meters from the base of the staircase they'd need to descend. They searched for an alternative route, but there was none.

"It looks like we're stuck, Chief," she commented.

"Maybe. Look, while we're working together, make it Kyle."

She nodded. "Okay. It's a weird place to get acquainted, but you can call me Amelia." She suddenly shivered, "You don't think...."

"What?"

"You don't think we're going to die here? Is that why you told me your name?"

He chuckled quietly. "Not in a million years. I was just being sociable as we've been thrown together."

I'm sorry, Amelia, but I had to lie to you. The truth is, we could be in too deep here, and there may not be any way out.

He unslung his rifle and sighted on the fighters below. Viewed through the optics, each man was lit up, and an easy target at short range. The problem was the SWS Mk 11 was a single shot rifle, and at no time were all six men visible. They'd disappear behind the truck or close to the wall of nearby house, invisible from the roof. If only one man ran, and reported a sniper with a silenced weapon was shooting from the rooftop, it would be as good as sending them a radio message announcing they were in town.

Yet, how long can we wait here? It will be dawn in around four hours, by which time we need to be long gone.

He looked down on the Somalis. They were chatting in loud, excited voices. Khat, they were chewing it just like the men they'd run into earlier.

Why don't you get out of here and go party somewhere else?

"What do we do?"

"I'm thinking."

But there was only one thing to do. They had to get past, had to join up with Grant's fireteam and reach Nabil Barre. These men had to die. That meant using Amelia down on the ground to pick off anyone who tried to run. She still wore her camo wetsuit, but on a nearby washing line strung between chimneys, he'd seen a brightly colored African dress.

"How's your marksmanship?"

She thought for a moment. "It's pretty damn good."

"Ever killed a man?"

"No."

He gave her his P226.

"You're going to have to start now. This is what I want you to do...."

He waited while she donned the dress, pulling it down over the rubber of her wetsuit. It was a tight fit, hugging her curves. For the job he had in mind, it was perfect. She crept down to the ground level. He heard her report in his earpiece.

"I'm in position."

"Roger that. You know what to do."

He watched her walk out casually into the square,

garishly clad in the multihued garment.

Is it my imagination, or has she introduced a sexy sway to her hips?

It caught the attention of the Somalis, who reacted immediately. He heard a torrent of the strange language directed at Amelia. She was of Somali descent and wore a Somali dress. A woman looking like her, and out at this time of night, meant only one thing. Provided they didn't notice the wetsuit underneath. Or the suppressed pistol she held behind her back. There was little fear of them noticing anything other than what they wanted to see, a sexy young woman, a woman who was obviously available.

She went to meet them, moving closer, but not too close. He'd stressed that. He needed a clear field of fire. He could hear the men's voices, thick and throaty with desire. Good, they were blind to anything other than the tasty dish in front of their eyes. He could see four men, which was not ideal. He'd just have to hope the others came into view, or she was able to kill them before they made any noise. Once again, he sighted carefully on the group, choosing his targets. She was only three meters away from the first man when he pulled the trigger. And again, four times, until four bodies lay bleeding on the ground. One man rushed into his sights, and he pulled the trigger a fifth time, and then a sixth. The double tap knocked him straight down, and he immediately began searching for number six.

A voice called out from behind the truck. A frightened voice, and yet filled with aggression. She managed to whisper on the commo.

"He said whoever you are, come out or I'll kill the girl."
Shit!

"Okay, keep calm. I'll stand up so he can see me. As soon as he comes out to take the shot, take him. Can you do that?

"I think so."

"Do it, or we're dead."

"Okay." Her voice was a frightened whisper, but as a Federal Agent, she must have known this moment would come.

"Get ready. Whatever happens, don't let him get off a shot. He does that, and we're finished."

He stood up in full view. The man stepped out, keeping the girl between him and Nolan, with his AK-47 raised. She brought her pistol into view and stepped toward him. He glanced around, saw she was holding a gun, and his mouth dropped open in astonishment. For several seconds, it was like a frozen tableau, and neither of them moved. Then he started to swing his rifle barrel around, too late. She squeezed the trigger, and up on the roof Nolan heard for distinct 'thunks' as she fired. The Somali stopped moving, stared at her, and then slowly toppled to the ground. Nolan raced down the staircase and out into the square, checking for further targets, but it was clear. He went toward the girl and took his pistol. She was shivering, her eyes wide with shock.

"You did well."

"I killed a man."

"He was about to kill us both. You saved our lives."

"Yes."

He pulled her to him, trying to inject some of his strength into her body, to protect and reassure her. She clung to him, as if he was her only anchor in a huge storm. A storm that was all in her mind, yet no less powerful because of it, a raging fury threatening to eat her up with guilt and despair. She had to get over it, and fast. He pushed her away from him, yet still held her in his strong hands.

"You want to get everyone killed? The guys in Bravo have wives, kids, mothers and fathers. You want those people to see our guys shipped home in body bags?"

"No, no!" Her eyes were wide with astonishment, but not fear.

Good.

"Then pulled yourself together. We have a job to do here. If you go all weak on me like a schoolgirl, you may as well start writing the letters to the widows."

She stiffened, her expression changed to one of anger, and then comprehension.

"I get it. It's just…"

"I know you feel bad now, but save it for later. Move out."

He made the last words harsh, as loud as he dared in this hostile town. She reacted at once.

"I get it. I'll be okay."

They had to leave the bodies where they lay. The town was alive with militia, and there wasn't time to hide them. She pointed in the direction of their target, and they went forward. Once again, their way was blocked. They were walking along a wider street when the headlights of a truck appeared around the bend, almost catching them in the bright wash of illumination. The truck came nearer and nearer, and this time, there were no recessed doorways to hide in. A few seconds more, and they'd be lit up like ducks in a shooting gallery. Nolan glanced around frantically, but the other end of the street was too far. He raised his rifle, ready to fight it out. And then turned, as a voice called to them.

"In here, quick!"

He didn't stop to consider. The man had opened a street door and beckoned to them. They raced through the opening, just as the headlights lit up the area they'd been standing in. He closed the door quietly, and they looked around the room. There was no hallway, just a living room lit by a dim oil lamp, with a door that opened to the street. The walls were lined with shelves, all of them bursting with books. The man was not militia. He was elderly, very tall and thin, with gray hair. He was dressed in jeans and a faded T-shirt with the emblem of some university barely visible on the chest. Nolan gripped his pistol and waited.

"My name is Ahmed, Ayub Ahmed."

Amelia stared at him with interest. "Of course, you're Ashe Ahmed's uncle. Dr. Ayub Ahmed. So this street is…"

"Avenue of the Prophet, yes. He told you about me?"

Nolan nodded. "He did, Sir. He said to come here if we were in trouble."

"I will do my best. It was obvious something was going on in the town, now I know why. Why are you here, what have you come for?" When he didn't reply, the elderly academic rephrased the question, "Or should I say, who have you come for?"

Nolan decided he could trust the guy. "Barre."

The man's eyes widened. "Barre? You've chosen the hardest target in Somalia, especially now that the town is alerted. How many of you?"

"Ten." He glanced at Amelia, "Make that eleven."

Ahmed raised his eyebrows at her unusual apparel, the gaudy dress over her camo wetsuit. "That's not enough men to take Barre. I've even seen tanks inside the town."

He decided not to mention the object of the mission wasn't to take the warlord. Nor did he let slip anything about the UAVs, or the M3 missiles.

Trust is one thing, but you can take it too far.

He stopped and listened as Grant's voice came into his earpiece.

"Bravo Two, what's your status?" Nolan explained where they were hiding, "Roger that. We're still holed up in the same place. We can see the target area, but we can't get close. There's been a development. That armor they talked about, a T54 just appeared and parked out front. They're pretty determined to stop anyone getting near Barre."

"Understood. Do you have the M3s?"

"Yeah, we have one missile system, so with any luck we could take him. But we only have one missile. Our spare got dropped while we were running for cover. The only other missiles are with Boswell, and he's still out of contact."

"What about the Predators?"

"Same problem. The Lieutenant has the tactical pad and the satcom, so we have no way of contacting the controllers."

"Roger that. Hold in place. I'll get back to you in a few minutes."

"Make it quick," Grant's voice sounded unusually tense, "The militia is starting to search inside the buildings. If they come across us, we'll have to fight them off and take on the tank. Some of the hostiles are armed with RPG7s, and I don't think one M3 missile is enough to handle them all."

"What about Merano, our other sniper?"

"He's with Boswell's team."

"Understood. Give me a few minutes."

He thought fast. With Boswell's fireteam an unknown quantity, Nolan was effectively in charge of those elements of Bravo he could reach. Which meant he had to make decisions, and make them fast. Time was running out.

And then it ran out. Someone started banging on the door and shouting in Somali.

Amelia stared at him, her eyes wide with terror. "They're here. They want to search the house."

* * *

Someone was shaking his shoulder gently. His eyes flicked open.

Is this the Americans come to kill me, like they killed Osama bin Laden in the compound in Abbottabad, Pakistan?

"My Sheikh."

He felt a sigh of relief. It was Osman Yusuf, one of his bodyguards. A huge man, built like a circus strongman, he'd enjoyed a career as a professional wrestler before joining the leader of Al Shabaab.

"What is it, Osman?"

"There is activity in the town, my master. People have caught glimpses of strange soldiers, and we may be under attack."

"Attack! What are you doing about it?"

"Sir, we have a hundred men scouring the town, looking for the intruders. It may be nothing, or perhaps an attack from a rival clan. But we have to be sure."

He thought quickly. That was the most likely scenario,

arrayed from a local faction who envied his success. It could also be the Kenyans, a commando raid across the border in revenge for the attack on the Westgate shopping center. But he had to consider the worst case, an attack by American Special Forces.

Is it possible they've learned about my plan to send the war to the American mainland? Yes, of course it is possible.

Perhaps he'd been foolish to send those shrunken heads to the President of the United States. But it had been wonderful thinking about their stupid faces, frozen with horror when they saw what was inside that cardboard carton. And since then, the turmoil inside Washington, as it dawned on them they were vulnerable to attack.

The purpose of terrorism is to terrorize.

But it was vitally important the plan went forward without problems. If the stupid Americans were alerted, their eyes were on Somalia, not on Washington. He smiled to himself.

The martyrs will carry out their attack as planned. Even so, it may be as well to take no chances.

"Contact Musse Daud, and tell him to move up the schedule by forty-eight hours. And then get outside and make certain the fighters are making a thorough search. My security is paramount. It is vital that no one gets inside this building."

"My Sheikh, moving up the operation at this late stage could cause problems. Will the martyrs have enough time to get into position?"

"They have to have enough time!" he flared, "Call them!"

"At once. Sir, if we are under attack, you should leave this house. It is not safe. We have a plan for these situations.

Do you wish me to..."

"Do it. We're leaving. Notify my personal guard at once, and make sure everything is ready for my departure."

"Yes, Sir."

The man hurried away. He smiled to himself, they would soon deal with these intruders, and in a few days, the Americans would feel the wrath of the Nabil Barre. And their President would be dead.

Life is good.

"My master, are you coming back to bed?"

He looked down at Saba. Another weak American bent to his will.

"No. Get up. I require you to dress me, and prepare my son, Mukhtar. Make sure he is ready to travel."

"Yes, my master."

CHAPTER SIX

"Here, take this, you may need it." Dr. Ahmed handed him a battered cellphone, "Go up to second floor, the room at the rear. You will find you can climb out to the balcony and down to the garden at the rear of the house. If you need anything, call me."

He was puzzled by the gift of the cellphone, but he nodded his thanks, and they raced up the staircase. The academic shouted to the men outside, attempting to delay them, but all he achieved was a renewed frenzy of knocking. There were two rooms on the second floor. Nolan led the way into the one at the rear and found the window that opened onto the balcony. On the first floor he heard a huge crash, followed by a splintering of wood. The militia had tired of waiting and had smashed down the door. He pushed open the window, and they climbed out onto a narrow, wrought iron balcony. It was coated with rust and wobbled alarmingly. Below, the garden was dark, yet the smell reached up to them, the fragrance of jungle foliage, mingled with the omnipresent sewage stench.

She stepped over the rail, and he lowered her down to the ground and then jumped himself, landing in the center of a clump of bushes below. They crept along the garden until they reached the rear and left through the gate. They were in yet another narrow lane, and the stink of sewage was much stronger, almost enough to stifle their breathing. Back at the house, he could hear the pursuers out in the garden, and he turned to whisper to her.

"We have to link up with Grant's team. Can you find it from here?"

"I think so. It's this way."

She indicated an almost invisible path to the left and started jogging along the soft, noisome surface. God only knew what they were stepping on. Nolan followed and constantly swept the area through three hundred and sixty degrees with his NV goggles. It was soon evident the militia had left the streets to conduct a house-to-house search, and he breathed a sigh of relief. The route to the house where Grant's team was hiding was clear. Four minutes later they were outside. He tapped lightly on the door, and it opened.

"It's good to see you," Lucas said as they entered the house. He glanced at Amelia's multi-hued dress and gave a half smile, "I see you treated the lady to a party frock."

Nolan waved away the comment. "Who do you have with you?"

"Murray, Rose, and Moseley. They're upstairs, watching the street."

"Anything from Boswell?"

"Nothing. And they have the satcom, the tactical tablet, the spare missiles, the works. We're isolated. We should pull out. This place is starting to wake up."

"Maybe. Let's go upstairs and take a look."

The interior of the house was an empty shell. Even the plaster had crumbled, leaving bare brick, stone, and wood to be attacked by the pervasive, dank jungle climate. He started up the creaking stairs, and Lucas called to him to be careful. Most of the treads were splintered and broken, and the rest were rotten with worm. Grant made to follow, but he stopped him.

"Wait here. We can't leave the first floor unguarded. They're conducting house-to-house searches, and I need you to keep an eye out for them. Amelia, come with me."

Even in the dim light, he saw the Seal vet flush and could almost read his thoughts. Before he joined Bravo, a place on the famous bin Laden raid, and now Nolan had relegated him to the position of sentry. He hesitated for moment and then gave a resigned smile.

"Copy that, Chief. You're the boss."

"For now. Boswell should be here, leading us. You worried about him, Lucas?"

He saw him jerk his head around in surprise. The question could have a double meaning, worried about him personally, or about his unit; except Nolan couldn't give a damn about any 'friendship', even if it existed.

"No."

He nodded and ran up the stairs. The three men on the second floor glanced around in alarm.

"It's okay. It's Nolan."

"Welcome back, Chief," Brad replied. The others nodded a greeting.

"What's going on out there?"

"Bunch of gomers, searching every building. Sooner or later, they'll get to this one."

"Can you see Barre's place?" he asked. Rose nodded, "Show me."

The trooper went to the window on the north side of the house and pointed.

"Assuming he's still there. He could well have pulled out when the shooting started."

"It's possible. But he may still be there. We'll assume he's in there until we know different."

It was easy to distinguish his place from the nearby houses. It was big, much bigger than the surrounding houses and in better repair. There was also a perimeter wall around the grounds. In front of the building was open space for what looked like a hundred meters on each side, a good defensive position. He was certain guards would also be posted at the windows of the house. However, they didn't just rely on guards armed with assault rifles and RPG7s. In the center of the space nearest them, he saw the tank. The 100mm main gun looked huge, but it was the secondary armament that worried him most. Two machine guns, a 7.62mm mounted on the bodywork, and inside the turret, a 12.7mm DShK heavy machine gun.

"We have to get past that bastard."

"We surely do," Brad replied.

With a start, he realized he'd been thinking aloud.

"Where's the M3 launcher?"

"Downstairs with Grant," Zeke told him.

"Get it up here. If we need to use it, this is the best platform to launch."

Zeke went away, and he continued gazing at the distant house. Finally, he made his mind up. Unless they heard from Boswell's team in the next ten minutes, he'd attack the target, locate Barre, and kill him.

If he's still there, but first, the tank.

He glanced at Zeke as he returned with the Carl Gustav. "What about explosives?"

"Plenty in my pack. Boswell didn't want to slow his team down with anything real heavy."

Boswell, there'll be time for him, but not now. Later.

"That's good news. At least we have something to fight with. We need to get those tankers out in the open where we can kill them. The only way I can think of is if something damages their vehicle, enough to, say, bust a track. That would bring 'em out; they'd need to replace it."

"Sure, that would do it," Zeke replied, "There's just one problem. Getting the explosive charge across open ground and setting it against the track. Unless someone's feeling suicidal."

He chuckled. "Nothing like that, but I want them out in the open. As soon as they're outside, we can take 'em."

"Why not use the Carl Gustav?" Brad objected.

"Remember the intel on armor inside Kismayo? I heard they had two of these T54s. We have the one missile. When it's gone, the chances are, the other one'll turn up around the corner."

"Yeah, but we kill the crew of that monster out there, and they'll still call for the other tank."

"I hope so. There'll be two of us inside the disabled tank, waiting to blow their ass off as soon as they show. Zeke, I reckon that'll be you on the gun, and you can take Dan to load for you. He's the automatic weapons specialist. Maybe he'll get a chance to practice with that DShK."

"It sounds like a plan, Chief, except for one problem. Getting the charge across open ground. That's the bit you missed."

"I'll take it across. I reckon I can make it."

They stared at him. Amelia approached and touched his arm. Her face was strained with terror, terror for him.

"No, Kyle. You can't do it. It's like they said, suicide. There has to be another way."

"There isn't. Zeke, get that charge together. We sit here any longer, and we may as well invite them in for breakfast. I need to talk to Lucas. We have to have a diversion so I can get over there and plant the charge."

* * *

He crouched behind a low stonewall, clutching the package Zeke had put together. A block of C4 plastic explosive, enough to destroy one of the tracks and disable it, but not enough to put the main and secondary armament out of operation. They hoped. In front of him, he could see the open square, dominated by the threatening bulk of the T54. Beyond the tank lay their target, the house, and inside the murderous leader of Al Shabaab, Nabil Barre.

He glanced at the rooftop on the far side of the square. Through his night vision goggles, he could make out the shape of Lucas Grant waiting with their M249. The plan was a simple one. On his signal, Lucas would open fire and pepper the hull of the tank with a stream of 5.56mm bullets. It should be enough to divert the attention of the crew, and they would start to return fire. It was up to Lucas to judge the time to get off the roof. That would be when the 100mm main gun began to target his position. An explosive shell would be more than enough to ruin his day.

He took the final glance around, but there was only the

tank and a few guards visible inside the perimeter wall of Barre's house. He knew Amelia would be watching from the window of the house behind him. She'd continued to plead with him to come up with another plan, but there was no other way. When infantry had to deal with a pair of main battle tanks, the options were severely limited. He touched the transmit button.

"Open fire."

Lucas didn't say a word. His response came from the machine gun. A hail of bullets lashed out, and most of them hit the tank. He shifted his aim briefly to pepper the guards in front of Barre's house, and then refocused his aim on the armored behemoth. At first, they opened fire with the 12.7mm machine gun mounted in the turret, and Nolan watched the Seal duck behind the stone parapet as the heavy slugs chewed masonry from the facade of the building. The gun stopped firing, and he put his head back up and sent another burst down to the T 54. It was more than enough for them. Their patience was exhausted, and the noise of the turret motor was loud in the sudden silence as the giant barrel began to turn and elevate, to seek out and destroy the insolent machine gunner.

He got up to a crouch and waited. Lucas had disappeared, hopefully far enough from the edge of the building. Then the gun fired an explosion that echoed around the town, and almost at the same second the entire front of the building exploded in chaos of broken masonry and timbers. The initial flash lit up square, but he'd been waiting for it and averted his eyes. When he opened them, everything was in darkness, except for a few fires where the wood of the target building was burning. He knew he'd never get a better chance. Anyone watching would have had their night vision crippled by the enormous flash. He sprinted out from behind the wall and ran straight toward the tank.

He estimated afterward he could have come close to an Olympic qualifying time. Except for the weight of his weapons and armor. But he made it to the side of the Russian built T54 and crouched down. Zeke had prepared the timer and set it for three minutes, enough time to get clear. He jammed the package into the iron track, pressed the button to start the timer, and turned to run straight into a mountain.

It wasn't a mountain. It was a man, a Somali, and jet black. He'd just come up behind Nolan and stood with his hands hanging by his sides and a relaxed sneer on his face. He must have been almost seven feet tall and broad in proportion. Yet there was no fat. He was all muscle, like a champion shot-putter. His head was bald, and beneath his low forehead he had two small, staring pig eyes. The lips were like cycle tires, thick and rubbery, and his sneer had exposed his teeth, both of them. It was an eerie, gruesome sight, yet the man was more than a visible threat. The physical threat was even more real, as he brought one huge fist to slam into Nolan's body armor.

It was like being hit by an artillery shell, and he felt himself tossed back to the ground. His back slammed against the tank track, and as his arm swung around and hit the heavy iron, his hand gun flew from his fingers. The giant moved in with a huge boot lifted ready to strike, and he was barely able to throw himself to the side to avoid the monster damaging his organs. It spoke in a voice pitched surprisingly high for such a huge specimen.

"You are American, yes? You think you can come here and attack our leader, even though the last time you came, we sent you away with a bloody nose. I will send you back to your country in little pieces, but before you die, you should know it is Yusuf Osman who has sent another Western infidel to hell."

Nolan staggered to his feet, trying not to retch from the agony in his guts. He desperately needed a weapon to fight with, any weapon. He'd left his rifle with Zeke in the house, not that it would have been any use in a fight like this at close range. His handgun had vanished in the dark, and all he had left was his combat knife. He snatched it out and assumed a defensive posture. The man laughed.

"You cannot be serious! Throw down your knife, little man. I will kill you quickly, to show mercy. When you're dead, you will not feel your limbs being torn from your body. Otherwise, I will dismember you while you are still alive. Don't be stupid."

He closed and reached out a huge hand to snatch at Nolan's knife hand. He jerked back, feinted to the left, and went right, slashing across the man's eyes as he went past. The monster let out a shrill scream of pain and anger, staring at the Seal through eyes that were already misted with blood.

"Enough. It is time to finish this."

He moved in again, and this time he was fast, demonstrating skill with footwork that could only have been acquired in a martial arts gymnasium. He narrowly avoided a massive punch that would have taken his head off, and then the giant clamped a hand around his neck. He began to squeeze, and Nolan's vision began to go dark. The only thing that saved him was the high collar of his vest. The hand had gripped his neck outside of the collar. Even so, the pressure mounted, and it was only a matter of seconds before his air supply cut off altogether. The big man moved his head down to look for a better grip on Nolan's neck, and for a brief, fraction of a second, the pig eyes were within range.

He didn't hesitate. He stabbed forward, straight into the man's left eye. The blade traveled a long way in before the screaming victim clamped a hand over his own hand on the hilt, stopping it going in further to his brain. For a few chaotic seconds, they fought for control of the hilt. Blood and mucus spurted out, but although the huge man was weakening, he possessed superhuman strength. Nolan fought to pull the fingers apart, fingers that were like thick steel rods. It was a losing battle, and he felt himself losing the fight as blackness overcame him. And then the grip loosened, just as he heard the rattle of machine gun fire only meters away.

It all happened at once. The main gun began to turn and drop lower to seek out the new target, just as the bullets smacked into the back of his opponent. The man went limp as his last breath whooshed out of his body. Nolan disengaged himself, but the huge man was partly on top of him. He realized he'd lost track of time, the explosive charge on the track. It could only have seconds before it detonated, a half minute at most. And then someone was next to him, helping to drag the huge body off him. Through his returning consciousness, he realized it was Grant who must have run out and across the open ground to shoot the giant.

"Lucas! The charge, it's about to detonate."

Before the man answered, a rattle of machine gunfire chewed up the earth close to them, and he looked up to see the secondary machine gun was trying to lower sufficiently to target them. He realized at once there was no way they could escape across the open ground. The second they showed themselves, the gun would shred them. He searched around for cover, any cover from the explosive charge, and his eyes fixed on the massive corpse that lay only inches away.

"Get behind the body! Quick, we're out of time."

Grant didn't need any more urging. He dived to the ground next to Nolan, and between them, they pulled the huge, heavy corpse to cover their bodies. The machine gunner in the T54 had finally managed to correct his aim, and a dozen rounds smacked into the inert corpse that protected them. And then the world exploded.

The charge he'd placed was only partly hidden behind the steel track. It was enough to destroy the massive iron links, and the track parted immediately. The blast, instead of being directed inward, blew out, and an enormous shockwave picked up all three of them, the two Seals and the massive body, and threw them up in the air. In the strange explosive vortex, the blast that should have throwing them outbound from the steel hull sucked them in, so that all three of them, two alive and one dead, were held against the steel monster.

For the second time in as many minutes, Nolan felt consciousness slipping from him. He could hear the roar of an engine. The tank commander had ordered his driver to advance, and he was trying to propel the vehicle forward. With a smashed and destroyed track, nothing happened, only a tortured grinding of steel as the undamaged track tried to turn in opposition to the broken track. Abruptly, the engine note faded to tick over as they realized the futility of the maneuver. Then the hatch clanged open.

Grant was shaking him.

"He's coming out. You have to deal with him, Chief. I'll go up and take the rest of them inside the hull."

Lucas thrust a pistol in his hand and understanding came to him. He managed to spit out the words, "I can deal with it. You go."

Then Grant was gone, and he was on his own. A man had climbed out of the forward hatch and was walking around to where he lay, to inspect the track. Grant crept around back of the tank and up onto the deck.

Nolan was lying prone, tucked well into the side of the wrecked track. At first, the man didn't see him. He was examining the twisted and broken steel when he almost stumbled on the Seal waiting for him. He opened his mouth to shout, but the Chief shot him with a bullet at close range into his head and a second to the chest. The rounds punched him to the ground, dead. Nolan checked the body to make sure, and then went around front and up onto the deck.

Through the hatch, he could see a scene of bloody chaos. The interior was lit with a dim red battle light, and crouched in the center of the cabin Lucas Grant was checking the bodies littered over the steel floor. As he made the checks with one hand, he held a combat knife in the other. The blade was wet and dripping with blood.

"You got them all with a knife?"

Grant looked up. "Yeah, like lambs to the slaughter. Their shooting was second rate, but their security was terrible. I guess they thought I was their crewman on his way back to report. I had to take them down fast. We don't want these gomers to suspect we've taken their toy."

"No. Good job, I'll call Zeke and Dan over to get these

guns working."

He pressed the transmit button and told them to get their asses over to the T54 mighty fast. Less than a minute later, they were climbing through the hatch. Immediately, Zeke began reloading the main gun, and Dan commandeered the 12.7mm in the turret. He left them to it and began familiarizing himself with the interior of the armored vehicle, just as the radio erupted into a torrent of Somali. If they didn't answer, the militia would come out to check. And if they did answer, all hell would break loose.

He let them gabble on, and after a couple of minutes, the speaker went silent. Nolan popped his head out of the turret, but there was no sign of the militia coming to check. Probably, they assumed the explosion had killed the crew. Yes, it had to be that, for in the distance, he could hear the roar of another tank engine warming up. He ducked down inside the turret and slammed the hatch closed.

"You need to hurry it up. The other T54 just started up. It can't be far away."

"I'm working on it," Zeke replied, "This main gun is not like anything I've encountered, so I'm having to do it by the seat of my pants."

"Do what you can."

He looked down at Lucas, who'd finished checking over the bodies. He sat in the center of them, a gruesome sight, covered with his victims' blood.

"Grant, can you help Zeke out? He could do with a loader."

"Sure." He managed to thread his way through to the loader's seat close to the breech of the big gun. Nolan opened the hatch a fraction, in time to see the second T54 round the corner and advance. Its gun pointed right at them, but they couldn't do a thing about it. If they began to traverse the main gun, the Somali tank crew would know something was up. And at a range of one hundred meters, there'd be no warning, no time to get clear. They'd be on the receiving end of a massive high explosive shell.

The tank came closer and closer, and they waited. A sudden thought hit Nolan like a hammer blow. If Barre's men had taken Boswell's fireteam, the enemy could well have extracted the details of their operation from the prisoners. If that were the case, no matter the outcome of what happened in the square when they fought the second T54, penetrating Barre's house would make no difference. He'd be long gone. Everything hinged on that single factor.

Where the hell is Boswell?

The big diesel engine roared. The echo bounced around the square, and all of a sudden the cloud moved, and a shaft of moonlight lit up the square. It also cast a monstrous shadow on the buildings, a shadow in the shape of a monstrous T54 tank, heading right at them.

* * *

The door opened, a shaft of light lit up the dark cellar, and they threw Dave Eisner back inside. The door slammed shut, the lock rattled, and once again they were sealed inside the black pit.

"Dave, how are you, buddy?" Will called across to his friend and fellow Seal.

"I've been better, but I'm breathing, so I guess I'll live."

"What did they do to you?" Lieutenant Boswell

demanded. His voice shook with fear. It was obvious he'd allowed the terror of the coming torture to overcome him.

"Busted a couple of ribs and two fingers of my right hand."

The cellar was hot, excessively hot, and it stank like a cesspit in a leper colony. Will groped his way through the darkness to come alongside the wounded man.

"I'll strap up the fingers. There must be something I can use. Does anyone have a bandage they didn't take?"

He'd come up with Boswell's fireteam as they'd been advancing toward the outskirts of the town. A few minutes later, the Somalis fell on them. There must have been forty of them, all experts in the art of concealment. One moment, the jungle was a silent, dark wall of green, and the next it was alive with men. They'd kicked and punched the Seals to subdue them, and ripped off their webbing, equipment, and vests. All they had left were the wetsuits. Before they were incarcerated in the dark pit, they'd separated Ashe Ahmed. Maybe because he was a high value prisoner, a UN commissioner was a rare catch. Or maybe to kill him as a supposed ally of the Western influenced United Nations. Bryce cursed to himself. So far, they knew nothing. Nothing of who had taken them, no idea of the location of Ashe Ahmed. Nothing.

We need info. We have to have some answers, if we're to get out of here.

No one replied to his request for a dressing. "Okay, search around, men. Feel with your fingers. There must be something here I can strap up his fingers with."

He waited while they groped around the dark space, with his arm around Eisner to support him. Despite his making light of it, Bryce knew they'd roughed him up real bad. He was cycling between consciousness and unconsciousness, and the tough PO1 was determined to keep him awake, even if it was only to meet a worse fate. He dismissed that thought as quickly as it came.

We're getting out of here, no question. Besides, Chief Nolan is still on the loose. We have to hold out, just a little longer.

Vince Merano had been first, and he was lying in a heap on the floor, his left arm dislocated.

Who will be next? Will wondered.

But they didn't have long to wait. The door opened again, and the Somali beckoned toward Boswell.

"You. Come."

The Lieutenant surprised them all. He climbed to his feet and walked out of the cell, with his head up.

"If that don't beat all," Dave murmured.

"Yeah. Unless he has a plan for them to go easy on him."

"A plan? How would he do that?"

Vince had asked the question from the corner where he lay. After a moment, he supplied the answer as well.

"Oh, yeah, got it. He could tell them everything."

The room was silent as they digested the import of his words. Sure, selling the mission may save him from a beating. But if they knew about Nolan and the other fireteam, it could be enough for them to plant an ambush, and either kill them all or consign them to this dark, sweating hell. With Nolan's team gone, there'd be no chance of getting out.

Once more, the door opened, and they pushed a prisoner inside. Even in the dim wash of light that briefly lit up the room, they could see it was Ashe Ahmed. His black face was battered, one eye closed, and blood poured from his knee. Bryce helped him to sit on the floor. The man was working hard to contain his agony. His shirt and pants were in rags, and it was obvious they'd worked him over hard.

"I'll fix them up for you. We're looking for some dressings."

"Use my shirt," he gasped, "You may as well finish it off."

Will ripped off the last of the cotton fabric and swiftly shredded it into strips. He passed two of them to Weissman, who they hadn't beaten so far. Then he started work on Ahmed. He cleaned away the worst of the blood and felt with his fingers around the wound. He bunched up the rags and tied them down the best he could. While he was working, he took the opportunity to question Ahmed.

"What do we know about these Al Shabaab people? Anything that could be useful to us?"

Even through his pain, the man chuckled. "Al Shabaab? No, this group is nothing to do with Al Shabaab. The man in charge is General Mohammed Hersi. He led the JVA, the Jubla Valley Alliance until recently. When he fell out with the current government, he formed a new group, the Movement for the Liberation of Somalia."

"What's the difference between them and Al Shabaab?"

Another chuckle, this time it was more forced. "Very little. They want the same thing, power. And they don't care who suffers or dies in the process. I suppose the main difference is the MLS promotes a socialist agenda, offering food and land to the hungry and poor. Al Shabaab has only one message."

"Religion."

"Death. Theirs is the religion of death."

The room was silent for several minutes, and then Ahmed had a question of his own.

"They asked me how many men we came with, and I said I only knew of the men I was captured with. Obviously, as long as your other men are at large, there is a chance they could help us. Your Lieutenant will keep the secret?"

Their silence was his reply.

"I see. Then only a miracle will save us."

A quarter of an hour later, the door opened, and they tossed Boswell back inside. He didn't look bad, as if they'd gone easy on him. A few minutes later, they heard the sound of a truck engine starting up, and it drove away. No one looked at Boswell. No one spoke. They knew. He'd sold out the other fireteam, Nolan's fireteam.

* * *

Musse Daud peered through the grimy, soot-streaked window and surveyed the street below. They'd landed at New York's JFK International the night before and checked in with legitimate student visas. When their contact wasn't there to meet them, he had used up most of their reserves of cash to pay for cabs into the city. As instructed, they'd gone to the Malcolm Shabazz Mosque in Harlem. Amongst so many black faces, they'd felt more comfortable, but when they knocked on the door and announced they were Al Shabaab brothers from Somalia, the Imam had adopted a furious expression and told them to get out before he called the cops.

"You people have caused us more then enough trouble in New York. The mosque is raided twice a week. We've had enough. Get out of here and don't come back!"

Bewildered, they'd spent the night in an abandoned subway tunnel in West Harlem. The young men were all tired and dispirited, but Daud pointed out to them their target was less than eight kilometers distant.

"Tomorrow, we'll take a walk through the city and take a look. It will be an opportunity to make certain we're not under surveillance. As soon as we know we're in the clear, I'll call the contact Sheikh Barre gave me, and arrange for them to deliver our martyr's vests to us that same afternoon. Remember, the schedule has been put forward. We have to carry out the attack on the following day."

It was dim in the unlit tunnel, but he could feel their eyes on him. One of them, Amin, plucked up the courage to question him.

"Musse, it's crazy to put forward the schedule. It means we'll have to change the ambush site to the UN Building. It's madness. We may not even get near him."

Musse smiled to himself. *What does he think could happen to us? We're all going to die anyway.*

"I don't care. The order came from Sheikh Barre. When the President of the United States arrives at the UN Building, we will find a way to get near him and kill him. The plan has already been made. All we have to do is get there and, well..."

He glanced around at their faces. They were all tired through lack of sleep, and fear.

"The UN is heavily protected," Amin persisted.

"I don't fucking care!" he lost his temper, "Those are the orders, and we will obey them. It is the will of the Prophet."

They were silent.

Is it the will of the Prophet, or the will of Nabil Barre?

He put the thought out of his mind. He had dedicated his life and his death to this operation. The day after tomorrow, the President of the United States would die. The original plan was to hit him as his cavalcade emerged from the New York Met, but there wasn't time. They'd use the back up plan. Eight men, each wearing a martyr's vest, would detonate simultaneously as the President's limousine passed between the tunnel of death they would create. The blast would be enormous. Nothing could survive. Nothing. No one.

"It is definite, Musse, the day after tomorrow?" Amin asked him, in a voice that quivered with fear.

"Unless the Sheikh calls to postpone for some reason, yes, it is definite."

He reached in his pocket for the cellphone they'd given him. Would it ring to cancel before the appointed hour? No. Soon, they would be in Paradise. It was true. Everyone said it was so.

How do they know? No one has ever returned to tell of what they'd seen.

He dismissed the thought. It was blasphemy. The President would die, as the Sheikh had decreed, and for the eight martyrs, Paradise. He thought of Maryam, the girl he'd said goodbye to in Somalia.

If only.

CHAPTER SEVEN

They watched the shadow come nearer. It loomed large in the eerie moonlight, and then the roar of the massive engine faded.

"Where did it go?" Zeke asked.

They were keyed up and waiting for the fight. Nolan didn't reply. He was watching to see if they'd come at them from a different direction.

But why? They don't know their enemies have captured the crippled T54. There has to be another reason, but what?

They heard the growling echo of the powerful engine and the grinding clatter of the tracks from somewhere behind Barre's house. Then the track noise stopped, and the engine note dropped to a tick over. The guards protecting Barre's house had started to melt away, and then it struck him.

"The bastard's getting away! That other tank isn't to reinforce the defenses. It's his transport out."

He frantically thought through the options. There must be something they could do. Yet they only had one M3 missile with which to take on the armor. To deploy the missile, they'd have to race through to the other side of the house, and it would mean dueling with the remaining guards. Time, the old, unbeatable enemy, was against them. There was nothing they could do. Nothing. Even as he was trying to come up with something, anything to turn the situation around, the tank engine roared and the grinding of the tracks started up again. He was leaving.

He was aware of Zeke, Dan, and Lucas all watching him.

What do they think? I'm some kind of a miracle worker. He squashed the thought. *Yes, that's exactly what they pay me to be, a miracle worker.*

He pressed the transmit button.

"This is Bravo Two. Brad, you there?"

"Yep, nothing happening back here. What's going down?"

"We think Barre just pulled out. We're going into his house and see if we can find out where he went. We'll launch a frontal attack from here. I want you to use the M249 and give us covering fire when we go in."

"Copy that. Chief, I can see a few guards over there. You sure a frontal attack is the best plan?"

"Watch me. Just be ready with that machine gun. I'm leaving my SWS in the hull of tank. Grab it as you come by. I need something smaller to fight with inside that house."

"Sure."

He clicked off and unclipped an AK-47S, the shorter, folding stock model, from the rack inside the tank. He grabbed a canvas bag and filled it with the distinctive banana shaped clips, and then turned to Zeke, who was in the gunner's seat.

"Are you loaded with HE?"

"High explosive? Sure, the shell's in the breech. What's the target?"

"Take a look at the militia defending Barre's place. We're going in there. I want to clear them away."

His lips curled up in amusement. "It'll only take a minute."

Nolan gestured to the other two men. "We need to get outside. As soon as the shell hits, there's going to be dust and debris everywhere. It'll give us a smokescreen to go in."

"Roger that."

They climbed out of the hull and waited. The turret whirred as Zeke used the controls to rotate and elevate the big main gun. At the last second, the men opposite suddenly understood what was about to happen. Several of them started to run, and then the rest followed. The futility of trying to outrun a high explosive tank shell was demonstrated a second later. Zeke fired, and the shell slammed into the front of the building.

The devastation threw up a sheet of flame and smoke, and the fragments and debris scythed through the ground between the house and the perimeter wall, destroying everything in its path. It was a golden opportunity; the entire area was shrouded in smoke and dust. Nolan took it.

"Charge!"

They ran forward, and the same time Brad Rose opened fire with the M249 to deter any of the defenders who managed to recover. As his 5.56mm bullets peppered the windows of Barre's house, Nolan led the Seals past the wall, and they ran straight through the main door that had been left open. They entered the hallway, and simultaneously Brad stopped firing. A silence descended upon the house as the debris settled. Abruptly, a set of footsteps sounded in a room at the side of the hallway. He nodded to Lucas, and they ran forward to the open door.

There was no obvious sign that anyone was inside, except the footsteps had disappeared in there. He didn't want to waste a grenade. They were already low on ordnance and facing an uphill battle. He picked an ornament from a niche in the wall. It looked like a bust of Osama bin Laden.

At least the infamous terrorist commander can do something useful, he reflected as he tossed the heavy piece into the room. It clattered to the floor, and a burst of automatic fire slashed across the room.

He immediately threw himself through the doorway, rolled over, and came up with his weapon ready to fire. He brought up the borrowed AK-47S and fired a burst at a man sheltering behind a sofa. He ducked behind the upholstery, but the fabric did nothing to protect him from the heavy 7.62mm bullets. He heard the thump as the man's body hit the floor and ran around to check him, but he was dead. As he ducked, the burst had caught him in the head and throat, killing him instantly.

He looked up and nodded to Lucas. "Let's go. And remember, we need to find out where Barre's gone. I don't want you to kill them all."

Grant grimaced. "That's a pity."

They rushed back out in the hallway, and this time Lucas led the way. Straight into a burst of machine gunfire from the second floor. Several rounds smacked into his ballistic vest and punched him to the floor. He rolled around to the side of the staircase, clutching his chest, but he'd lost his HK 410, dropping when the bullets smashed into his armor.

"Chief! Watch out..."

"Relax, I've got it. Stay where you are, and leave the gun. You can pick it up when I've aced these gomers."

"Roger that. Christ, those Russian rounds sting like hell."

"Yeah."

Nolan poked his head around the doorway and identified the position of the shooter. A guy was up on the landing clutching a PK, the Soviet made light machine gun. A second man was crouched next to him, feeding an ammunition belt into the gun.

He ducked back inside the room and switched clips. He needed to hit them hard and fast, and he knew he'd need every single one of the thirty rounds in the magazine of the AK. When he was loaded, he happened to glance down and see the statuette of Osama lying on the floor where he'd tossed it.

I've got another job for you, pal.

He picked up the bust and suddenly remembered Brad Rose coming in from the front. He keyed his mic.

"This is Bravo Two. Brad, what's your location?"

"I'm outside the house, just come past the perimeter wall. All clear out here. Zeke did a solid job with that tank shell."

"Yeah. Be aware there's a machine gun up on the second floor. He can see the front entrance, so don't come in that way."

"Roger that. The windows are all blasted out. I'll go that way. You need a hand?"

"Negative. What I need is a prisoner."

"Do my best. Out."

Nolan heard a burst of machine gunfire from further inside the house where Zeke and Dan were cleaning up.

Good, it'll divert the gunner's attention.

He tossed the statuette into the hallway, aiming for a patch of marble floor. It hit with a loud crash and split into scores of small fragments.

Fish food size, he smiled to himself.

But it gave him the chance he needed. A burst of machine gunfire tore through the air and chewed plaster off the walls. The gunfire only stopped when the belt came to the end.

He heard the gunner shouting at his loader to hurry. They spoke in Somali, he assumed, but he didn't need an interpreter to know what they needed.

Too bad, pal. You should have used a longer belt.

He stepped out into the hall and stared up at the machine gunners. They stared back at him, a frozen moment in time, and he could see in their eyes they knew they were about to die. But still, they were trained militiamen, probably veterans of a number of clashes with local tribal factions. The gunner pushed the machine gun away, and both men clawed for the pistols tucked into their sashes. Nolan pulled the trigger and sprayed them with fire, using their own bullets.

The AK-47 range of weapons had a good reputation for reliability, even in the roughest and most difficult terrain. It was one of the reasons they were popular across Africa. And gave it the nickname 'the troubled continent', that and their wide availability and low price. His AK-47S maintained that reputation.

The 7.62mm round was a rifle cartridge designed during World War II, and first used in the RPD machine gun. The ammunition was designed to function well in a wide range of temperatures, from extremely cold Polar Regions to hot desert climates. It was a warm night, but well within the tolerances for the ammunition. Every single one of the thirty rounds left the barrel, and at least half of them impacted the two Somalis. The kinetic force and heavy weight of lead tossed them back several feet, and their bodies finally hit the floor.

He was about to race up to check them when he heard footsteps, and a face appeared at the head of the staircase before he had a chance to change clips.

"It's okay," Dan shouted, "I was clearing the second floor. I found a prisoner, Chief. A woman."

"Good work, bring her down."

He finished reloading as Brad entered the house with Amelia. She carried his long SWS Mk 11. He shouldered the AK47S and took the sniper rifle, enjoying the familiar feel of the butt, molded to his exact specifications. It was like an old friend. Reliable.

They turned as Dan came down the staircase, leading a woman. She wore traditional Somali dress, a colorful dress, with a matching scarf wrapped around her head. She'd been attractive, once, but that was a long time ago. Her jet-black face was lined and careworn.

"She speaks English," he told them, "Says she's related to Nabil Barre."

"I am his wife!" she spat, "His first wife."

"We need you to help us," Amelia said in soothing tones. The woman relaxed and seemed to warm to her. At least the African American FBI Agent was the same color,

"We're looking for your husband, Ma'am," she continued, her tone soothing.

"To kill him? Is that right, you'll murder him when you find him?"

Her eyes were wild, almost crazy. Yet Nolan detected something there that wasn't madness.

It's...anger.

"We need to find him," Amelia hedged.

"Hah! You want to kill him, these American soldiers. You think I'm stupid? Don't worry; I want to see that bastard dead for what he's done. He..."

She stopped, and her eyes filled with tears.

"Tell me, Ma'am," Amelia prompted her gently.

In between sobs, the story came out. "It is my son. My name was Daud before we married. Fatima Daud. We married when I was very young, only thirteen years old. My husband is a hard man. He leads the militia in this area. At first, he was kind to me. Even when he took other wives, he found time to spend with me, and I was happy. Until the American girl."

They stared at her. "An American girl? You mean she's some kind of convert to Islam?"

She laughed. "A convert? Oh, no. She was twelve when he took her. At first, she hated all of us. She fought and struggled to escape, but Nabil locked her away in a basement for several months. Then he beat her until she submitted to his desires. He became so infatuated with her he took her for his new wife. And he spends all his time with her. She even gave birth to his son, Mukhtar. The only words he has for his other wives are to command us to carry out menial tasks in his household." Her eyes misted, "The poor girl, he calls her Saba, begged for him to release her when the baby was born. She wanted her son to be brought up as an American. He just laughed and beat her. She is a slave, just like the rest of us."

"We'll do what we can. She's definitely an American?"

"Yes, she was taken as a prize from a captured yacht. He killed her parents, but he fell for her youth. She was only twelve, you see. To him, the rest of us were old women."

Nolan recoiled in horror.

Twelve years old! A young girl, he murdered her parents and then kidnapped her, effectively raped her. The fucking pedophile!

"She was so young, so pretty," the woman continued, "Blonde hair, a beautiful child. That was four years ago, of course. She's aged since she came into his house."

I be she has.

Lucas interrupted. His face was like thunder. "Ma'am, this American girl? You say he won't let her take her son home?"

They all looked at Lucas in surprise. Something about the story had touched a nerve, but what?

"That is correct."

His face was hard and cold. Nolan remembered to have that conversation about what was bugging him. When there was time.

"That sounds like hell," Amelia sympathized, "Not much fun at all." The good-looking Special Agent had managed to gain a degree of empathy with her.

"No, it wasn't fun." She glared up at them, her face reflecting a thousand miseries, "I know what you're thinking. Why would I want him dead, just for giving me a few extra chores, and for all the beatings? But it's not that, it's my son. He killed him."

"I'm sorry," Amelia shook her head, "That's terrible.

When did it happen?"

"I don't know, but it will be soon."

"Will be? I don't understand."

"Nabil sent out a group of our young people on a mission. He ordered all of them to become shaheeds, martyrs, in the name of the Prophet. One of them is my son, Musse Daud."

"Shit, that's a rough deal," she soothed, "Do you happen to know the target, or when it's going down?"

"The target is in America, that's all I know. That's all I know."

America! So Al Shabaab was planning to hit the US sooner rather than later. It meant the intel was correct. But they were too late, Barre had already let loose his dogs of war, unless they could find out the when and the where.

"America is a big place, Ma'am. Could you be more specific? We need to know the timing, and the target, if you can help us."

She shrugged. "That's all I know, America. There are eight of them. Eight martyrs, including my son. Please, I want to stop him, but I don't know how to reach him."

Amelia nodded. "Okay, we'll do what we can."

"Please, try to stop them. I do not want them dead."

"One more thing, Ma'am. Where is your husband now? Where can we find him?"

"To kill him?"

Amelia looked at Nolan. After a few seconds, he nodded.

"Yes. After we find out what we want to know. To kill him."

"Good. Jidka Jaamacadda."

"Excuse me?"

"It is the name of the street where he has a house. I do not know which house is his, but that is where he will go. It is close to Mogadishu University. Although the government does not support the aims of Al Shabaab, many of the students do, and so they help him. I wanted Musse to study at Mogadishu University," she sobbed again.

"Thank you. We will do our best to..."

"Kill him!" she shouted.

This time, Nolan replied. "We will, Ma'am. That's a promise."

Zeke returned from mopping up the last resistance inside the house, and Nolan sent him outside with Brad and Dan to watch the perimeter. While Amelia turned to help a protesting Lucas Grant, who insisted his wounds were 'nothing', he thought about their next step. Without Boswell's fireteam, they were sunk. He needed men, communications, and weapons, and they had them all. He had an idea how to locate them. He dug out the cellphone and called Ayub Ahmed.

"We need your help again, Sir."

"Anything, if it's to get that bastard Barre."

"Our informant tells us he's gone to ground in Mogadishu, at a street called Jidka Jaamacadda, close to..."

"Mogadishu University, yes, I know Jidka Jaamacadda. He has a house in that street? That's the first I heard of it, but still..." he stopped, thinking, "Yes, it's possible. There are a score of big houses past the campus. They're all big places, surrounded by high walls with guards and security cameras. The owners value their anonymity. Wealth can attract a lot of envy in this country."

"Can you find out which house is his? We don't have

much time. It seems he has help from students in the college. I wondered if you could ask around."

"Certainly, I can try. So you're headed to Mogadishu? You know that it's three hundred kilometers?"

"I know, but first we have to locate our people. They disappeared inside Kismayo."

He explained they'd skirted around the north side of the town and then vanished.

"MLS. Has to be."

"I'm sorry, MLS? What's that?"

"Movement for the Liberation of Somalia. They control the north side of Kismayo, so if your men disappeared, that's who would have taken them. Their leader is Faisal Askar, a man who is feared across the whole of Somalia. They'd have taken them for ransom, probably. They know foreign soldiers will be worth a lot of money from their government. They'd want their weapons as well, to use themselves. What about my relation, Ashe Ahmed? Is he with them?"

"We assume so. We don't know anything for sure until we find them."

"I will see what I can find out. There is someone in the town that may know more. He is a civilian who works for the police."

It was five minutes before he came back. "Yes, they took over a transport depot in Farjarno. It's three hundred meters past the bus station."

"Can you give me the coordinates?"

"Yes." He read of a series of numbers, which Nolan fed into his GPS.

"Got it. So they're holed up inside this old transport depot."

"Not old, no. My contact says it's still running, and they use the vehicles to convey drugs and weapons around the country."

"The place is still running? You mean they have trucks?"

"Yes. It would be a useful front for their activities, and very profitable. Think about it, who would dare set up in opposition to the MLS? They'd soon find their trucks hijacked, their buildings burned, and their drivers beaten or killed. By the way, he said the company is called SLM Trucking."

MLS reversed, yeah, very droll.

"Thanks. We'll do our best to protect Ashe if we come across him."

"I hope so. I'll do my best to find out if they are holding your men, and I'll call you when I know anything."

He ended the call, and Nolan passed on what he knew. There was a big problem that prevented them moving straight through Kismayo undetected. It was starting to get light outside. When the town was fully awake, and they realized what had gone down during the night, the place would come alive with cops, militia, and God only knew who else.

"We'll retreat to the house across the square. We'll move right now. We have to wait until tonight to make our move. In the meantime, we all need to get some rest."

They started to move out, and when they reached open ground, sprinted across the square to get inside cover before daylight revealed them to the Somalis. It was only when they got inside the derelict house he realized the woman, Barre's wife, was with them. He went to eject her, but Amelia stopped him.

"She has to stay, Kyle. She's the only one in that house

who would have known where to find Barre. If we send her away, they'll kill her."

She was listening, standing a few meters away.

"I can cook," she called over to him, "If he didn't want me for anything else, my husband always valued me for the meals I cooked for him. Look," she pointed out an old solid fuel stove, "I can get this working and make a good meal for your men. My husband always said men fight better after a good meal and a good woman."

I'll bet he did.

He hated the idea of having someone from the enemy camp with his tiny unit, but Amelia glared at him, and he knew he had no choice.

"Okay, you can stay."

"I will make a good meal. You'll be happy you kept me with you. I can do other things for you as well, American soldier."

"The meal will be fine, Fatima."

She pulled a face and then spoke rapidly to Amelia in Somali, who turned to him.

"We need to go to the market. It's not too far away. They open about now, so we can pick up some fresh stuff."

He looked at her. She looked ethnic enough. "Right. You got a gun?" She patted her multi-hued dress, "I'm still packing the Tokarev."

They left, and he looked around to see the men were staring at him, Lucas, Brad, Zeke, and Dan. They were probably wondering had he lost his head, letting the two women go into a town in the most dangerous country in the world; to get ingredients for a meal, of all things. He'd wondered the same thing, before he thought it all through. They were stuck in the house and had to lay low. They couldn't move until nightfall, and most of the furor over the military activity had died down.

So far, every person who'd seen them and identified them as Americans was dead. If the locals discovered the truth, there was an American Special Forces unit in their town, God help them. He reminded himself where they were. Somalia. A name synonymous with nightmares in America, the subject of a movie about the whole fiasco, Black Hawk Down, and the pirate capital of the world. A place to stay out of sight; they would wait.

While they waited, they needed rest and food for the next stage. He'd made up his mind to attack the MLS headquarters after dark and free the prisoners, assuming they were still alive.

They have to be alive. There's no way I can contemplate their deaths. It hasn't happened. They'll be there. Will Bryce, Dave Eisner, Vince Merano, Jack Weissman, and even Boswell. They have to be there, and Ashe Ahmed, if he's lucky. Surely, they won't kill a UN Commissioner? Only if it suits them. They're alive, all of them.

His plan was to free them, take a truck, and make straight for Mogadishu in the same night, a four-hour drive to Barre's hidey-hole. And then kill the bastard, a murderer, a thug and, a pedophile. Except...there was the question of the attack on the US. Before he died, the terrorist leader would tell them all about it. All he needed was the right persuasion. He glanced at Lucas Grant.

Yes, Lucas will know how to handle it.

There was something about the enigmatic Seal. Something dark, more brutal than was the norm for Special Forces. Nolan resolved to make sure Grant didn't kill Barre. Not before time.

* * *

Four hours later, when they were resting after the hot stew that Fatima Barre had cooked up for them, they'd changed their minds. The women had returned after collecting armfuls of meat and vegetables. The older woman had prepared a fire in the wood-burning stove, and the old derelict house came alive to the smells of cooking. The meal was every bit as good as the odors promised, and afterward they relaxed for the first time in a long time.

In the mid afternoon, Nolan was on watch on the second floor at the front of the house. Most of the men were dozing downstairs, except Lucas who was checking and cleaning his weapons. There was movement outside, men running in and out of Barre's house, searching the grounds and climbing all over the disabled T54 in the center of the square. But none came near the house in which they sheltered. Why should they? It was derelict and assumed to be empty. He got the impression that people had no idea where Barre had disappeared to, which was unsurprising. When a man in Somalia with a big price on his head decided to go to ground, he'd want it to be kept as secret as possible.

He turned as someone came into the room behind him. The FBI Special Agent, Amelia Stowe, strolled over to him and sat down next to where he crouched beside the window.

"What's going on out there?" she asked him.

"Nothing to worry us. They're running around like ants, and they haven't a clue what happened in the night. As we're out of sight, I'd guess they believe it was a rival bunch of militia that hit them. Maybe even this Movement for the Liberation of Somalia."

"It's possible," she murmured, "Kyle, we've been lucky. After what we kicked up in the night, it's amazing they're not hunting the town for American soldiers."

He took his eyes off the square for a moment and smiled. "Amelia, why don't I feel lucky? I mean, trapped in this shithole, and surrounded by Somalis who would slit our throats if they thought we were here."

"I'm a Somali, don't forget," she pointed out.

But he shook his head. "You're American, same as me, same as the rest of Bravo. Just because your origins are here, doesn't make any difference. I have Irish ancestors, like a few million Americans, but it doesn't make me Irish. Why would you want to claim to be a Somali? Look at this place. These people live in a toilet, literally. Christ, they don't even dispose of their sewage."

She grimaced. "I know, but it's not their fault. The country has been ravaged by wars for hundreds of years. The poor devils don't stand a chance, ripped between different tribal factions, and in the old days, it was colonial overlords."

He was keeping his gaze on the square outside, watching through a small hole he'd wiped in the grime of the window. Even so, he smiled. She was sincere in her beliefs and concern for the country of her forefathers, but like most people with idealistic theories, hopelessly wrong.

There was something else, something that was bothering him. She was a beautiful young woman, and the fragrant musk of her wafted toward him, and he felt almost overcome by it. With an effort, he turned his mind back to her argument.

"There's another country with a similar history. It's called the United States of America. Sure, we had constant battles between warring tribes, armies of colonists pouring into the country, and fighting each other as well as the tribes. Yet as I recall, we managed to shake it off and do rather well. Somalia is rich in resources, agriculture, telecoms, manufacturing, even airlines and finance. Enough to give these people a good life, if they just stop shooting at each other."

"So why doesn't it happen?" she asked plaintively. He could hear the agony in her voice for these people, most of whom had no interest in anything other than feeding their families.

He grimaced. "There's another resource Somalia is also rich in. Perhaps richer than any of the others."

"Islam," she said quietly.

"Islam, yeah. You find an Islamic country, and you'll find most of the population living like paupers. Even in the oil-rich countries, where there is no excuse for letting people starve, it's no different."

"You think Islam is the problem?"

"I don't say that. What I'm saying is, it's a common factor. I'll leave someone else to work out the rest of it."

She didn't reply for a few minutes and spent some time staring out the window with him, watching the people outside. Most of them were ragged and obviously in need of a good meal. Yet someone had found the resources to equip most of them with weaponry. It didn't take a huge leap of imagination to work out that if they spent the money thrown away on weapons, on food, clothing, and education, Somalia would be a better place. She turned her head toward him.

"Why don't they do it? Lay down their guns and live a better life."

"Ask the Mullahs."

She sighed and moved nearer to him. "What's going on over there?"

He followed her gaze to a vehicle tucked into the end of a narrow lane at the side of the square. The place where they were parked was under a clump of palm trees. Normally, they'd be laden with branches and leaves, but the explosions had stripped them bare.

A man in the robes of a Mullah was hammering on the roof, and a militiaman was banging on the driver's side door with the butt of his rifle. The door opened slowly, and a man looked out. He was a young Somali, good looking and clean-shaven, with well-trimmed hair. The Mullah raved and shouted, and the militiaman ran around, raised his rifle, and brought it down on his head. The kid screamed in pain as the Mullah dragged him out of the car and tossed him on the ground. The passenger door opened, and a girl got out. She was young and pretty, and it wasn't too hard to work out they'd been making out inside the vehicle. Nolan smiled.

"The poor bastards thought it was a quiet spot at the end of that lane. All that shooting and shelling last night stripped it bare. Looks like they're in trouble."

The boy was on the ground, and now the militiaman was using his boot to kick him. The Mullah had turned his attention to the girl, and he was screaming at her, only inches from her face. Abruptly, he took a step back, and slapped her so hard she fell sprawling to the ground. Nolan heard Amelia gasp at the ferocity.

"Bastard, they weren't doing anything bad. Usually,

Somalia is not so rigid about boys and girls making out. Maybe it's because Al Shabaab is more active in this area."

"Or maybe the girl is the Mullah's daughter, and he's real pissed."

She turned him and grinned. "Good point. You could be right."

He felt her eyes meet his, and a shiver went through him. It was almost like magnetism, or more like an animal magnetism. The attraction between them was strong, and she swayed toward him, and then their lips met in a long and passionate kiss. He felt himself becoming aroused and inhaled the sweet scent of her body, as his instincts almost overcame him. Almost. He broke away.

"Jesus, I nearly…"

"Yes," she agreed. She fixed him with those deep, dark eyes again, "Kyle, why almost? We're on our own."

"I'm supposed to be keeping watch. If I took my eyes off the square to ravish the most beautiful girl I've set eyes on in a long time, the enemy could be all over us while we were otherwise engaged."

"So don't take your eyes off the square. We can arrange it."

"How?"

She put her finger to his lips, and he went silent. She swiftly removed her dress; the wetsuit was no longer under it. All she wore beneath it was panties and bra. A few seconds later, they were lying on the floor. She went to work on his camo wetsuit and pulled it off him. He felt relief at losing the clammy garment, which wasn't design for lengthy operations in climates like Somalia.

"Damn, that feels good."

"You mean me undressing you?"

"Well, yeah, but getting that wetsuit off."

"Right. Maybe we can fix up some ordinary clothing for you. You wouldn't look like a bunch of invading American Special Forces. Let's see how we can work this out."

She pulled an old wooden chair to the window, and he sat down in it, feeling strange on sentry duty with no clothes on. Then she knelt on the floor and put her head over his shaft. He enjoyed the exquisite ecstasy as she gently stroked him with her mouth, and when he was rock hard, she climbed astride him and guided him inside her. They started to rock back and forth, a slow, sensuous rhythm that was unearthly. Especially since he never took his eyes off the square.

Her hands caressed his body, and she licked his neck, but still he kept his gaze firmly rooted ahead, even when she tilted her head sideways and managed to engage his lips in a kiss that was more passionate for the strange circumstances. He was moving to a new plane. His mind soared to the very heights of the highest mountains and the depths of the deepest valleys, as he sailed the ship of ecstasy.

He never knew if it was her, or a combination of such weird circumstances with his brain split into two parts, one part on watch, and the other enjoying an experience like never before. You want it to last, forever. It was as if all his life had been pointed toward this unique and incredible experience.

Sadly, it is a truism that the very best things in life are usually very fleeting in nature. Like seeing in the street the face of a beautiful girl as she strolls past, or exquisite cuisine that is quickly devoured and rarely repeated. So it was with making love to Amelia Stowe. All too soon, he climaxed. She sensed it coming, and her hips writhed almost as if she was in agony, and she joined him at the summit of their lovemaking.

They kept their lips clamped firmly together, determined not to make any kind of a sound that would give away their secret tryst. Instead, they held each other, with their hands clamped over the other's shoulders to hold their partner close. Yet not so close to prevent him carrying out his duty.

Finally, she disentangled her body from his and pulled on her underwear and dress. She handed him his camo wetsuit, and still staring through the hole in the grimy window, he pulled it back on, wincing at the clammy damp of the rubberized fabric. She grimaced at his discomfort.

"You need to find some real clothes to wear, Kyle."

"Yeah, right. You think I should go raiding the washing lines?"

She glanced down at her red dress. "No, really, there are markets everywhere you can buy jeans and T-shirts. You wouldn't be so conspicuous."

"Lady, with my skin, I'd need more than a T-shirt to blend in. You'd be okay with anything. You look like a local."

"True, but I intend keep this dress anyway. I'm growing fond of it. It brings me luck."

"It brought me a fair bit of luck, too."

She grinned. "Don't think it's going to become a habit, buster."

"No, I...hold it." He leaned forward, "Jesus Christ!"

"Trouble?" She was at the window, peering out beside him.

"Not trouble, no. It's Dr. Ayub Ahmed. He's coming

here."

* * *

Several minutes later, the academic was standing inside the building. He stared at Fatima Barre.

"What's she doing here? I recognize her. She's..."

"We know. She's his wife, or one of them. She fed us the info about her husband, and now she's keeping out of the way, in case they discover who ratted him out. Besides, she's a damn good cook."

"Cook?" He looked mystified.

At that moment, Brad came in from the stove in the kitchen, carrying a bowl of stew.

"You ought to try it, Doc. Better than an apple a day."

He looked bewildered.

"American humor," Nolan explained, "What's happened?"

"I found out some more some information about the MLS. One of their fighters let slip to his wife they're holding a bunch of foreign soldiers at the SLM Trucking depot in Farjarno. I thought she might help. She's a second cousin of the woman who cleans my house. She doesn't know about Ashe, but I would imagine he's held in the same place. They're definitely there."

"Now we know, Dr. Ahmed, is there any chance you could borrow a car? Even after dark, we could run into trouble getting there on foot."

He thought for a few moments, and then his face brightened. "Yes, yes, there may be something. The journey is only five kilometers."

* * *

The car arrived just before nightfall. They heard an old gas engine chugging toward them. At least, it looked something like a car. The paintwork was red. Once. Now, it was a combination of rust and pitted, faded red. When they went outside, Dr. Ahmed was switching off the engine.

"It's a Moskvich," he said brightly, "It was built in 1987 and imported to Somalia by a Russian oil exploration company. When they went bust, it came up for auction, and I bought it. It's very reliable."

"Yeah, right."

"It will reach Farjarno, never fear."

"Doc, you need to transport five Seals and Amelia Stowe. Look at it. We have our gear as well."

"It will fit in the trunk."

Nolan shook his head. The trunk was little bigger than a shoebox, but as the light faded, they gathered their gear together and found they could wedge it inside with the lid tied down. The nose of the M3 launcher poked out, and they covered it with a piece of canvas.

They were making final checks on their weapons when Fatima Barre approached him.

"What about me? You can't leave me here."

"I will return for you," Ahmed said gently, "Never fear, we will get you out of Kismayo this night."

She nodded uncertainly.

"Time to rock 'n' roll," Nolan told them, "Let's load this tin can and get the show on the road."

They crammed into the tiny vehicle. Amelia Stowe sat in the passenger seat, as she could pass for a native. The rest of them, five men, squeezed into the back in a space barely big enough for two adults. The journey to Farjarno was a nightmare. The ancient springs were pushed to their limits by the extra weight, and every bump and pothole shook the frame of the old vehicle and transmitted the jars to the occupants.

They reached the outskirts of Farjarno, and Ahmed braked to a halt five hundred meters from the MLM headquarters. He drove away before any of the fighters noticed a strange car in the area, and Nolan's squad deployed into the brush at the side of the narrow track. They reached the edge of the foliage; the nearest they could get to the compound without taking the risk of the defenders seeing them. The ground around the outside had been cleared of foliage, to make a two hundred-meter wide kill zone. Overhead security lights also lighted it up, and guards were pacing around the top of the five-meter high perimeter wall. The main gates were made of reinforced steel and locked shut.

"It reminds me of a fort," Brad murmured.

"That's the way they designed it. We need to…"

Before he finished, a searchlight clicked on and played around the open ground. It stayed on the several minutes before it clicked off. They watched and waited, and a few minutes later the light came on again. This time, it stayed on.

"You think they suspect something?" Zeke said.

"Wouldn't you? Last night we created hell inside the town, and they'll be on alert for more trouble tonight. They'll be watching for an attack from a rival gang, Al Shabaab most likely."

He grunted a reply, and they settled down to watch

and wait. After an hour, when nothing changed, and the searchlight continued to play around the kill zone, Nolan decided they had no choice.

"We have to go in."

"Chief, the wall's pretty high, which leaves the gates. How do we get through them?"

"We use the M3. As soon as they blow, a fireteam will go over the wall at the back. We'll need a boarding line with a grapple."

"I'll do it," Lucas said, "I can be over that wall before the dust from the missile hit has cleared."

"I'm counting on it. Brad, take the M249 and go with him."

Lucas immediately began to worm his way toward the rear of the compound. Dan and Zeke went the opposite way to position themselves with a good view of the front gate. Nolan waited in sight with the girl.

"Bravo Two, this is Grant. We're in position."

A moment later Zeke called in. "Bravo Two. M3 ready to shoot."

"Wait for my order," he replied quietly.

"What are you waiting for?" Amelia asked.

"Listen."

She heard it a few seconds later. The sound of an engine, a heavy truck engine. Ten seconds later it appeared, driving at high speed toward the gates. An open Fiat truck, and sitting in the rear were militia. A dozen men in all, and armed with an assortment of weapons, AK-47s and RPG7s.

"But...how could they know we're here?"

"They don't, but they're taking no chances."

"We have to call it off. Kyle, what can we do? How can

we rescue those men?"

Without turning away from watching the truck, he muttered, "Watch."

The truck slowed as it neared the gates. He touched his mic. "This is Bravo Two. Zeke, you know what to do."

"Copy that."

"Lucas, I'd guess about ten seconds."

"Copy that."

The vehicle came to a stop, and the gates started to swing open to allow it to drive inside. When they were wide, a trail of fire streaked across the open ground and impacted the Fiat. The explosion was massive, lighting up the sky in an enormous fireball of flame and smoke. A score of small fires started, and the entire compound was engulfed in smoke. Lucas called in first.

"This is Lucas. We're inside the compound."

"Roger that."

He climbed to his feet and stared back at her.

"Time to go. We'll join Zeke and Dan by the front gate."

He was already walking away, and she leapt to her feet and followed him through the wisps of smoke that swept around the area for hundreds of meters. He linked up with Zeke and Dan, who were ready and waiting.

"That was good shooting. Time to go and finish the job."

They jogged toward the smoking wreckage of the truck jammed in the center of the open gates, with its grisly load of charred corpses. Amelia caught up with him.

"What about the rest of the defenders inside the compound? They'll cut us to pieces as soon as we get inside."

Before he could answer, they heard the sound of

automatic fire from the M249 chewing up the compound.

He smiled. "I guess they have a few things on their mind right now."

CHAPTER EIGHT

The day came to an end, and their tempers were more frayed than ever. They'd managed to rent a shabby hotel room for their last night on earth, and it was hot and crowded. And stank of fear. The eight martyrs' vests were ranged around the floor, and it was impossible to look in any direction without seeing the obscene garments.

They were crudely constructed of canvas with rough stitching. The pockets around the vests were filled with blocks of plastic explosive and connected to the main detonator with a wire to the circuit board. A thin cable extended from the circuit board to a small button for each martyr to conceal in his hand. At the moment he gave them the signal, they would press the button and detonate their explosives, the first part of their journey to Paradise.

Or so they thought. The reality was rather different. In order to create an explosion great enough to destroy the President's armored limo, the buttons were dummies. Except for his. The vests were linked by radio to each other, so when he detonated, they would explode as one.

Anyone within a fifty-meter radius would die, armored limo or not. Including the martyrs, whether they wanted to or not. The problem was, the decision was his, and his alone to make. And he didn't want to die.

He thought again about Nabil Barre. The Sheikh had convinced them all of the holy nature of their mission, butt Barre hadn't been to Paradise himself, so how could he know? There was another problem. Musse's beloved mother, Fatima, was married to the Sheikh and lived in Barre's household, although it had been a long time since he'd taken her to his bed. The Sheikh had made it clear the penalty for failure would mean the life of his mother.

No, I will have to go through with it.

It would mean honor for his mother and a pension for life. The alternative was too terrible to consider.

"Musse, can I have a word?"

Amin again. He had a sly look on his face, as if he'd been scheming with some of the others.

"What is it?"

"It's about Rageh."

One of the martyrs, the youngest, was only fourteen years old and consumed with religious passion.

"Go on."

"I think he's having second thoughts. It's the way he's been talking to the others. He could be a security risk. I think we should kill him."

Musse stared at Amin for a few seconds. "Kill him? Is that your answer to everything, Amin? Death?"

He shrugged. "In his case, yes. We're all going to die anyway. He'll just be a little," he grinned, his thick lips formed a sneer, "a little premature."

"No! If he wants to back out, that's up to him. Amin,

you may wear his martyr's vest. After all, you are going to Paradise, what difference one or two vests? We will lock him in this room until it is over. Use the plastic ties we brought with us."

"I still think we should kill him."

"No. We are martyrs, not murderers."

"Are you afraid, Musse, afraid of killing? I mean; you're not going to back out of this?"

He flared in anger. "Of course not. Besides, you know what is at stake."

"Your mother, yes, I know. Why did Sheikh Barre not acknowledge you as his son?"

"Because he and my mother were not married. It was difficult, at the time. See to Rageh, and no more talk of murder."

"Yes, Musse."

Mother, I wish it did not have to be like this. I wish there was some other way, but there isn't. And when I am dead tomorrow, the Sheikh will give you special honor as his preferred wife, and at long last name me as his son.

* * *

They hurtled into the compound, weapons ready, straight past the gruesome wreck carrying its load of smoking corpses to hell. Nolan carried the AK47s. This was not work for a long range, semi-auto sniper rifle. He needed the brutal bark of the Soviet made assault carbine. A guard was picking himself off the ground, still groggy from the explosion, and Nolan shot him dead with a three-shot burst. Behind him, Zeke fired to the side, taking out a militiaman who was standing on top of the wall, about to line up a shot. They ran on toward the rear, and the sounds of the firefight where Grant and Rose had infiltrated the compound.

They came upon the bulk of the MLS force of almost a score of men crouched behind a single story building, a storehouse probably. 5.56mm rounds from Brad's M249 sprayed the building, preventing them from taking their attackers head on, but one of the men was walking out of the door of the building with an RPG7 mounted on his shoulder. He saw the men go into a huddle, making their plans to kill the intruders. There was no time to finesse it. If they launched that rocket at Brad and Lucas' position, they'd be wiped out. He slapped in a fresh clip and turned to the men behind him.

"We have to hit them now. If they use that rocket..."

"What are we waiting for?" Dan grimaced.

"Let's go."

They went in running, firing from the hip. At first, the defenders failed to understand the danger, until it was way too late. Four of them went down, amongst them the missile shooter; then two more, and they turned to face the new threat. Three more fell, one of them screaming in his death agony enough to chill the blood of his comrades. They threw down their weapons and began to raise their hands. Zeke glanced at him, his eyebrows raised.

"What do we do, Chief?"

"Don't kill them. They could be useful. Find somewhere to lock them away. That building looks possible." He walked into the building, which was constructed of stone, with no windows and a thick wooden door with heavy iron bolts. The only materials inside were old engine and vehicle parts.

"It'll do. Lock them in, and put the injured out of their misery. I believe it's called Somali Healthcare."

He grinned. "Right."

They shepherded the prisoners inside, slid the bolts across, and went about their grisly work terminating the wounded. He called Lucas and Brad.

"This is Bravo Two. Cease fire, I say again, cease fire."

"Copy that. What do we have left inside?"

"We're not certain, not yet. We have to search the buildings and locate our men. We're sure to run into more hostiles, so stay alert."

"Roger that."

Two minutes later, they joined up with Nolan. Lucas gave a casual glance at the heap of bodies.

"That's a few less to take pot shots at us."

"Yeah. They're locking the survivors in that storeroom."

He looked surprised. "Survivors? Is that a good idea, Chief?"

"We're not murderers, Lucas. We only kill when it's essential."

Grant darted him a strange glance. "We should be, after what these people do."

His voice dripped with venom.

"What is it, Lucas?"

"My sister. She killed herself a couple of weeks ago. Her Saudi ex-husband took her baby son. She couldn't live with it."

"I'm sorry."

"Yeah. So will these bastards be sorry."

So that explains the problem.

He shook his head. There were more important matters to attend to than Grant's bitterness. There'd be time to help him later. In the meantime, there were the hostages. Zeke and Dan returned, and he told them to start looking for them.

"Remember, they could be guarded by militia, so don't do anything to get them killed. Lucas, come with me. We'll take this end of the compound. Zeke, you two take the other. We'll meet up in the center in around fifteen minutes. Call in if you find anything."

"Copy that."

They jogged away, and he led Lucas to start searching the buildings. They scored zero with the first three structures, which were huge garages where the valuable trucks could be locked away. All they found were trucks, lots of trucks.

They came to an open space with a couple more trucks parked either end. At the side stood a two-story building with an engineering workshop on the first floor, and an office on the second with an outside metal staircase.

"We'll check this out. I'll go up first. Cover me."

"Roger that."

Whatever else he was, Lucas Grant was an efficient Seal. He positioned himself so that anyone coming out to take a shot would be in his sights. Nolan started up the metal stairs and looked through the window set in the door. A man was inside, sitting behind a desk, a huge man, bald, and with a heavily scarred face. When he saw Nolan, he gave him a small wave and beckoned him in.

The Seal inched open the door and poked the barrel of his AK inside.

"Who are you?"

The big man gave him a lazy smile. "I'm the man who can kill your friends, if we don't make a deal. My name is Faisal Askar, and I own these premises, so it looks to me like you're trespassing."

"It looks to me like you're looking at the wrong end of a gun barrel."

The big man laughed out loud. "You kill me, and they all die."

"Where are they, Askar?"

He shook his head. "Oh, no, not until we have a deal. I don't mind you killing my men. It'll save me paying them, and they are always plenty more looking for work. But my trucks, that's a different matter. I want you out of here. Leave me alone, and when you're gone, you can call me, and I'll tell you where to find them."

Nolan thought quickly. He knew if he left the compound, the guy could call in an army on the way within minutes. Now that the Seals had killed his men, he'd want revenge, without a doubt. Besides, he couldn't leave, not without his men.

They have to be here somewhere, but where?"

He keyed his mic. "Zeke, this is Bravo Two. Get back to those prisoners, and ask them where our people are being held. I'm with their boss, Faisal Askar, and he's not talking."

"Roger that. What can we offer the one who talks?"

"Tell them the one who talks can go free, the rest die."

"For real?"

"No, but make them think it."

Something was wrong. Askar had glared at him as he spoke, so the man knew it was only a matter of time. Yet there was something else, a defiant 'this isn't over' look Nolan had seen many times before.

What am I missing?

Ten minutes later, Zeke called back. "We found them,

Boswell and the rest, Vince, Will, and Eisner. They're okay. Vince is knocked about pretty bad, but he'll live."

"What about Commissioner Ashe Ahmed?"

"No sign of him. He was with them, but they separated him some time ago, and they don't know where they took him."

"Understood. Zeke, you know where we're going. Find the best truck you have, and get the men aboard. I need to talk to..."

There was the sound of a struggle, someone arguing.

What the hell?

"Chief Nolan," Boswell cut in.

He's taken Zeke's headset.

"Good to hear your voice again. What is it, Lt?"

"You remember who's running this outfit? I'll give the orders when I decide where we're heading. Until then, hold your position."

Lucas had come up the stairs and was grinning at him from the doorway.

"Lt, listen. You've been incarcerated, so you don't know what's going down. Zeke will find us a truck. We'll need that to get clear of the town. We'll worry about chain of command when we're out of here. Would you put Zeke back on, Sir."

He grunted, and a few seconds later, he heard Zeke's voice.

"Chief?"

"Get us that truck, Zeke. And tell Dan and Brad to keep their eyes peeled. This place could still be hot. There's no sign of the UN Commissioner. I'm trying to locate him. Let me know when you've got the transport."

"Yeah, roger that. I'm sorry about Boswell. He..."

"I know. "

He turned his attention back to the grinning Somali. Nolan realized his crazed, grinning expression wasn't Khat. He'd seen it before, in the grim backstreets of the US Crystal Meth. It made sense. Somalia wouldn't be the first country to use the drug to enhance the martial abilities of their fighting men.

Nazi Germany led the way, when the drug was branded Pervetin, and given to the troops in large quantities to help with alertness and combat fatigue. Common on the Eastern Front in the snows of Russia, it was unlikely most of its adherents lived long enough to become seriously addicted.

"Okay, Askar, here's how it goes. I have my men. I only want the Commissioner. Hand him over, and the place is yours."

He shook his head. "No, Mister, no way. You'll never find him, and in another couple of hours, he dies. He's in a room with air for twelve hours maximum. He's been in their ten hours already. He won't last much longer."

They argued, and he pushed the man as far as he dared, even promising to leave some of their weaponry when they left, anything to recover the Commissioner. He seemed to consider, looking around the shabby office, and finally, he agreed.

"Okay, Mr. American, it's a deal. I'll give him to you, but I'll want those M3 missiles in return. You leave them here."

"Okay, I'll leave everything we have left. Where is he?"

Lucas had left the room, and Nolan was alone. Askar glanced at him, then around the room. Then he smiled, showing a grinning row of white teeth. It was not a pleasant smile.

"Right here, in the strong room."

What is it with this guy? He's too confident. He's not acting like a loser.

He moved aside a row of filing cabinets. They moved as one block on rubber shod casters. Behind them was a steel door, like a safe door or strong room door. The big Somali dialed a combination, moved the brass lever, and the door started to swing open. A body dropped out, Ashe Ahmed, UN Commissioner. As his body hit the floor, he made a slight noise. He wasn't dead.

Nolan ran forward and put down his AK to help him. He didn't notice Askar put a hand behind the row of filing cabinets. When the hand emerged, it was no longer empty. He held a weapon, a snub submachine gun. It all happened in less than a second. He recognized the deadly shape of an Intratec TEC-9, more commonly known as a TEC-9, a blowback-operated semi-automatic handgun, and at short range as deadly as an assault rifle.

This was at short range, less than four meters. The Somali raised the gun, his smile becoming a deep sneer as his finger tightened on the trigger. His eyes were wide, the eyes of a man who is super-powered by Crystal Meth.

The crack of the shot was loud in the room. Only a single shot, which was strange, as was the absence of any pain. He looked up. Amelia Stowe was standing nearby, holding a pistol. A tiny wisp of smoke escaped from the end of the barrel. Askar didn't make a sound. He breathed out loudly and dropped his TEC-9, but still he stood, motionless. He turned to face the black woman in the bright patterned dress and took a step toward her. Nolan braced himself to lunge at the big man, but it was unnecessary.

He crumpled slowly to the floor, falling at the feet of his killer. He looked at her. She was trembling, and he crossed to her.

"Hey, are you okay?"

She nodded dumbly.

"You're something of a guardian angel, Agent Stowe. I reckon I'm getting plenty from my tax dollars."

She tried to smile, but it was forced and quickly disappeared. Lucas raced into the room and swept his gaze around for a target.

"Any problem in here?"

"Nothing, we're good."

The Seal glanced at the body of Askar and left. Nolan gave Stowe a gentle shake.

"Ashe needs help, Amelia. Do what you can for him. I have to make sure the compound is secure."

She nodded. "I'll do what I can." Her voice was thin and reedy, but with a job to do, he reckoned she'd be okay. He left the office, descended the metal staircase, and walked over to the parked trucks. Zeke was inside the cab of a big eight-wheeled curtainsider. Outside, Dan and Brad were patrolling the open area, and he could see several bodies scattered around. Brad saw him glance at them.

"They put up a struggle when we came to take one of their trucks, so we had to put them down."

"Are we clear now?"

"Yep, we've swept the entire area. We're good."

"Roger that."

They looked up as the big diesel engine roared to life. Zeke left it on tick over and jumped down."

"She'll get us to Mogadishu, no question. The engine

sounds sweet, and the tank is full of fuel."

"Good work. Brad, you and Dan give Amelia a hand to lift Commissioner Ahmed down the staircase. Then round up everyone, and we'll load up and get on the road." He told them where to find Amelia and Ashe Ahmed, and they raced off.

There had to be something he was missing. It had all happened so quickly. He needed to think like a Seal, think on his feet.

Sure, Dr. Ahmed and the woman, Fatimah Barre.

If they were to complete the operation and kill Nabil Barre, they'd need local intel, and those two people could be worth their weight in gold. He remembered the cellphone, dug it out, and pressed the speed dial. It answered right away.

"Dr. Ahmed."

"This is Nolan. We've secured the compound. Where are you?"

"On the way, me and Fatima. We had to take a wide detour. There's shooting in the streets. Some of the factions are trying to take advantage of the chaos to grab territory."

There's a surprise.

"We'll be leaving soon. Make if fast."

"A few minutes, and we'll be with you."

He clicked off. Boswell was striding toward him, his face red with anger.

"Chief, they tell me you've decided we're going to Mogadishu. I told you, I give the orders around here. What's the reason for heading north? You know about Mogadishu, yes? Operation Gothic Serpent, a fucking disaster."

He did his best to keep cool. "I know. We had intel that Barre is holed up there."

"We're not going to Mogadishu, no way. I'll contact Jacks and arrange for exfil. Jesus Christ, are you trying to get this unit killed? Some of us have plans for the future, and none of them include burial in a shallow grave in this African shithole."

Nolan glanced at Lucas, who stood listening, his face neutral.

Fuck Boswell's pet dog. It's time to explain the way things work.

He took a deep breath to control his anger, but it failed. He was boiling.

"Lt, with all respect, we came here to do a job." His voice was calm, but like ice. And dripping with contempt, "And I don't intend to pull out before it's done, so fuck the cozy political careers in Washington. We're Seals, not ass-kissing chair polishers."

He realized his voice had risen.

Fuck it! It's time the man heard the truth.

Boswell went white and turned to Lucas.

"Grant, I'm putting you as my number two. Chief Nolan will stand down from command, as of now."

His voice was shaky, but he gathered confidence as he spoke with the Seal vet beside him. There was a long silence as he waited for Grant to acknowledge.

"Well? Is that clear, Grant?"

"No, Sir."

"No!" His voice was a shriek, "What do you mean, no?"

"Chief is right, Lt. We came here to do a job, and we have a way to do just that. We have transport, equipment, and weapons; you name it. As soon as we locate the satcom, we can relocate the UAVs to the area around Mogadishu, and go in and finish the job."

The Lieutenant shook his head in exasperation or maybe fear. Nolan pressed on with the clincher.

"There's something else, Lt. Our source told us Barre sent a bunch of suicide bombers to the States. They're due to hit a vital target very soon."

He glared at Nolan. "Which target?"

A pause. "She doesn't know."

He sneered. "Doesn't know, uh? That's some intel, Chief."

They stood silently, as Boswell appeared to mull it over. But it was obvious he was trying to work out the best way for them to pull out. He looked at Lucas Grant again, but the vet refused to meet his gaze. Then they looked at the entrance as a small car chugged up to the smoking wreckage that blocked the gates, and two people got out, a man and a woman. The car was a Moskvich. The two people were Dr. Ahmed and Fatimah Barre. They ran forward, and with a cry of relief, Ayub Ahmed went across to where Amelia was tending to Ashe. Mrs. Barre hesitated, but Nolan beckoned her forward.

"Lt, this is Barre's wife, one of 'em. Ma'am, this is the man in charge, Lieutenant Boswell. Tell him about your son."

She explained about the suicide bombers who'd left for the US. But she was unable to supply what really mattered, the where and the when. Boswell sighed with exasperation.

"So this is all a crock of shit. We know nothing. There may not even be any plot to bomb the US."

"There is a threat," she affirmed quietly.

"So you say. Lucas, get the men together. I'll call Jacks and we'll pull out."

Grant didn't move. "It could be true, Lt. Think about it. If something happens, and you failed to act, well..."

The Lieutenant was silent for a moment, and it wasn't hard to work out how he was thinking. A terrorist attack on the US, even another 911, and he'd failed to do anything about it. He looked around at them all.

"Okay, what do you suggest? Not this suicide mission to Mogadishu, surely?"

"It's the only way," Nolan told him.

"The truck's ready to leave?"

"Yep."

"Maybe I was wrong, and we have to do this. Chief, get the men mounted up. We'll do it." He looked around for Zeke, "Did you locate our gear, weapons, and satcom?"

"We did, yeah. Even the Carl Gustav and the Raven."

He nodded. "We'll probably need more than that, but it's a start."

Amelia came over to him with Ayub Ahmed. He stared at her native dress.

"Some kind of disguise, Agent Stowe, or did you lose your wetsuit?"

She gave him a stony glance. "Lieutenant Boswell, this is Dr. Ayub Ahmed. He's related to Commissioner Ahmed."

They shook hands. "How is the Commissioner?"

"Recovering after his ordeal locked in that strong room. He'll be fine after some rest. I assume you still want me to guide you to Barre's house in Mogadishu?"

Nolan interceded. "Lieutenant Boswell doesn't know the details yet, Doctor." He turned to the Lieutenant. "Dr. Ahmed will lead us to his place, Lt. It should be a straight in and out, if everything goes well. You'll be home in time for the nominations."

Boswell gave him a sharp look, then grunted. "Let's do it. I'll call Jacks on the way up there."

* * *

The road to Mogadishu was like most highways in Somalia, a road in name only. The big truck bumped and lurched continually so that they even remembered fondly the discomfort of the C-17 hold. At least it didn't crunch into every pothole. Boswell rode in the back with the men, in spite of his protests.

Will Bryce drove, as he needed Dr. Ahmed to navigate. Amelia Stowe rode with them in the front so that anyone coming across the truck would only see three black faces in the cab.

As soon as they were on the road, Boswell ordered Zeke to get Jacks on the encrypted satcom. It took a few minutes, and the Admiral answered. They chatted for a few minutes, and then he gave the handset to Nolan.

"He wants you."

He took the set. "Sir, Nolan here."

"Chief, good to hear your voice. Is this all true, this Mogadishu thing?"

"All true, Sir. Barre is there, and before we kill him, we need to find out where the attack is going down."

"No ideas, not even a guess?"

"No, Sir, but it's something big."

"Got it. I've ordered the UAVs to be located over the target zone, so they'll be ready for you. Tell me, how is Boswell doing? Any complaints?"

A pause. But he was a Seal. And Boswell was Bravo. "None."

"Yeah, right. I'm getting a picture of what's been happening, and from my end, it doesn't look like he's covered himself in glory. A pity, I thought he'd sorted himself out after his problems at the start."

"So did I."

"Yeah. Very well, good luck with Mogadishu. Anything you need, you call. Boswell has a direct feed to his tablet from the UAVs, so you'll know what's going down around you. We'll be watching every step of the way. And let me know the second you hear anything about that attack. Jacks out."

* * *

The truck rumbled on through the night. Twice they were stopped, and twice the black faces and Somali voices in the cab saved them. After four hours, Will's voice came through on their headsets.

"Heads up, people. We're nearing the outskirts of Mogadishu."

Nolan checked his wristwatch. It was just after 0300 hours. They had maybe three hours of darkness in which to go in, find out about the attack, and kill Barre. After that, all bets were off.

"I'm passing the headset over to Dr. Ahmed. He'll give you a commentary on what we see."

A few moments later, "Hello, hello?"

"Just talk naturally, Doctor. Press the transmit button to speak."

"I see. We're about ten minutes out from the University. His house is just past the main campus."

They checked their weapons, checked again, switched

on the NV goggles, and loosened knives in sheathes. Eisner prepared the M3 launcher, just in case, and Weissman prepared the M248 machine gun. Nolan considered once again, which rifle to carry. In the end, he slung the SWS Mk 11 on his back and carried the compact AK47S in his arms. Lucas grimaced.

"You're packing a lot of hardware, Chief."

It was a fair point, with his P226 in his leg holster and the big combat knife in his belt; it was a weight of metal.

"Barre could be packing a lot of firepower, Lucas."

He grinned. "Good point." He shouted across to Weissman. "Hey, Jack, you want me to carry a spare box mag for that machine gun?"

"Sure."

Boswell called them together. "We'll be there shortly. I propose to split the platoon into two fireteams again, and..."

"No, Lt. Not again. We stay together," Nolan told him grimly.

He looked at his second-in-command for a long moment. Then his shoulders sagged slightly. "Yeah, okay. Maybe that's a good plan. We'll stay together."

He tried a grin, but it didn't come off. Nolan noticed the glare the Lieutenant gave him when he thought he didn't notice. Boswell would bear watching.

Then the platoon leader went to talk to Commissioner Ahmed.

"We're alongside the University building, coming up on Barre's place now," Ahmed's voice came to them from the cab.

They waited. "We're outside his place now. Will says he'll drive past and stop around the corner, about eighty meters away."

Soon the big truck braked to a halt, and Will came around to open the tailgate so they could climb down. He addressed himself to Nolan.

"The road is clear, no sign of anyone. Bad news is there's no sign of any life at Barre's house. It doesn't mean he's not there. It is the middle of the night, and they could all be asleep, but I doubt it."

Fatimah Barre climbed down to join them. "There's no one there? That's strange. Unless..." They waited, "Unless he's in the basement."

"Under the house?" Boswell asked, surprised, "Why would he be in a basement? He'd be trapped like a rat if anyone came for him."

"Not under the house, under the university. When they erected the main buildings, they came across an ancient cave system. The construction workers covered them over with concrete, but some of Barre's supporters, students at the University, heard of them and found them. At the nearest point, they were only twenty meters from my husband's house, so they dug a tunnel for him to reach them."

"So this tunnel starts inside his house?" Boswell asked.

"Yes, in the kitchen. There is a wine cellar, and the entrance is behind the bottle racks."

"I thought he was a Muslim." Ahmed sounded astonished.

"He is," she affirmed, "but he likes fine wines. He says Mohammed would approve if he returned to Earth."

Ahmed frowned. "That is blasphemy."

"Okay, so we need to get into the house," Nolan interrupted, "We'll enter the tunnel system and locate him, but what about an exit? Can he get out from inside the University?"

"Yes." She pointed across to a cone shaped structure close to the main building, "There, it cannot be accessed from outside, but from inside. They can unlock the roof and escape in an emergency."

"Understood." He turned to Boswell. "We need to cover the exit, Lt."

"Yeah, I know that. Bryce, you can cover it. Use the M249."

"No." He turned as Nolan spoke. "No? What do you mean, no?"

"I mean Will is too useful to leave out here, just in case. Vince, he'd be a better bet. He's still not fully recovered from the beating they gave him, and he could snipe at the enemy if necessary. They may not come out in a bunch, even if they come out that way at all."

Boswell seemed to be fighting to control his temper, but finally he nodded.

"Agreed. If there're no other arguments, we need to get in there and flush this bastard out before he does something real bad. Jesus, he could even have a plan to kill the President. Even if he is a Democrat."

No one laughed.

They made Fatimah Barre comfortable in back of the truck with both of the Ahmeds. Then they melted into the darkness.

Vince went off first, to seal off any chance of the hostiles getting out the back door. He went into the front yard of Barre's house, actually a small mansion, and worked his way through the darkness to the University grounds, where he found a suitable stand behind a bunch of tall, steel garbage containers.

Boswell led Bravo Platoon across the yard to Barre's house. The front door was close and locked, before Will Bryce stepped forward and rammed a shoulder against the area of the lock. It was quicker than using a key. The door sprung open and they were in. Using NV goggles, they quickly checked out the dark interior, but it was empty.

They reached the kitchen, and Boswell nodded to Lucas, who opened the door to the wine cellar. Racks of bottles lined the back wall, and Lucas simply gave it a wrench and ripped the entire metal structure out of the wall. The secret entrance was behind a concrete portal that fitted almost perfectly to the surrounding wall. If you didn't know it was there, you wouldn't find it. Lucas found a narrow ring lying flush with the door, and pulled it out, then used it to pull the entire portal open.

"I'll be damned," he muttered.

The space behind was an anteroom, a small hallway. It was furnished with a narrow cot, surrounded by iron rings set into the concrete, enough to hold a prisoner for eternity if they were gagged and couldn't cry out.

Nolan though of the American girl he'd held captive.

Is this the basement he kept her hidden in for long months, alone in the darkness. Yes, probably.

He vowed more than ever to get her out safe and back home. And to make Barre die a thousand deaths for what he'd done.

On the far wall of the grim anteroom was another door. He crossed the room and pushed down on the handle. It opened instantly, and he led the way into a low, dark tunnel. It had been cut through the ground and reinforced with timber props, like an old time gold mine. There was no illumination, but the NV gear made it unnecessary. He reached the other end of the tunnel, a distance of about thirty meters, and this time it was locked, just an empty slot for a key. They had ways of bypassing locked doors, without alerting an enemy.

"Zeke, I need you to open this."

Zeke Murray was a man of many talents, electronics, communications, and demolitions, anything mechanical, electrical or electronic. He was also a first class shot with his HK410 assault rifle. He walked forward and extracted a pair of small tools from his belt pack. Then he knelt down to take a closer look.

"Yeah, it's no big deal. Two minutes tops."

It was a minute and ten seconds later they heard the soft 'click' and he stood up.

"It's open."

Nolan turned and pushed the door. It opened without a sound. He crept through into a rocky cavern. This time it was lit by armored electric lights fastened to the walls, and he removed his goggles. In the distance, further into the cavern, he could hear voices. He turned back and gave a hand signal for silence.

They grouped together in the cavern, preparing for the assault.

"What do you think this place is?" Will murmured.

He was looking around in awe. The walls were not just bare rock; some were decorated with cave paintings. Primitive cave paintings, depicting animals, people, birds, even the sea.

"Prehistoric," Zeke offered, "I visited some caves in Europe once, in the Pyrenees between France and Spain. There was stuff just like this on the walls, almost identical."

"Thanks for the history lesson," Boswell whispered, "I'm more interested in the whereabouts of Barre. It's long past the time we kill him and go home."

He has a point, Nolan considered. *Except for the little matter of a huge plot to bomb America, and an American girl he's holding hostage.*

Amelia had gone to the far side where there was a further tunnel, to try and make sense of what they were saying. After a few minutes, she came back to tell Nolan what she'd heard.

"Ma'am, if there's anything you can tell us, you can tell me," Boswell murmured.

"Right. I can hear a crowd of men talking, speaking Somali of course. They were discussing the trouble in Kismayo, and what it meant. That's about all. I've no way of knowing who's in there."

"I'll go forward and check it out," Boswell whispered, surprising them.

They watched as he crept forward. He was back three minutes later.

"Okay, it's not going to be so easy. There's a guard about thirty meters along that passage. We'll have to take him, but the slightest sound will stir them up. Further along, it's like a meeting room. People coming and going, and a half-dozen men sat around the rock floor. One of them is Barre. I don't know about the others, but we can assume they're all Al Shabaab. There's also a woman. She's serving them food and drinks."

"An African woman?"

"A veiled woman, Chief, covered head to toe in a black robe. Could be black, white, brown, yellow, you name it. She's not the problem. It's that guard. He's out in the open, and there's no way to reach him."

Nolan picked up his SWS rifle. "I'll take him. They won't hear a thing."

Boswell frowned. "If he drops his weapon, they'll hear it. I have a better idea. Agent Stowe, you look like a local. You're even dressed for the part. Can you distract him?"

She stared at him. "And just how would a Somali girl suddenly appear in this passage? You think they called for a takeaway pizza? The second I walk around that corner, he'll be on to me."

He scowled. "Maybe you're right. Okay, it'll have to be a long rifle. Chief, it's all yours; go take a look at your target."

Nolan edged toward the bend in the tunnel. When he peered round, he could see the guard thirty meters away as Boswell had said. Barre and the rest of the Somalis were much further along the tunnel, maybe another forty meters.

Impossible.

He crawled back to the men.

"It won't work. The distances are too great. The only way is a frontal attack. Go straight in."

Lucas cocked an eyebrow. "And if they have a dozen guards down there, maybe a machine gun? You want to get us all killed?" He crept back to the tunnel, muttering, "I'll keep an eye on things."

Will intervened. "He's right, Chief. It's the wrong approach. Let's do this right, the Seal way. Make sure we know what we're up against."

Reluctantly, he nodded. "Maybe the guard will go for a piss."

"Maybe," Will nodded, "There is another way. A

Hellfire missile would open the escape shaft that Vince is covering."

"And we'd never know what Barre is planning."

He inclined his head. "Right."

Lucas' voice came over the commo, a faint whisper. "Someone coming, a woman. I'll duck into the shadows and let her pass. You can take her when she reaches you."

They flattened themselves against the walls. In the dim light, there'd be a short time before anyone who entered realized they weren't alone.

She walked slowly into the cave. Her clothes were the typical Muslim black garb; veiled from head to toe. She could only see straight ahead, and when Will stepped out, she didn't know he was there until a hand clamped over her mouth.

"Keep it quiet. We're not going to hurt you." He looked at Agent Stowe. "Tell her, Ma'am. She may not understand English. And tell her when I release my hand, if she speaks in anything louder than a whisper, I'll break her neck."

Amelia grimaced but moved close to the woman and spoke rapidly. Then she turned to explain.

"She doesn't understand English. She's the wife of one of Barre's lieutenants. She says she won't make any noise. She hates them all. She wants us to allow her to escape when we're finished here."

Nolan nodded. "No problem. Tell her she can go now."

Another conversation in Somali, "She won't leave until they're dead. If her husband comes after her, he'd kill her. But I have an idea. We need to know the layout of that cave system, yes?" He nodded, "I'll swap clothes with her. We're about the same size, and as I'm black, it won't be obvious. She was coming out to collect a couple of bottles of wine from the cellar. I can take those in to them and take a look around."

"No!" He glared at her, only just remembering to keep his voice down, "They'd find out and kill you."

"It's a good idea," Boswell told him, "Agent Stowe, find out what they expect from her, and do it. Make sure your commo is hooked up, and you can let us know what's in there."

Five minutes later, the black robed woman prepared to go into the cave system, into the lair of Nabil Barre and his gang of armed fanatics. Her own weapon was not fitted with a suppressor, and Nolan gave her his P226 to hide inside her robes. She handed him her pistol.

"We'll give it ten minutes, and if we haven't heard from you, we'll come in after you. Anyone looks at you the wrong way, shoot first, and then call for help."

She stared at him for a moment. Then she bowed. "Yes, my master."

He didn't laugh. She held the wine bottles and started forward, around the bend, and past the guard.

Ten minutes later, there was no word, and the radio was still silent. She'd disappeared.

CHAPTER NINE

"What the fuck's going on here?"

Musse Daud glared at his fellow martyrs. He'd been out for a walk to check the route to the UN building. At least, that was his excuse. The truth was, he'd had more than enough of this roomful of squabbling Somalis. His fellow martyrs, to be sure, but they were also unbearable.

The room stank of sweat. More than sweat. It was a stink of fear, body odor, unwashed bodies, and stale food. It made him want to vomit. Or perhaps that was just his own terror of what lay ahead for them, only twelve hours from now. For the thousandth time, he found himself wondering was there a Paradise. Were the other boys thinking the same thoughts, as the hours counted down? Of course they were. Their tension had finally cracked, when Amin lost his cool with Rageh.

"This sniveling bastard, he was trying to escape."

He had the younger man's collar held in his grip, and Amin was a strong man. Rageh was a youngster, a frightened boy.

We're all boys, aren't we? Not one of us has reached adulthood.

"Let him alone, Amin. Is that true, Rageh?"

The boy sagged to the floor as the bigger boy released him. He looked back at the faces in the room. They were staring at him. Accusing faces. His eyes filled with tears, and he shook his head.

"No, I swear it."

Musse shrugged. "There you are, Amin. He has..."

"But if I wanted to leave, there's nothing to stop me. Nothing in the holy books."

The room went quiet. "The truth. Are you thinking of backing out of this?"

At first he wouldn't answer. Then he dried his tears and gave them a defiant look.

"Yes. I don't believe this is right. It's not the way, not for any of us."

"You fucking shit," Amin snarled, "We ought to kill you now."

"No!" Musse stepped in front of him, stopping him from reaching the boy, "This is a mission for volunteers. Sheikh Barre said so himself. No one may be compelled to martyr himself if he does not wish to."

"That was back in Somalia. Even then, we had little choice, and you know it. What would become of your mother if you refused, Musse? And my own parents, hungry and my father dying of AIDS for want of medicine. Rageh here, they offered to buy his family a new fishing boat." He stared at the youth. "You want them to go hungry, just because you're a coward."

"Shut up, Amin. If he doesn't want to do it, I won't make him."

"And what about if he gets caught, and rats us out to

the cops?"

I pray to God that happens. It would be wonderful, a way out that would at least leave me some honor.

"He won't talk to the cops."

"You're damn right he won't."

He hadn't seen what the other boy was doing, until he drew a long, sharp filleting knife and leapt forward. Before he could stop him, Amin gave him a hard, savage shove that sent him reeling to the floor. The boy raised the knife as he went forward to Rageh. He slashed down once into the boy's chest.

The room was silent. Except for the faint sound of blood mixed with air, gurgling out of the deep chest wound. Musse climbed back to his feet.

"You bastard. You didn't need to kill him."

"I did, and you know it. He could have finished us all."

Musse knelt down and checked the pulse. It was faint at first and then stopped as the last thread of life flowed from the boy's body. He looked up.

"You killed him! One of our own people, a martyr."

"Not a martyr, Musse. You heard him. He wanted out."

"Even so..."

"We couldn't risk it. We have to go through with the plan and make certain out families get their rewards. As we will be rewarded, in Paradise."

Will we? I have to do it, but if only...

They bundled Rageh's body into a closet. It would have to stay there for the night. After that, it wouldn't matter.

* * *

She'd taken the wine into the cave, past the guard who took no notice of her. She entered the larger cavern and recognized Barre immediately. He grunted at her to open the bottles and pour for them, and then join the women. She did as he ordered, then left the cave. She had no idea where the women were, but she had no intention of joining them. She started walking along the tunnel when she reached another, smaller cavern. As she entered, a man appeared, an older, gray haired Somali, armed with an AK-47.

"Where are you going, woman? You know you are not allowed outside the women's quarters! Come, I will escort you there."

He took her arm and led her through yet another side tunnel. They reached a heavy door at the end. He gestured at her to enter and stood aside. She briefly considered drawing her weapon and killing him, but it was deep inside the folds of her robe, and he'd have ample chance to stop her before she got halfway. She walked into the room, and he closed the door behind her. She noticed he didn't lock it, but his post at the end of the tunnel meant there was no way out, other than past him. When she needed to leave, she'd have to kill him.

So be it.

There were two women in the dimly lit room, sitting on the floor on threadbare and tattered cushions. They'd removed their veils, and with a shock she saw one of them was white. She was very young and clutched a baby.

So it's true.

They looked at her, not noticing she wasn't the woman who'd left earlier to fetch the wine.

"Yasmin, how are they? Still worried about an attack?

They're like a bunch of frightened old women," the black woman scoffed. She looked at the white girl. "Saba, make space for our sister."

"Yes, Hawo." She moved to one side and patted the cushion, "Yasmin, please sit here."

Amelia decided to take a chance. But first, she found the butt of her pistol and gripped it ready to draw. With the other hand, she pulled off her veil.

"You're not Yasmin!" the black woman said nervously, "Who are you? What did they do to her?"

She put her finger to her lips. "All in good time. But first, do either of you two girls wish to escape from this place and from these men?"

The white girl, Saba, answered, "With all my heart. You know how long I've been here? It's like asking if I wanted to be rescued from hell."

The black woman nodded. "It is true. We are no more than slaves for our husband, Nabil Barre. But if we try to escape, he will kill us. You don't know him."

"I know him. My name is Amelia Stowe, and I work for the FBI."

Saba's eyes widened. "But you speak Somali."

"That was my family. Believe me, I'm as American as apple pie. I'm here with a group of people trying to put a stop to Barre's terror attacks."

"Hah!" Hawo muttered, her voice laden with scorn, "You'd have to kill him to do that. It's in his blood." She stopped, as realization hit her, "You are going to kill him."

"Yes. Do you want to help me or not?" Saba nodded eagerly, the other woman a second later, "Good, here's what we need to do."

She glanced at her wristwatch and realized she was late

in calling in. She moved her hand toward the transmit button, but when she called there was no reply. The solid rock made transmissions all but impossible. She tried again, and a third time, but the sound of machine gunfire stopped her.

They're coming in. God help them.

She took out the pistol and opened the door to retrace her steps. As she stepped into the tunnel, she came face to face with the guard, who'd come to secure the women when the shooting started. He saw her face and then looked down at the gun.

"You're not Yasmin!"

He raised his assault rifle. Amelia began to raise the pistol, but the barrel was fitted with a suppressor, making it long and unwieldy. It caught in the unfamiliar folds of her robe, and she tugged desperately to free it. The Somali smiled.

"Whoever you are, lady, this is the end of the line. Time to say goodbye."

She saw his eyes dilate, as his drugged mind savored the moment, the killing. Saba passed the baby to Hawo and became a dark shadow, slipping around Amelia to plunge a dagger into his stomach. As he went down, the FBI agent managed to free the Sig Sauer, and she popped a bullet into his head. She picked up the victim's AK-47 and turned to Saba.

"You saved my life. And we gained an assault rifle."

The girl's eyes were wide with horror. "I killed him."

"No, we both killed him. Would you have preferred to die down in this dark pit?"

The girl shook her head, unable to say more as the shock of her knife attack on the fighter paralyzed her.

Agent Stowe was about to speak when she heard a fragment of static in her earpiece.

* * *

"That's it, I'm going in."

They looked around as Nolan spoke.

"Give her more time," Boswell said quietly, "You could wreck everything if you go charging in there.

"And they'll kill her if I don't. Cover me."

He slung the AK47S on his back and took out the SWS rifle. He checked the load, ratcheted a round into the breech, and crept silently to the edge of the room. When he peered into the tunnel, the guard was in the same place, sitting on the floor. He'd put down his assault rifle to pull out a canvas bag. Khat. He watched the man take out a handful of leaves and start to chew them. Then he relaxed as the drug began to take hold.

He took careful aim and squeezed the trigger. The bullet took the man in the center of his forehead and bore through his skull, and into the brain. He was dead a microsecond later. He slumped down to the rocky floor. There'd been no noise. Nolan checked they were ready to follow him, then stepped forward.

The men in the far room were talking loudly in Somali and concentrating on a map they had placed on the floor. They didn't see him until he was abreast of the dead guard's body, and then one of them looked up and called out. But the man wasn't there. Instead, there was a man wearing a wetsuit, carrying an unfamiliar weapon. He reacted fast and catapulted to his feet, shouting to the others.

They scattered in an instant, and Nolan charged

forward. The rest of Bravo was right behind him, and for one exultant moment, he thought they'd get there. Then the shooting started.

They had a machine gun already covering the tunnel in a pre-prepared position, with just the barrel visible through a hole in the rock. Whoever was behind there knew his business. It was less than two seconds since they'd realized they were under attack, but a hail of lead swept the tunnel. He heard screams from behind but kept running. He had to get there, had to knock out that gun before it finished them all. He ran, his legs pounding, every muscle stretched to the maximum.

The opening ahead was narrowing. He realized with desperation they were closing a heavy steel door to seal off the tunnel. He tried to run faster, his lungs searing with desperation; but with a 'clang' that echoed through the cavern, like the gates of hell swinging shut, the door locked into place, and his body crunched into the hard metal. The rest of them came storming along the tunnel and stopped.

"Fuck!" Will growled, "That's one we hadn't counted on."

"We have to get in there, Will. She's in there, Amelia. And Barre, we have to know about this attack."

"But how?"

Boswell pushed him aside and examined the door. "It was all for nothing, Chief. We won't get past it. I'd guess it's an inch thick. Our first priority is to get the wounded out. It's time we arranged for an exfil."

"The wounded?"

"That machine gun cut through us. It missed you, but we were right behind. Brad took one in the leg, and Dan

Moseley's not too good, took one high in the shoulder. I guess he'll live, which is more than Weissman managed."

"Jack Weissman? He's dead?"

"A hit to the head, he was dead before he hit the ground."

Nolan went back to the end of the tunnel. They'd dragged the dead and wounded back to the cavern they'd started from. Weissman lay on his back, his sightless eyes wide, and his mouth open in an angry snarl. The two wounded, Brad Rose and Dan Moseley sat nearby while Dave Eisner put dressings on their wounds to staunch the bleeding. Eisner saw him and looked up.

"Don't worry, Chief. They'll live."

"Weissman won't."

"No."

"It's my fault, Dave. I should have waited."

"Probably," he agreed," And if you were perfect, they'd likely make you the President of the United States. Then again, you really would be the number one target for these Al Shabaab types. No, you're not perfect, none of us are. We're just men, trying to do a job, and do it the best way we can. If you..."

"Hold it, Dave."

It hit him like a sledgehammer, the number one target for Al Shabaab.

The President of the United States, is it possible? Yes, of course it is.

On Friday, the 22nd of November, President Kennedy was fatally shot in Dallas, Texas, by a lone sniper, Lee Harvey Oswald, while traveling with his wife Jacqueline in a presidential motorcade.

A lone sniper! And Fatimah's son is traveling with several companions, all suicide bombers.

He ran back to Boswell and explained his theory. The reaction was incredulity, with a healthy measure of disbelief.

"The President? I don't think so, Chief. That's just a wild guess." He looked around at Lucas Grant for support. "There're a thousand and one targets in the US. It could be any of them."

"One of them could be the President," Nolan persisted.

The Lieutenant was shaking his head. "I doubt it, no. It's a crazy idea."

"There's only one way to check it out," Grant murmured.

"Yeah? What's that?"

"Blast through that door, and ask the guys the other side. I'll get answers from them."

"Blast through the door," he sneered, "What with, you gonna bring a Caterpillar down here? Or maybe we have some demolition charges I've forgotten about."

"With the M3 missile, Lt."

His mouth dropped open. "The M3, down here? It'll kill us all, and bring the roof down."

"It's the only way," Will agreed, "There's no alternative, Boss. We have to try it."

Nolan thought about the effect of a Carl Gustav in such a confined space. The appalling blast would catch the women as surely as the Al Shabaab defenders.

The missile could kill them all, Amelia, the American girl. And if we kill the hostiles, we'll never find out about their attack on the US. If the attack is on the President, we'll never find out the truth, the when and the where until it's too late, and he's dead.

Lucas had already brought up the Carl Gustav and was preparing the missile to fire, as Boswell tried to reason with him.

"Grant, this is crazy thinking. I can't let you do it. Chief, what do you think?"

If we use the missile, we could kill them all.

Lucas ignored the Lieutenant, and Will Bryce started to pull everyone back to the tiny room at back of the wine cellar. Nolan made another desperate attempt to get through to Amelia Stowe.

Have they uncovered her disguise? Is she dead, or just sitting in the line of fire?

"This is Bravo Two, Amelia, do you read?"

Nothing. He tried again, and there was something.

"This.....Stowe. We're...."

She's alive!

His hopes soared. But still, they had to survive the M3.

"Amelia, fire in the hole! Do you read, fire in the hole. Hit the dirt."

Nothing. No reply. No acknowledgement. He swung around to Lucas.

"You have to wait. If you shoot that thing now, you'll kill them all. The women are inside. I need time to get through to them. They have to get under cover."

He turned to Boswell. "Lt, you have to stop this, at least postpone it. I can get through to them. I just need a few minutes."

The officer glanced around at the men, at Will, at Nolan, at the others, and at Grant. His mouth opened, but at first no sound emerged.

"Lt, just a couple of minutes!"

"I don't know." He looked again at Grant. "What do you think, Lucas?"

Nolan exploded. "For fuck's sake, Lieutenant Boswell,

you're supposed to run this platoon, not Lucas Grant. There're women in there, just give me a few minutes to get through to them and get them under cover. Otherwise you could kill them all."

"Hold on there," Grant interrupted, "I know you're worried about your girlfriend, but we have to get in there and pin down those Al Shabaab gomers. Every minute we hang back is another minute we're giving the enemy."

"No," Nolan shook his head, "Two minutes, that's all I'm asking."

Don't they get it? There's a girl in there, an innocent American, kidnapped by Somali animals and kept in slavery, as well as Amelia.

Finally, the Lieutenant made up his mind. "I'm sorry, we're going in now. Nolan, pull everyone back to the wine cellar. Lucas, can you fire that thing and get behind cover in time?"

"I reckon. Just pull them back, Lt. We need to do this thing."

Nolan hesitated for a couple of seconds, and then gave in to the inevitable. He led them back the way they'd come to the tiny anteroom with the bed, and the door through to the wine racks. They came out into the kitchen. Boswell was last and about to close the door when an idea occurred to him.

"Lt, the mattress. Grant could use it. It'll give him some protection."

He nodded. "Yeah, good idea, take it into him. He's about to fire."

Nolan rushed back behind the wine racks, grabbed the mattress, and dragged it through. Lucas was searching for the best firing position to give him some cover from the massive blast.

"I brought this. It'll protect you from some of the blast debris."

"Yeah, thanks. Hey, Chief, I'm sorry. I mean; I know this is the only way. If there was some other means to get through that door, I'd do it."

"You'll kill them all. You think this'll earn you brownie points with your pet Lieutenant?"

He stared at Nolan. "You think this is what it's all about? Me looking for promotion, or some nice cozy job with his family's brokerage firm?"

"Isn't it?"

He laughed. "I was sent to help the guy out, sure. He made me an offer, and I did consider it. You know he wants me to take over from you as number two in the platoon?"

"It's no surprise, yeah, I knew."

"I've decided not to take it. You're the best man for the job. When this is all over, I'll tell him. As for the job offer, I reckon I'm not going anywhere. Navy Seal pensions don't get paid out too often, do they?"

He's seen his death somewhere along the line. Soon.

"We'll get out of this, Lucas. You're not going to die."

"Like Weissman?" he grated, "We'll see about that. Get out of here, Chief. I'll give it two minutes. Try and contact your girl. Then I shoot."

Nolan nodded and raced back through the wine cellar to the kitchen. He kept trying to raise Amelia, but there was nothing. He checked his wristwatch. Thirty seconds before Grant's two minutes was up. In his guts, he knew the missile would kill them all in the cave system, and there was nothing he could do about it. Navy Seals wasn't a democracy. Never had been, never would be.

Boswell glanced at him, his gaze suspicious. "Why hasn't he fired?"

"He will."

He checked his watch. Fifteen seconds until all hell was let loose and that cave system became a roaring inferno, as the immense pressure of the blast destroyed everything in its wake. And then he turned to look at the three Somalis who poured into the kitchen. The men raised their rifles, but he snapped, "Stand down!"

Ashe Ahmed, Ayub Ahmed, and Fatimah Barre.

"Lieutenant Boswell, Mr. Nolan, we may have some information that will help!"

"Yeah, what is it?"

Fatimah Barre stepped forward. "Did you encounter a steel door down in the cave system?"

"Yeah, we did, Ma'am. We're about to blast through it."

"There's no need. I can tell you of an emergency release mechanism. It was installed in case there was a rock fall that jammed the lock. If you want..."

Nolan was already racing through the cavern. "Lucas, stop! There's no need. We can get the door open."

His body was in the relaxed, yet focused position. Wound up tight ready to take the shot, crouched behind the mattress. Slowly, he turned. Nolan was shocked. His eyes were almost empty. He'd expected to die in the blast. Yet knowing it, he'd gone ahead. No wonder he wasn't concerned with Boswell's career plans. He truly did expect to die.

"How?"

He explained about Fatimah Barre. "She's coming through now to show us the lock override."

"Is that right? You have any idea what'll happen when

we open that door? They'll hit us with everything they've got. It'll be like shooting ducks in a gallery."

"Better than dying when the missile hits."

"You ever seen one of these things underground?" Grant asked him.

"Never. It's not something you'd see during training."

"Right. We went into a cave system in the Pakistan boonies. A bunch of Taliban holed up in a cavern, and they brought the roof down to stop us going after them. It was obvious they had a back exit, and time was running out. Our platoon leader decided to hit the obstruction with a missile. Did it himself, poor bastard. But at least we finished off the hostiles and got home, all except him."

"Yet you were still ready to launch the missile."

He grimaced. "There's always a chance I'd have survived. But sooner or later, we're all going to get it, you know that."

"No, I don't know that. Stand down, maybe we'll have a better use for that missile later."

And when we get home, this guy needs to talk to our shrink. He has a death wish.

Fatimah appeared in the tunnel with Boswell and Will. She went directly to a niche in the rock, a meter from the steel door.

"It is here, look."

Nolan played his flashlight on the niche. Inside, hidden in the darkness, was a small metal lever.

"When you push the lever down, the lock will disengage, and the door will open. There is an identical override on the other side."

We'll need to position the machine guns here," Nolan said, almost to himself. "When the door opens, they'll hit us with everything they have. We'll need something strong to protect the gunners. Will, get the men to bring up loose rocks, the bigger the better. A couple of dozen chunks of stone would do it."

Bryce nodded and raced away.

"They could have grenades," Grant warned.

"Yep. We'll need to be ready for them. I'll join the machine gunners with the sniper rifle, and if anyone looks like they may even be thinking about tossing a grenade, they go down, RPG7s, too. These Somalis love 'em. Lt, you'll need a fireteam ready to storm in as soon as we've suppressed their defensive fire."

"Yeah," He looked back and forth, at the door, back along the tunnel, and came to a decision, "I'll lead them in. Lucas, bring two other men and follow me in."

Grant looked surprised. Something of the old Boswell had returned. The man who'd made a decision to the job right, before concerns for his career and his skin changed his outlook.

There's hope yet.

It only took a few minutes of relays of men carrying rocks to set up the machine guns behind a barrier. They made three firing loops, two for the M249s and one for the rifle. Boswell gripped his gun and looked around at his team.

"Ready?"

Lucas was right behind him. Eisner and Bryce brought up the rear. Fatima Barre was standing at the niche. She'd insisted she'd be the one to release the door lock. Then she'd duck behind cover with Nolan.

He checked his stance for the last time and took up the pressure. He'd decided against using NV. Too much light in the cave when the door opened, and he'd be blinded. Better to shoot at shadows.

Both gunners acknowledged. "Ready."

Fatima's voice, strong and determined. "Ready."

Nolan kept his voice calm. They were about to open the door to hell.

"Ready."

Fatima Barre hesitated only a fraction of a second. Then she pulled the lever, and the door started to swing open.

CHAPTER TEN

It was two in the morning. In New York the city that never sleeps, they could hear the nighttime noises, sirens bleating their strident appeals to clear the carriageway. Someone, somewhere, was sick or injured; the constant murmur of traffic and in the distance, a big jet taking off from Kennedy. It was enough to keep them awake. They were still unused to the big city bustle. They were a long way from home, a long way from Somalia.

He stood at the window, watching a young couple stagger home after a night out. Partying, maybe, perhaps dinner after a show, and too much wine with the meal. Doing the things that normal young people did in this country, but not those who had committed their lives to martyrdom.

Is there a way out?

He wished to Allah he had chosen a different path. Nevertheless, he had made his choice, and more importantly, his mother depended on him. She would receive honors and rewards after the event. But if he stumbled and failed to carry out the attack, Barre would treat her harshly. He may even kill her to send a message to other martyrs.

"Musse."

He didn't turn around. It was Amin, and since he'd killed Rageh, Musse wanted to slit the throat of the arrogant, stupid fanatic. If he could have exploded his suicide vest, he would have ordered him to try it on and then detonated it. But that would kill all of them. Besides, the cops would come running, and they would be arrested.

What would the penalty be for exploding a bomb in a hotel room? Ten years in prison maybe? Then again, the penalty for what we plan is for eternity.

"What do you want?"

"Look at me, Musse." He turned and saw Amin had donned his explosive vest, "I shall wear this for every moment until we carry out our sacred mission."

"Yes. Was there something else?"

"I think we should all wear them. Wake up the others if they're asleep. We should commit ourselves once again to Paradise. I sense there may be one or two waverers. It is time to remind ourselves of the glories that await us."

"Let them sleep, Amin. For one last time."

"But..."

"Leave them alone!" He hadn't meant to shout out so loud, but the youth made him angry, "Are you so keen to die?"

And then Amin surprised him. His eyes filled with tears, and he hung his head.

"I have no choice, Musse. I shamed myself, my family, and I cannot go home. Paradise will give me back the life I have thrown away."

"What do you mean?"

"I fell in love. It was impossible, forbidden. My family went crazy. My father almost dragged me out of the house and shot me dead. Then I found the alternative, blessed martyrdom, and eternal peace in Paradise."

Musse stared at him.

Maybe.

"All this, over the love of a girl your family found was unsuitable?"

A pause. "It wasn't a girl."

"I see." He looked out at the city for a few more moments, "Homosexuality isn't frowned on here, in America. It isn't in most places, only in the Islamic world."

"So the Prophet commanded, blessed be his name. We must obey."

"I understand the punishment was decreed later, in the Hadiths, the interpretations. The Prophet said it was sinful but did not decree extreme punishment. Besides, our understanding of many of the ancient texts has been shown to be false."

"Sheikh Barre said it was a crime punishable by death."

"Sheikh Barre is not a homosexual."

They went quiet. Musse could sense the other man's agony.

"Don't worry, Amin. We will carry out this mission."

"And we shall go to Paradise?"

He thought about that for a long time.

Everyone says it is so, but who knows for certain?

Yet again, he agonized over the question. Finally, he smiled gently at the embarrassed youth.

"I cannot say, Amin, but our families will be proud of us. Tomorrow is the end of everything for us, and the start of a new journey. As for where it takes us, Paradise or not, I cannot say. We must accept the outcome, whatever it is."

"Are you a homosexual, Musse?"

He thought of his girl back in Somalia.

"No."

"Oh, I just..."

Musse realized, with a sense of horror that the youth wanted to take his hand, for him to take the younger man into his arms. And then he laughed to himself.

What the hell difference does it make?

He pulled Amin to him and held him close, calming some of the terrors that shivered through the youth's body.

* * *

They were waiting and had anticipated them finding the lock release. Even before the door was wide open, lead began to slash out of the darkness, to hiss and ricochet around the tunnel where they sheltered. The heavy bark of Soviet made PK machine guns, slower than their M249s, but firing a heavier 7.72mm bullet. They couldn't see the Seals but relied on blanketing the tunnel with a fast rate of fire.

A man darted out from a side tunnel, his arm raised, ready to throw. Nolan hit him, once, twice, and he went down. His grenade exploded, and the screams of the defenders caught in the blast echoed through the cavern, even over the roar of the gunfire. One of the PKs was out of action, the gunner shredded by grenade fragments from his own man. But the other kept up a steady rate of fire.

He was an expert, and short bursts targeted every living creature in that tunnel. Nolan felt a graze to his cheek as one of the bullets buzzed past him, removing a strip of flesh. It was lower than his eyes and didn't obstruct his vision with pools of blood, and he kept firing.

The SWS sniper rifle came into its own. As the Seals' gunfire sliced into the defenders, more Somalis rushed forward to take their places. Some hid behind the bodies of their fallen comrades, and they were more wary. Nolan took his time, and the moment the smallest part of a human body came into his sights, he fired. Doing what he did best.

Elbows, ankles, even ears, he fired and scored. They didn't expose themselves enough for a kill, but he took a terrible toll of their extremities, and men with shattered ankles and elbows, or with blood running down their faces from a shot off ear, lost their enthusiasm to keep up the fight. Gradually, they fell back, and the firing slackened, but it was still taking too long. There were friendlies in there, Agent Stowe, and the American girl. Maybe more.

Then Lucas ran forward, an almost suicidal charge to hurl a grenade into the defenders' positions. As soon as it left his hand, he dropped flat to the rocky tunnel floor, but not before he was hit. Nolan noticed his body jerk as one round took him low in the side and another high in the shoulder, both on the same side of his body, the right.

He ducked as the grenade exploded. Debris cascaded over them, and he darted out to drag Grant to safety. He looked down into his eyes. They were shut tight.

"Lucas! Talk to me, buddy!"

The eyes opened and he grimaced. "Jesus, that hurt, thanks."

"Yeah. Stay down until we can get those wounds treated."

The grimace turned into a grin. "I guess that's enough for a Purple Heart."

"We don't get medals, pal, so just keep your stupid head down before they blow it off, " He'd dropped his assault rifle, so Nolan plucked out the Tokarev, "Can you use this left handed? If they get past us, I mean."

They both knew he meant if it all went bad, and they were wiped out. If Al Shabaab came for him, he'd want to be able to defend himself, and maybe more. Prisoners of the psychotic Islamists fared badly, very badly.

"Sure. Thanks, Chief."

"Just stay down. We're going in. Look after this."

He didn't wait for an answer, and just put his rifle on the ground next to Grant and unslung the AK47S. He turned to see them waiting for his order. He turned back to the check the opposition. The air was still thick with dust, a perfect smokescreen.

"Let's go!"

He catapulted to his feet and ran. The only chance was to hit them before they fully recovered. Lucas' bravery had given them that tiny window. Will was right behind him, clutching one of the M249s, firing from the hip. Behind him, Dave Eisner was on their left flank, peppering the cavern ahead of them with short bursts from his assault rifle. Boswell was in the rear. Somewhere along the line he'd lost his assault rifle, and he clutched his handgun, like a junior officer in the trenches of the First World War, except they led from the front.

The second PK machine gunner recovered and made a grab for his weapon. Nolan gave him a burst from his

AK carbine as he ran past, and someone behind made sure with a half-dozen rounds. He ran on, swerving as a hostile appeared right in front of him. Three rounds in the guts, and he went down howling in agony, rage, and surprise. Another enemy was right behind him. He carried a huge pistol, leveled ready to fire. Three assault rifles spat out their message of death and tossed his body aside like yesterday's garbage. They were recovering, but too slow.

"Keep moving. Don't stop for anything," Nolan shouted to them.

They were on a roll, and as long as they surged forward, bringing death and misery to the cave complex, the defenders would find it next to impossible to recover. They reached a fork in the tunnel.

"I'll go left. Will, come with me. Lt, you and Dave take the right. Remember, we need Barre. We have to have him alive. Now move!"

The tunnel was quite short with a stout door at the end. On the floor lay the body of one of the defenders, his guts ripped by a jagged knife wound, and his head tattooed with a red bullet hole through the forehead.

There's something strange going on. None of us have got this far, so who killed the gomer?

He went to the right of the tunnel and signaled Will to cover him from the left with the M249. They reached the door and he listened. Nothing. He gave the hand signals and put one hand on the latch. It was unlocked. He glanced at Will.

"Now!"

Will's shoulder crashed into the door. It hurtled open. He went in to the right, and Will tumbled into the left side. They came up with their weapons ready to fire, and he found himself staring into the barrel of an AK-47. His finger tightened on the trigger, then stopped. There were three women in the room, and the person holding the weapon wore a black burqa, but her head was uncovered.

"Amelia!"

"Kyle!"

She ran into his arms. He gently disentangled himself and glanced at the other women.

"Are they okay?"

She smiled. "More than okay. Give them a gun, and they'll empty it into Barre's guts. Saba has already stabbed one of the guards, the guy outside."

"My name is Emily. Saba is the Muslim name he forced me to adopt. I hated it."

She'd spoken in English. Amelia nodded and smiled. "Emily."

The young white girl clutched her baby fiercely.

"You're American?" Nolan asked her.

She inclined her head. "Yes. Well, I was, before that animal raped me and forced me into marriage."

"You'll get your baby home, Ma'am. We'll deal with Barre."

Lucas had limped into the room, still clutching the pistol. His face was paper white, and it was obvious the wounds were agonizing. But for him it was a watershed, a chance to turn things around, and to make up a little for the hurt and damage done to his sister by an Islamic husband.

"Lucas, you should take it easy."

He shook his head. "I'll take it easy when that bastard is in hell."

"Hold it. We want him alive."

It was too late. He'd already limped away. Nolan debated sending Will after him but decided against it. He had a strong feeling the Al Shabaab commander was long gone. He turned to Amelia.

"You get these women along the tunnel and out into the house. We'll be leaving pretty soon, as soon as we've checked the place over for any survivors."

She nodded and spoke to the women in Somali. It seemed strange that Emily replied in the same language. She held her baby close as they left the room and started back. He and Will left and headed back through the tunnels, but there were no more hostiles. They were all dead. And no Barre. He tried to call Vince, to warn him that Barre could be coming out, but there was no signal below ground, not unexpected. They'd just have to hope he got him when he came out, although he wouldn't know how urgent it was to keep him alive.

"Will, we need to contact Vince. Tell him to keep Barre alive. He'll have to shoot to disable, not to kill. Go back through the tunnel until you get a signal and warn him."

"Roger that."

The big Seal went away in a crouching run where the tunnel was too low to allow his big frame to walk upright. Nolan went deeper into the tunnels and caught up with Lucas. It was a larger space, obviously used as an office. The rocky floor had a thick rug, and there was a desk, together with four chairs and a filing cabinet.

Grant nodded a greeting. He sat on one of the chairs and was going through paperwork on the desk.

"They didn't have time to clear this lot. Most of it's in Arabic, but there are some diagrams. I'm going through them."

"Anything we can use?"

"Maybe. There's a map of New York City, several pencil marks on it. JFK, Brooklyn Bridge, the UN Building, the Empire State Building, and some other stuff, yeah, Central Park. It looks like a target selection list. They were trying to work out what to hit, but it doesn't tell us what they decided, only the city."

"That's a start. We can get that back to...fuck! The satcom is shot. We can't contact Jacks."

"Unless we use this," he grinned. He handed over a satellite phone, "It'll work anywhere up on the surface, and it's almost as good as an encrypted phone. You can get a patch through to him from anywhere."

Nolan found a tattered backpack loose on the floor and stuffed the phone inside, together with the map.

"Anything else?"

Lucas was rubbing a pencil lead across a sheet of paper. Someone had written something over it, and it had indented the paper below.

"It's a cellphone number and a name, Musse."

"Musse. The name of Fatimah's son was Musse. It could be the same guy. I wonder if she talked to him. He'd listen to her."

"There are a few of them. How would you stop them all?"

"It's a start."

He jotted the number on a piece of paper.

"I need to find Nabil Barre. You should start back along the tunnel. We'll be pulling out soon. I'll link up in a few minutes when I've double checked."

"Yeah, I think I will. I don't think you'll find him. I went deeper into the complex, as far as the exit to the air vent in the University grounds. He's gone."

"Let's hope Vince nailed him."

"Yeah."

When he returned to the wine cellar and exited the cave complex, he'd drawn a blank on Barre. Boswell had posted sentries on the windows of the house, watching for any sign of hostiles.

"Chief, you took your time. Zeke mined the complex, and as soon as we get out of here, he's going to blow it. If they want to use it again, they'll need excavators."

"Right. Any sign of Barre?"

"Barre? No."

"I'll call Vince."

His answer was the same. Barre hadn't appeared. He wasn't in the cave complex. He hadn't escaped through the air vent, so where was he? Obviously, there was a third exit, one that was well hidden. Which meant he was long gone, and with him went their chance of uncovering the plan of the attack, which they now knew would take place in New York City.

"Fuck!"

Boswell stared at him. "What is it?"

"We're back to square one. That's what it is. We know an attack is imminent, but we still don't know the when and the where."

* * *

His anger was all consuming. The hated Americans had taken everything from him. Many of his most valued leaders and fighters were dead and his wives taken. And there was worse. Much worse.

They took my son!

He emerged in a basement storeroom of the university main building, mentally thanking the loyal students who'd uncovered the almost invisible portal to the cave complex. He wanted revenge for these impudent Americans who'd dared to set foot in his country. They'd done untold damage to his organization, but that could be rebuilt. There were always volunteers anxious to sign up, in return for the means to feed their families. And his donors would send more arms and money. He'd rebuild, yes, bigger and stronger than ever before. He'd also find a new wife. Perhaps the pirates would send him a juicy young captive, a pretty white girl for him to train in his ways. But there was one, huge black cloud on the horizon, something he couldn't plan to replace so easily.

They took my son!

No, he had to get him back. Mukhtar was too valuable, by far. The heir to his future planned Islamic Caliphate, an empire that would stretch across the whole of North Africa; even into the oil-rich Gulf States, so never again would he lack for funds.

He calmed his mind and began to make plans. First, he had to stop them getting away. They were obviously well armed and resourceful. He needed people, lots of people. Cannon fodder, prepared to make a barricade of their dead and wounded bodies to stop the infidels from getting away and stealing his son.

He left the storeroom and went up the staircase to the main floor. He knew where he would find an internal phone a few meters along the passage, and he called the number. A familiar voice answered; the man who coordinated Al Shabaab inside the University.

"This is Dr. Magan, how can I help you?"

"Sheikh Barre."

A pause. "Sheikh Barre? But, this is an internal phone. You are here, inside the building?"

"Yes. Just listen."

He rapidly explained about the devastating attack on his underground headquarters, and about his son.

"I have to have him back, Magan. He is the heir, and one day he will rule over a vast Islamic Caliphate. All our futures depend on him."

"You will have other sons, my Sheikh."

"I WANT MY SON!"

His rage silenced the other man. After a few seconds, he replied, "Yes, of course. How may I help?"

That's better.

"How many supporters do we have inside the University?"

"About fifty."

"Is that all? And inside Mogadishu?"

"Hundreds, perhaps five hundred in all."

"Get them all out. I don't care how you do it. If they possess a weapon, tell them to bring it. They are to stop the Americans from escaping."

"Many of them do not have weapons, and you tell me the Americans are well armed. They will not be able to fight Special Forces without guns."

"Just get them all out. If there's a battle, the unarmed can stand at the rear and take up the guns of those who fall. I don't care what it takes; get them to block the road. They have to be stopped."

"What about you, my Sheikh?"

"Come down to the first floor. I am near the basement

entrance. You can show me to your office, and when the crowd has gathered, I will speak to them."

"Yes, Sheikh Barre, but if it comes to a battle out there, you could be killed."

"My followers will protect me, never fear. But if anything should happen, you know everything. You will be able to carry on."

"And the operation in America?"

"All on course. Tomorrow the infidels will know what it is like to lose a leader."

* * *

"We need to get out of here," Boswell told them. He'd called them together for a briefing.

"We still haven't got Barre," Nolan pointed out.

"For Christ's sake, Chief. Haven't we done enough? We've given Al Shabaab a real bloody nose and recovered an American hostage. What more is there to do?"

"Get Barre, and pummel the crap out of him until he tells us what they're up to in New York," Grant snapped out.

The Lieutenant turned to his supposed ally in surprise. "Lucas, you can see the sense of getting out, surely? We're in Mogadishu, for Christ's sake. Before you know what's happening, they'll contact their buddies, and we'll have more people on the road outside than queue for a Red Sox game."

"I never was a Red Sox fan, Lt, and I didn't go to Harvard. We leave that sucker alive, and he'll keep doing his thing. Killing, rape, kidnap, you name it. We're here, so we may as well finish the job."

Boswell flushed red with anger. "I still say we should request an immediate exfil," he muttered.

They all ignored him, and Nolan started to weigh up the options. Barre could be in the university, which was a problem. Busting into a University mob-handed was way outside their ROEs, apart from the simple immorality of attacking an educational institution. And there was always the possibility of Barre escaping elsewhere. He called Vince.

"How're things looking out there?"

"Still nothing. Nobody came in, nobody went out. All I saw was a small delivery truck. It left a few moments ago. Looked empty."

"Copy that. Stay out there. Call us if you see anything."

"Roger that."

He ended the conversation and looked around. His eyes fell on Fatimah, the mother of that kid who was in the US in New York, if the papers they found were to be believed. He took them out of the rucksack, found the one with the name and cellphone number, and took it to her.

"Ma'am, this number could belong to the cellphone your son is using in the US."

She looked at the name, Musse, and her eyes filled with tears.

"It is a common name in Somalia, but yes, it could be."

"I want you to call and see if it's him. Try and get him to stop what he's doing. And find out exactly what it is, and when."

"If it's him," she said doubtfully.

"Give it a try, let's see. You'll need to go outside the house to make the satellite connection."

She looked at him, mystified. "It's a satphone," he explained.

She didn't get it, but she went out to the front of the house. Nolan went with her. She waited a couple of minutes for the satellite to connect and then dialed the number.

"Put it on speaker, Ma'am."

She looked puzzled, and he pressed the button for her. The button with the speaker icon printed on it. She heard the ringtone and understood. When the call connected, a voicemail message came though.

"I'm sorry, this phone is switched off. Transferring you to voicemail." And then, "This is the voicemail of Musse Daud. Leave a message, and I'll get back to you."

Shit. All the technology known to man, and he's switched off his phone.

She looked at him, and he nodded for her to leave a message.

"Musse, this is your mother. You must get back to me on this number. I'll be waiting, my darling son. Please, don't do anything foolish. Barre can't hurt me, not any more."

She hung up and passed the phone back to him.

"He'll call back. I know my own son."

Not if he's already dead, and a major target in New York City lies in smoking ruins.

He nodded. "We'll go back inside, and...holy shit!"

Past the university building, a few hundred meters toward the city of Mogadishu, a cloud of dust rose in the sky like smoke. But it wasn't smoke. He'd seen something like it before; the kind of dust cloud that was kicked up by a great mass of people walking along a dusty road.

Like this one.

He needed to see more, but his rifle with the scope sight was inside the house. He keyed his mic.

"Vince, this is Bravo Two. Coming up the road, what do you make of it?"

A pause. "It's people, Chief. Lots of 'em, and my guess is they're not planning on coming here for a church picnic. Or mosque picnic, whatever they have here."

"Right. Keep watching, and stand by for some fireworks."

Boswell was still inside the house, but there wasn't time to call him. Instead, he called Naval Base Coronado. NBC was a consolidated Navy installation, encompassing eight military facilities. They stretched from San Clemente Island, seventy miles west of San Diego, California, to the La Posta Mountain Warfare Training Facility and Camp Morena, sixty miles east of San Diego. It was also the same base for Seal Team Bravo and other Seal units. On this occasion, his call was intended for someone even further away from San Diego. Admiral Jacks, his boss.

It took several minutes to establish his credentials. There was a prescribed set of codewords for emergencies, but he managed to convince the operator he wasn't some teenage hacker.

"Sir, everything checks out, but it'll take some time to get through to Admiral Jacks. I'd guess about five minutes. I'll be as quick as I can."

"I'm not going anywhere."

He keyed his mic. "Bravo One, this is Two. Best get out here, Boss. There's something you all need to see."

A moment later, they came out onto the terrace. Boswell followed Nolan's pointing finger.

"Oh, my God. Is that what I think it is?"

"I reckon so."

A group of young Somalis exited the University grounds and turned away from them to join the oncoming throng. When they finally came into view, Vince was able to check out the numbers. He called them with the bad news.

"Maybe ten abreast on the road, at least twenty columns; two hundred, and more joining them. The guys at the front are armed, AKs, hunting rifles, couple of M-16s, three RPG7s. They mean business. You want me to stay here? I can take out the missile shooters."

The question was a simple one. Stay and fight, and he could be overwhelmed in his forward position. Or they could pull out, and try to escape across country.

"Hold your position."

"Hey, wait up," Boswell exclaimed angrily, "We can't fight those numbers. We're getting out. If we..."

The satphone was still on speakerphone, and it cut in, "This is Admiral Jacks."

Nolan seized the opportunity and walked away a couple of meters to stop the Lieutenant grabbing the phone.

"Sir, this is Nolan. We have a problem."

He described the crowd threatening them, the threat to New York, the rescue of the American girl, and the escape of Barre. And that he intended to fight them.

"So you called up for support."

That was as far as he got. Boswell seized the phone. "Sir, this is Lieutenant Boswell, the platoon commander. We need an exfil, right away."

"Hand the phone back to the Chief, Boswell. Now!"

He looked sheepish and passed it back to Nolan. The Lieutenant walked across to Lucas Grant, who'd just emerged from the house, clutching his wounded side.

"Sir?"

"Okay, we already have the UAV over Mogadishu, as you know. I can see it now, the crowd moving up that road. Yeah, I've got it. You're on that terrace. Any losses yet?"

"Weissman."

"Understood. Christ, I hate that place."

"You're not alone, Sir."

"I guess not. What're you looking for?"

"We need to disperse the crowd. A lot of 'em are armed. Some of them have RPGs. We can count three launchers so far, there may be more. We're still holding a Carl Gustav, but if we use it, the missile would go straight through the people at the front who're all armed, and detonate toward the rear. And some of them aren't armed. We need a Hellfire."

"That'll do it, for sure."

"Yes, but not in the center of the crowd. I want the operator to detonate at the front of them. He can fire as soon as he's ready."

"Understood, I'll pass on the order. Anything else? What about exfil?"

"Not until we've nailed Barre. We have to know about that threat to New York. As soon as that crowd has disappeared, we'll start looking for him. He can't be far away."

"Good luck with that. I'll pass on the order. Call me if anything changes."

The call ended. He watched the crowd for a few moments more as they drew nearer. It was time to retrieve his SWS sniper rifle and start looking for targets of opportunity, like the ringleaders, anyone who looked like they could whip a bunch of fanatics into frenzy.

And then Vince called. "Chief, someone just came out of the University building. They're walking toward the crowd. It could be our target."

"Barre! Don't shoot him, whatever you do. We have to take him alive."

"Copy that."

He raced into the house, slung on his AK47S, and picked up his rifle. Amelia was with the women. They were helping the wounded men, and it occurred to Nolan they should be ready to pull out as soon as they were done. He shouted at her to get out to the truck and get everyone aboard.

"We need to finish attending to these wounds," she objected.

"Do it in the truck, and take a look at the Commissioner while you're there. He had a hard time back in Kismayo. We've enough trouble with Al Shabaab, without upsetting the UN."

She nodded. "I'll get them moving."

He went back outside, focused the scope on the crowd, and there was the target, just like he'd seen in the images. Nabil Barre, self-styled 'Sheikh', bald and thin, almost to the point of emaciation. Wire rimmed glasses, and his chin sported a beard, not long, but ragged, as if he'd been on the run and too harried to groom his facial hair.

Good. You'll have a whole heap more to worry about before we leave this town.

As he watched, the man raised his hands and started speaking to the crowd. Haranguing the crowd would be a better way to put it, by the look of his body language.

At that moment, Nolan felt an icy realization tear through him.

The Hellfire!

He pressed buttons on the satphone and began the long, complicated process of security clearances to patch through to Jacks on the SSN Southampton, the submarine gliding through the Arabian Sea. Three minutes passed, then four, and still he was waiting, listening to a series of clicks as the call went around the world, passing from satellite to satellite. It finally reached the aerial trailed by the sub. And then they had to call Jacks to the communications center.

"Jacks."

"Thank Christ, this is Nolan. You have to stop the Hellfire launch. He's standing right in front of the crowd. If he dies, our last chance of finding out about the New York attack goes with him."

"The little bald guy standing in front of the crowd, that's Barre? We've been watching the feed from the UAV on the monitor. We wondered about him. Damn, I'll stop them. Don't..."

He didn't hear the rest of it. The weapon detonated, right on target, exactly at the front where he'd told Jacks to aim the missile. The AGM-114 had multi-target precision-strike capability and could be launched from multiple platforms, and in this case, a Predator UAV.

Not for nothing was the Hellfire the primary air-to-ground precision weapon for the armed forces of the United States. Powered by an M120E4 solid fuel rocket, flying at a speed n excess of Mach 1.2, and guided by a laser-aiming device, the twenty-pound high explosive charge detonated at the front of the mass of Somalis blocking the road.

The Hellfire was designed for use against hard targets; armored vehicles, fortified positions, and terrorist leaders, often when traveling in vehicles. It was the munition of choice for airborne-targeted killings of Anwar al-Awlaki, the American-born Islamic cleric in Yemen, and Abu Yahya al-Libi in Pakistan; and now of Nabil Barre.

Nolan watched the jet of flame roar high into the air, mixed with thick, roiling smoke. The explosion kicked up masses of debris, and for long minutes, the target area was obscured. But it didn't hide the sound of the survivors, wounded, panicked; many fleeing, many unable to flee, screams, shouts, and pleas for aid. They were the same in any language. Then the smoke cleared.

Where Barre had stood to encourage and enrage his followers, there was a deep hole in the ground. Scattered around the hole were bodies, scores of bodies, mixed in with the dying. The smell wafted toward them, the smell of battle, and the smell of death. The acrid stink of burned propellant and high explosive, mixed with burning clothes, and worst of all, the sweet stench of roasting flesh.

There was no need to check. He knew with a dull ache in his guts that New York was about to take a hit. A heavy hit, and the one man who knew the details that might enable Homeland Security and the FBI to halt it, or at least, clear the area so there were no casualties.

Jacks' voice came on the phone.

"Nolan? I tried, but it was too damn late. We watched the missile hit. It didn't look like there was any doubt."

"No doubt at all, Sir."

"Is there any way we can find out about that attack? There must be something."

"It's an outside possibility."

He told him about the cellphone number in New York. Jacks immediately said he'd get the handset triangulated, but Nolan told him not to waste his time. It was switched off.

"Shit. What next?"

Before he could reply, he saw two things happen. A man came out of the university building, probably a lecturer. He wore a short-sleeved shirt and colored tie, and sported thick round, black plastic glasses. He stared at the devastation, and then looked hard at the Seals standing nearby. His body language was suspicious, and when he ran out, he picked up a dropped assault rifle and ran back inside. Suspicions became a certainty. Lucas Grant was the first to react.

"Sonofabitch! That bastard is involved in all this. I'm going after him. He could give us the lead we need to stop that New York business."

"Lucas! That's a college. Those are kids in there."

"Yeah, right."

He ignored the warning and limped toward the University. Nolan gave Will Bryce the nod. "Go after him. I don't want anyone killed. Try and get him out of there."

"And if that guy is involved with Al Shabaab?"

"Yeah, bring him back, but no killing. There's been enough for one day."

Will ran after Grant, and Boswell watched him go. He glared at Nolan.

"If Lucas is hurt, I'll hold you responsible, Chief."

He ignored him, conscious of their failure. Timing had beaten them, had beaten him. It took him too damn long to cancel the fire order for the Hellfire. And a switch on a cellphone, if there ever was a chance Musse would listen to his mother. He tried to think of any way to retrieve the disaster, to stop what was going to happen in New York. But no matter which way he looked at it, he couldn't come up with a damn thing.

It's a fuck up, no matter which way you look at it. Sure, we rescued the American girl, assuming we can get her out of Mogadishu, and Barre is dead. A successful mission? Not when a heap of explosives detonate in downtown New York. There has to be something, but what?

CHAPTER ELEVEN

The room was filthy and stank of poor hygiene. Outside the window, the cacophony of New York City coming to life was like something from a movie, sirens, car horns, shots, screams, and heavy truck engines. In the distance, the clatter of the elevated railway. Inside, there was only silence, a silence that seemed more intense compared to the normal world outside. Amin had volunteered to go out and bring back pizza for breakfast. No one was inclined to think of any alternative. The boxes lay scattered on the floor where they'd thrown them, and the food lay congealing and cold on the plates, untouched.

"It's eight thirty," Ali informed them. He was two years younger than Musse, and the fear they all felt was reflected in his eyes.

"I know that."

"We need to be in position, ready for his arrival at one o'clock."

"I know."

"Shouldn't we, I mean..." he indicated the suicide vests,

stacked against the far wall.

Amin moved first, working hard to overcome his fear. He picked up his vest and fastened it on his body. He tightened the straps and went to admire his handiwork in the wall mirror. They all noticed his shudder when he saw his reflection staring back at him. Then he turned.

"Say something, someone."

Silence.

"I'm ready for this," he stated in a voice that only shook a little with fear, "I wish I could go now. The waiting is the worst part."

"You haven't been torn apart by explosives," Musse pointed out, "You may find the waiting is the best part, compared to your death. Or are you so keen to die?"

He stared back sullenly. Then he shook his head. "No. Musse, is there a Paradise"

"I don't know. I told you before."

He looked at Ali. The younger boy was weeping. For a moment, he felt like calling his mother. He'd left the cellphone switched off, as they instructed. It was in his bag, zipped into a side pocket. He could feel their eyes watching him as he took it out, felt the familiar plastic case. Then he shook his head and replaced the phone in the bag. If he switched it on, they could triangulate his position, if they knew the phone number. But how could they, it was a burner phone, bought in the US, and no connection with Somalia or Al Shabaab. Even so, he would follow orders.

I have to show them I can be strong.

He glanced at the heap of suicide vests, came to a decision, and walked over. He picked up his own vest, which was wired with an override that would explode all of the vests in one simultaneous blast. Then he strapped it on. It felt heavy, alien. It filled him with horror, but he swallowed his fear and nodded to the others.

"Get your vests on. We need to be familiar with wearing them, so when we walk to the target, we won't stand out as strange."

They didn't move for long moments. Then one by one, they picked up their vests and strapped them on. There was one vest spare, Rageh's. His body was stuffed into the closet, and they would leave it there when they left, an ignoble end. Perhaps that was true for all of them.

Is there a Paradise?

* * *

"Bravo Two, do you read? This is Bravo Three."

"Loud and clear. What's happening in there?"

"We lost him. Keep an eye out in case he tries to get away out the front."

Nolan looked at the heap of smoking bodies blocking the road. He could get past, but it would be a close run thing, and damn slow. If he tried it, they'd have him. Whoever he was.

"We're on it."

He passed it on to Boswell who was surveying the area through his binoculars. He gave him a sour glance. "Yeah, but what about that narrow track, looping around the back way? It joins the road a few hundred meters east, toward the city."

"Which narrow track?"

He pointed. "That one. You can see it now. There's a small delivery van driving along it now."

He snatched the binoculars and focused on the vehicle.

It was moving slowly, bumping up and down on what was obviously a badly rutted surface. The man in the driver's seat was wearing a short-sleeved shirt with a tie, thick round, black plastic glasses. Unusual for a delivery driver in this place, but a dead ringer for the guy who'd grabbed the AK, the man Lucas went after.

At that moment, Lucas came out of the building, supported by Will, who was almost carrying him in his huge, muscular arms.

"The bastard escaped," Grant croaked.

Nolan pointed. The vehicle was receding in the distance.

"He used the rear entrance. There's a track that joins up further along the road."

"Shit. Chief, the truck! We can go after him."

Boswell stared at his buddy. "Lucas, you're crazy. That piece of real estate down the road is named Mogadishu." Grant stared back at him with disdain. The Lieutenant looked at Nolan, appealing for some common sense.

He ignored the Lieutenant. He was already talking to Murray. "Zeke, we're going to need the truck. Amelia should be in the back with the wounded. Make sure they're all aboard, and drive down the rig down here to pick us up. We need to tail a target."

"In the truck? Tell me we're not following it to Mogadishu."

"The very same."

"Shit."

He sprinted up the road toward the big canvas sided truck. Boswell left Lucas and joined Nolan. His face was white, and it was obvious he'd had an argument with his sidekick.

"This is a bad idea, Chief. Chasing into Mogadishu, it'll

get us all killed."

"It's the only way to stop this thing, Lt! When that Hellfire hit Barre, everything he knew about the New York operation went with him. But it's a racing certainty he had someone working with him inside the university, and it's odds on that guy who just hightailed it is the same man."

Boswell considered for a few moments. They both knew it had gone beyond him calling rank on Chief Nolan. Jacks had made it clear who was running Bravo, and it wasn't the Lieutenant. They heard the truck engine start up, and it headed toward them.

"You could have a good future, Nolan. Stick with me when you leave the Navy, you'll be in easy street."

He'd been surveying the ground, checking for any sign of renewed enemy activity. He turned, startled.

"Excuse me?"

"A job, Chief. You know I'll be doing a short stint with the family brokerage firm, and then it's politics. All the way to the White House, who knows?"

"And if a suicide bomber decided to detonate right next to you when you're in a crowd?"

In his enthusiasm, he waved the comment away. "You could join me, be an important part of my team. Think about it, two former Navy Seals. We'd be unbeatable. We could make a difference, a real difference."

So he's fallen out with Lucas Grant. Tough titty.

"What about those poor bastards in New York? Something's going down there, and we still have a chance to find out the target, if we can catch up with that guy."

"He may not even know the target," Boswell blustered.

Nolan shook his head. "You keep the job, Lt. and I'll keep my honor. Sounds to me like the two don't mix."

Boswell reddened with anger but kept his mouth shut. The truck was almost with them. Nolan decided he needed a heads up.

"You know, Lt, there was a time when it looked like you'd be a damn good Seal officer. It looks like you blew it, but there's still time to pick it up. Forget the politics, and try being a hero. It's good for the soul. There's no one to vote for you out here. Just women and children, kidnapped and brutalized, and conned into becoming suicide bombers, or joining militia like Al Shabaab. This is where it's at, the frontline. This is where we make a difference, not kissing babies and taking bribes from political lobbyists."

He left him open mouthed and started to get the men aboard the truck. Ayub Ahmed was in the passenger seat next to Zeke. The rest of them were sprawled over the truck bed, hidden from view by the canvas roof.

"Will, take over the wheel from Zeke. We're heading into Mogadishu."

"Not too many white truck drivers down that way, Chief?"

"Not many, no. You'll need to drive through the university grounds and pick up that track to get on his tail."

"Right."

Boswell had one last try. "You know after that explosion, this place will be crawling with cops before long. We should clear the area fast."

Ayub Ahmed smiled. "Lieutenant this is Somalia, Mogadishu. If you were a cop here, would you come as soon as you heard the sounds of battle, explosions, and gunfire? No, they will wait and sound out their local contacts, get a better idea of what is happening, before they walk into a hail of bullets. Then they will come, when they know it is safe. Maybe tomorrow, or the day after."

He didn't reply. Instead, he moved to the front of the truck, as far away from them as possible. Nolan glanced at him.

Maybe the guy is thinking things through.

Seconds later, Zeke jumped into the truck as Will started up and lurched away. He gripped the side rails next to Nolan.

"Chief, something interesting. I described that gomer who got away, and Ayub said his name is Dr. Magan. He is a known Al Shabaab supporter in the university. According to Ayub, most of the staff detest him. Trying to persuade the kids to take up arms and fight, become suicide bombers, you know the kind of thing. All the poor bastards want to do is earn a living as engineers and teachers. They don't want to be involved."

"Dr. Magan, got it. What's he teach, asymmetric warfare?"

"Islamic studies."

"Same thing."

They broke through the gateposts either side of the track. The big truck was a meter too wide to fit, and Will swung the wheel over to head toward the city. One of the women screamed, the vehicle went up on one side, and the baby started crying. Lucas groaned. His injuries were by far the worse. Brad Rose was visibly gritting his teeth, and Dan Moseley had his eyes tight shut. It was about the worst treatment they could get for their bullet wounds, but the alternative was to leave them behind. In Mogadishu, Somalia, it was no contest.

They almost missed the little delivery van. Will jammed

on the brakes and stopped. His voice came on the commo.

"Guys, we just went past him, so I guess he doesn't know we're following. It's a building about four hundred meters back. What do you want me to do?"

"Find somewhere to turn around, then go back past this place, and we'll take a look. What sort of building?"

"A mosque."

"Right. It figures."

He put the truck into gear and drove a few hundred meters, then swung around in a huge circle to go back. They watched through tiny holes in the canvas sides, and the delivery van came into view, parked casually and in the open outside an overly ornate mosque. Even the domed roof was painted gold, and the entire building was decorated with gleaming ceramic tiles. Every piece of metalwork shone, as if it was coated with real gold. Will drove a short distance past and parked where they could observe the mosque.

A few of them whistled. This incredible sight was on the outskirts of Mogadishu, Somalia, yet it would have been more at home in Las Vegas.

"The Mosque of the Islamic Martyrs," Fatimah told them. She was peering through a slit in the canvas, "It was constructed twenty-five years ago with money provided by the Saudi Sheikh Fahd bin Massam. They have a reputation for sending suicide bombers to the West. They also have an affiliated mosque in Kismayo, which I expect Musse and his friends attended."

"I guess they don't preach all peace and happiness," Zeke commented.

"They preach death, death for our sons, for our young people. Even for some of our girls."

Nolan ignored them. His mind raced through the options open to them. To storm a mosque was not likely to go down well with the locals. The rapid appearance of the crowd at the university illustrated how volatile the Somalis were when it came to foreigners invading their turf, and a mosque; that would be something else, even if it were the Mosque of the Islamic Martyrs. They'd likely find bomb-making literature in there, materials for suicide vests, explosives, and Dr. Magan, the Islamic hate-monger. Local Islamists wouldn't give a shit. Probably contributed to the fund to pay for it all. They had to know, had to grab Magan, and shake it out of him. Unless.

He turned to Fatimah Barre and handed her the satphone.

"Your son, try him again. If it goes to voicemail, make the message stronger. You have to try and stop him."

She looked back at him. "You think I don't want to stop him with all of my heart. I will do my best, believe me."

She went to the rear of the truck, pressed the redial button, and waited. After a few minutes, the ringtone started.

For fuck's sake, Musse, pick up!

The ringing stopped. "I'm sorry, this phone is switched off. Transferring you to voicemail." And then, "This is the voicemail of Musse Daud. Leave a message, and I'll get back to you."

Amelia translated her words that were in Somali.

"Musse, this is your mother. By all the love you have for me, and me for you, please don't do this. Call me back on this number. I am safe, quite safe. And Nabil Barre is dead. There is no need to go on. Please, my darling son, stop it. Come back to your mother. I need you."

She ended the call and went to hand the phone back to Nolan, but Boswell interceded and took it off her.

"Thank you, Ma'am. I'll be needing that."

Nolan didn't argue. There was only one way now. They had to go in. He went and sat next to Boswell.

"Lt, we have to get that guy Magan. You know that. We have to go in there and pull him out."

The other man sucked in a breath and sighed. Then he nodded.

"You're right. And Chief, I haven't given this my best shot so far. I know that. There're a lot of things going on Stateside right now, a lot of things. It's just..."

"Forget Stateside. We're here, at the sharp end. Let's finish this. Besides, if we prevent a major terrorist attack in New York, it won't do your election prospects any harm."

Boswell smiled. "Yeah, I'd thought of that, but it's not the damned election. I've let people down, and it ends now. Let's do this right."

"Good." He turned to the Bravo troopers, "Gather round, guys, we're about to go to pray."

They chuckled and sprawled at the rear of the truck. Nolan keyed his mic.

"Will, this is Nolan. We're setting up the assault. I'll leave the channel open so you can hear."

"Roger that."

"Okay." He turned back to the men and shuddered. They were a pitiable sight. There were injuries he hadn't been away of, flesh wounds with hurriedly applied dressings. Brad Rose and Dan Moseley were in no shape to fight, and Lucas Grant was going down fast. If he didn't get medical attention soon, he'd be in serious trouble.

He looked at Boswell. "You mind if I do this?"

"Go ahead."

"Right. The three badly wounded will stay in the truck. There are civilians that need guarding, and besides," he held up his hand to stop the inevitable protests, "If the nasties get their hands on this vehicle, we're in deep shit. That's final. Vince, how are you, after that beating you got from those MLS guys?"

"Bruised, sore, and ready to hit back."

"Right. You stay in the truck too. I'll ask Dr. Ahmed to drive around back, let us out, and then park it the other side of the street opposite the front door. Anyone comes out you don't like the look of; pop them. If it's Magan, shoot to wound. The rest of you," he glanced at the three badly wounded men, "You'll be able to give support if necessary."

"Copy that."

"With you covering the front door, it frees the rest of us to sneak in the back. Now it's broad daylight, our white faces are a problem. Will Bryce can lead us in, and as soon as he's called it clear, we'll come in fast. One problem, we don't know the layout inside."

"I will go with you," Fatimah spoke up. She'd been following the briefing, which was no surprise, "I have been in that place before. I will guide you."

He hesitated for a few moments. He didn't like it, not at all.

But what choices do we have? None.

"Thank you, Ma'am. In that case, you'd better go in with Will. Stay with him. He'll keep an eye on you. That leaves four of us. We'll split into two-man teams. Lt, take Dave Eisner and the M249, in case you run into any trouble. Zeke, you come with me. The place has two stories, so we'll take one floor each. Lt, take the second floor. Zeke, we'll work through the first. And everyone, remember, this is our last chance to grab someone who knows about the New York attack. Or may know," he corrected himself.

"It's all we have. That's it. When we're done, we'll fall back to the truck, hopefully with Magan in tow, and retreat toward the shore outside of Mogadishu. We'll call for exfil. I guess the Southampton will take us off with their rubber boats. That's all. Let's do it. Will, you ready?"

"Yep, on my way. Ayub is moving to the driver's seat to take over the wheel."

Will appeared at the rear and helped Fatimah Barre down to the ground. They walked together around the rear of the mosque. A few seconds later, he called in.

"It's clear, you can ask Ayub to bring her around."

Nolan went to the front and stuck his head through the canvas. Ayub Ahmed was waiting.

"That's it, Dr. Ahmed. Drive around back, let us out, then go back across the road, and find a position where my men can cover the front entrance."

"As you wish. You are taking a huge risk, storming a mosque. Especially that mosque."

"We don't have a choice, Sir."

"No, perhaps not."

He turned away, put the vehicle in gear, and drove back to the mosque. The building was set on a large lot on its own. There was space either side for vehicles to approach the rear areas.

Probably for deliveries, Nolan thought to himself, *explosives, detonators, weapons, whatever; the growth industry created by the Islamists.*

Will and Fatimah were waiting outside a hardwood

door. It hung askew on its hinges where the big Seal had wrenched the lock open. Bryce was the lead breacher and always carried a small tool to jimmy open doors, when a full on shoulder charge or demolition explosives were not possible.

Nolan unslung his AK47S, put the SWS rifle on his back, and jumped down from the truck. The rest of them followed. They raced inside the building, weapons held ready. Eisner was in last, covering them with the machine gun.

They were in a small kitchen at the rear of the mosque. Further into the building, they could hear voices, some kind of prayer chanting. It didn't sound like there were more than a half-dozen men inside. Boswell opened a side door, found a staircase to the upper floor, and started up with Eisner following close behind. Nolan peered through the door that led into the main prayer hall.

The room was huge, the floor covered with a thick carpet, the ceiling with ornate paintings and carvings. Something about it reminded him of a New Orleans brothel. He'd seen other mosques, and this one was different. Tacky, designed and built by someone with more money than sense. At the top, a balcony ran all around the building, and he saw Boswell and Eisner creeping along it, staying low.

The place was dim. It smelt of incense, perfume, and old sweat. The voices were louder, and he peered further into the room. To one side, the worshippers were on their knees, occasionally bowing down with their asses in the air, making the verbal responses to the Imam. He stood out of sight, close to the rear wall. There was no sign of Magan. He pulled back before anyone turned and saw him. Fatimah was waiting, guarded by Will.

"Where would he be, Dr. Magan? I couldn't see him with the worshippers. Unless he's the Imam."

She chuckled. "Magan?" She shivered with hot anger. "He is one of the those I would like to kill. He helped persuade Musse to become a shaheed. He is not an Imam, just a peddler of hate and death. He will be in the library if he is not in the prayer room. It is a room at the side of the prayer room, and there is no other access. If you want him, you will have to get past those worshippers."

"Is there a window he could climb out of?"

"Yes, but it is barred, to prevent thieves. Even a mosque is not safe."

A mosque isn't safe from thieves in Somalia. Who would've believed it?

"Understood."

"Mr. Nolan, when you catch him, I would like to kill him," she added, her face screwed up in fury and misery, "I must have some revenge for what he has done to my son."

"I get it, but it's not the way to go. We need him. You know why."

"I will kill him," she muttered.

"Yeah."

He called Boswell and explained what she'd said. "We'll have to go through the prayer room, Lt, so I want you and Dave to cover us from up on that balcony."

"Roger that," was the whispered reply, "Chief, I'm not sure about starting a fight in this place. It could cause more trouble than it solves."

"Then don't start one. But if they make a move, they've already started it, and we have to defend ourselves."

"Yeah, okay, ready when you are."

"We'll enter through the door at the rear. Give us a minute."

"Roger that."

He turned to Will, who clutched the second M249.

"We're going into the prayer room, about six gomers, and the priest, Imam, whatever. As soon as Zeke and me go in, cover us from the doorway. Fatimah, stay behind Will. There's a chance someone will start shooting."

"I will stay behind him. Good luck, Mr. Nolan."

"Yeah."

He glanced at Zeke. "Ready?"

"Yep."

Murray held his HK410, barrel slanted upward, ready to bring into the firing position in a microsecond. He nodded.

"Let's go."

Nolan shoved the door wide with his shoulder and barged into the prayer room, his AK pointed at the men kneeling on the rug. Zeke came in behind him, his HK410 leveled at their bodies. And then Will poked the barrel of his M249 through the door, in case there was any room for doubt. Their jaws dropped open in astonishment at the miraculous appearance of the 'American Devils'; devils in wetsuits as battered, grimy, and bloody as their faces. But their weapons were clean, oiled, and loaded. The Imam, who'd been out of sight, said something in Somali. The words were gibberish, but the meaning was clear. 'Who the fuck are you? And get out of my mosque.'

Nolan ignored him. He noticed Boswell and Eisner come into view on the balcony, but the Somalis were too shocked to notice.

"Zeke, Will, cover me, I'm going through to bring Magan out."

"Roger that."

He ran across the floor, his feet sinking into the thick rug.

Saudi money, he reflected.

The cost of this mosque could probably have rescued the sinking Somali economy. The poor bastards needed medical care and work. Instead, they got a tacky mosque, a mosque that preached the philosophy of death, a martyr's death, but only for the young. Always young people, and led by the nose to a fate their teacher's leaders wouldn't dream of inflicting on themselves.

He reached the door, which was locked. He jiggled the handle, but there was no doubt whoever was in there had bolted the portal from inside. The wood was solid, carved hardwood, not easy to kick in. But the lock didn't look bulletproof. Fortunately, he had his suppressed Sig Sauer back in his possession. He unholstered it, aimed, and fired three shots at the area around the lock. It didn't give, and he readied the gun to fire again when a burst of gunfire from inside the library shattered the shocked silence of the building.

He flung himself to the side, narrowly avoiding the last few shots as the shooter worked his gun in an arc, designed to kill his attackers. He was working at an advantage. He could kill as many of the Americans as he could find, but they couldn't kill him. Not yet.

Nolan stood back and aimed again. This time, he emptied the magazine into the lock, and the door sagged open. Another volley of shots spewed out into the mosque, and one of the kneeling worshippers screamed in pain as a stray round clipped him.

They call it friendly fire, but it always seems pretty unfriendly, Nolan smiled to himself.

Will was out of sight of the shooter, and Zeke had flattened himself on the floor, lying prone and watching the Somalis. Boswell and Eisner were watching, but held their fire.

"Magan, we want to talk to you. That's all."

"Fuck you, American. You're here to kill me. If you think you'll get away, you're wrong. I've made a call to our Al Shabaab people in Mogadishu. They're already preparing to come here and paint the walls of this sacred place with your blood. The sacrifice will be a testament to the power of Islam."

Yeah, right. Has he called them? Maybe. So we need to wrap this up fast.

"I promise you, Magan, we're not here to kill you. I just need some information."

"What information?"

"Put down the gun, and we'll talk."

"Fuck you. Make your peace with your God, infidel. My people will be here soon to hang your intestines from the branches of the trees along the street."

I have to get in there and disarm the mad bastard, without getting myself shot.

He keyed his mic.

"Lt, I'm going in. I want you and Eisner to pepper the door with gunfire, but aim low. If you do hit him, it'll only be in the legs. Aim low, clear?"

"We're clear, Chief. Say the word."

"Do it."

The huge prayer room echoed to the thunder of the

shots. Eisner's machine gun chewing huge chunks out of the wooden door, and Boswell's HK adding to the awesome damage to several thousand dollars of rich, carved hardwood.

"Cease fire!"

The noise stopped, and he was on his feet, ready. Straight through the door, and a half roll to the side. He needn't have worried. Magan was sprawled on the rug, clutching his foot where at least one bullet had gone straight through. His blood soaked into the expensive Afghan weave, and his voice was a loud squeal of agony and hatred. His assault rifle lay across the other side of the room where he'd thrown it when the gunfire came through the door.

Nolan checked around the room. The four walls were lined with wooden bookshelves from floor to ceiling, apart from the opening of the barred window and the door. In the center, there was a low desk, no chair. Apparently, readers were expected to sit on the rug. In Magan's case, lie on the rug, screaming in agony, as his lifeblood leaked from a large hole in his foot.

He knelt next to him. "Dr. Magan, I meant what I said. We're not here to kill you. We just want some information."

The man stared back at him, his eyes scrunched up in pain. "I heard you the first time, and I still don't believe you." He glanced down at his leg and back at Nolan.

"Yeah, that was a mistake. The attack in New York, when's it scheduled to go down?"

"I know nothing of any attack in New York. Nothing!"

He was lying. Maybe without the painful wound he could have pulled it off, maybe not. But with the wound, he was fighting to hold it together, and his eyes looked away as he spoke.

"I have to know, Dr. Magan. People will die, innocent people."

"There are no innocent people. They are all part of the global struggle between Islam and darkness. And we will win, American. We will win."

"Sure. Listen, Magan, I know you have that information. We can do this the easy way, or the hard way. For the last time, when does it go down?"

The Somali glanced at the clock. He couldn't help himself. Nolan felt a chill. It would be soon. He checked his wristwatch. Almost midday, and New York City was eight hours behind Somalia, so it was 0400 hrs back there.

What time will the attack take place?

The attacks on the World Trade Center began at 0846 hrs, when American Airlines Flight 11 out of Boston Logan, en route to Los Angeles with a crew of eleven and seventy-six passengers, flew into the North Tower. And changed the world, at a stroke.

If this new attack involved suicide bombers, he reasoned it would be more personal. Besides, hijacking aircraft was a non-starter in these security conscious times. No, a building, an embassy maybe, or even the President. They'd want plenty of people around, collateral damage, so it would likely be from 0900 onward. It wasn't enough.

The guy has to spit it out, whatever it takes.

He tapped the barrel of the AK on the injured foot, and the man screamed.

"I have to know, Magan. You're gonna tell me, one way or the other, so it may as well be now. While you still have one foot that's uninjured."

He gave him another tap so there was no

misunderstanding, another shrill scream.

"Where is it?"

"No! I will not tell you."

Now we're getting somewhere. The bastard knows.

"You'll walk with a stick for the rest of your life, Magan, but at least you'll walk. I'm about to put a bullet in the other foot. And here's the thing, recognize the gun. It's one of yours. I took it off an Al Shabaab fighter. He won't be needing it anymore. Your bullets, too. Where is the attack to take place?"

He was weeping in agony.

"I need treatment. You must take me to a hospital."

"Where?"

"The hospital first."

And give them time to detonate? Thanks, but no thanks.

"Last chance. Where and when?"

He shook his head. Nolan put the barrel of the AK against the other foot and pulled the trigger.

The scream almost took the roof off. Outsider in the prayer room, the Somalis were shouting in rage at the treatment he was meting out, and the Seals were holding them down under the muzzles of their guns. But it was getting bad, and sooner or later someone would do something stupid, and there'd be a bloodbath. Or reinforcements would arrive, and they'd be trapped. Another tap on the shattered foot.

"Where is it, Magan? When does it go down?"

The man's face was contorted with extreme agony, and he looked to have lost all will to resist. He was breathing in short pants, gasping each breath in and out of his lungs as he fought to cope with the pain.

"All right, yes, I will tell you. But after, you will take me to a hospital?"

"You can go to a hospital. Your buddies can take you. Where is it? When?"

"I have it all here."

As he watched, Magan's face changed almost in an instant. With an effort of will that was almost superhuman, he pulled himself slowly off the floor, to rest on one elbow. Nolan assumed he was easing the pain. But his other hand dived behind his back, and with a sickening realization, he knew the man was about to pull a gun.

He couldn't stop him. The only way was to kill him, but he couldn't. No way. In a fraction of a second, he knew the indecision was about to kill him, when a burst of shots from the doorway tore into the stricken Somali. He slumped back to the rug, and this time, he wasn't getting up.

Boswell charged into the room, clutching his assault rifle. He ran to the body, flipped it over, and exposed a flat, black Tokarev automatic.

"He nearly had you, Chief."

"Yeah, he did. Thanks, but you should have winged him. He was the last link with the attack on New York City. Now we don't have any way of stopping it."

The other man was silent, as he understood the implication of killing Magan. He shook his head.

"Shit. There has to be another way, Chief. What about the mother? She could try calling her son again."

The satphone. She could try it till hell froze over. If he didn't switch it on, it was academic. And the signs were he wasn't about to switch it on. The guy was a suicide bomber on the run in a strange city, and about to spread his guts over some poor bastard's sidewalk. Social chitchat would be the last thing on his mind. Besides, he'd be wary of the authorities triangulating his position. No, the phone would stay off, most likely.

"It's a possibility."

Leave him some hope.

"We need to lock the Somalis somewhere they can't see us leaving in the truck and contact their buddies to send us a calling card, like an RPG up our asses."

"We'll take a look around."

He called Zeke and Dave, and told them to find a secure room and herd the Somalis inside. Five minutes later, they were finished. The expanse of the prayer room was empty. Only the smell of gunfire remained, and underneath, the faint tang of spilled blood from the library where Magan's corpse lay on the rug; a testament to their failure.

"We'll go out the back way." He called Vince and told him to ask Ayub Ahmed to bring the truck around.

Three minutes later, he climbed aboard, ready for the journey out of Somalia. Boswell took charge of the satphone. He had a quick conversation with Admiral Jacks to arrange for a pick up that night from a beach five klicks south of the town. He ended the call and told Will to take the wheel and head south, away from Mogadishu.

The engine roared, the gears crunched, and they began to move.

Someone, somewhere, is about to get blown to hell. We've done everything we can, but it isn't enough. Not by a long way.

He glanced across at Emily. She was nursing her baby, and for the first time, her face had relaxed, no longer stretched to harsh lines by the awful terror under which she'd lived the past five years. She saw his gaze.

"We're going home? I mean, really."

He nodded. "Yep, we're going home."

She relaxed even more and smiled. A moment later, she began singing to her son. It was a tender scene, and her freedom one success they could chalk up. At least before the Al Shabaab suicide bombers hit New York City.

Another 911? Could be.

Even Boswell looked relaxed. He grinned at Nolan. "We did it, Chief. Mission accomplished."

He recalled the last person who said that got it as wrong as it could be. George W. Bush, after the fall of Iraq. May 1st, 2003, on he deck of the aircraft carrier USS Abraham Lincoln. And where was Iraq now? In a deep, dark hole, tearing itself apart. And now the shaheeds were in New York.

We've failed. It's a total one hundred percent fuck up.

CHAPTER TWELVE

The room stank even worse than the evening before, worse than during the long, sleepless night. The pizzas had congealed on the table, the warmth of the room causing them to start to decompose. Just another reminder of what awaited them. The sudden blast, after they cry out, ' Allahu Akbar', so the infidels knew why they martyred themselves.

God is great, that was the meaning of the phrase.

Yes, God is indeed great.

Musse had no doubts, no doubts at all. His only reservations were for the message given to his representatives on Earth.

Who is to say if they tell the truth, the Imams, the Mullahs?

The vest irritated him. It was heavy, and the chemical stink of the explosives were nauseating. Perhaps they should improve the quality, so it didn't offend the nostrils of the shaheeds. He'd heard the sound of movement during the long night from behind the couch. Amin was now resting back there with another boy, Farah. He had no doubt they'd found a way to satisfy each other. They need have no worries about their being exposed. Or any worries about anything else. Death was the great problem solver.

He checked his watch and found it was 10.30. They would have to leave soon. No need for any preparation, any packing. Just don their coats to hide the vests, walk to the UN building, and line up each side to wait for the President. Back home, it would be 18.30, people basking in the late afternoon sunshine. He thought of Somalia with deep longing. If only...but it was too late for that. He thought of his girl and his mother.

My mother!

He'd give anything to call her, to hear her voice one last time. But it wasn't to be.

If I switch on the phone, they could track us down and kill us. Kill us!

He realized how ludicrous it was, worrying about imminent death. His death was ordained, and there was nothing to worry about, nothing at all.

Amin climbed to his feet from behind the sofa, and the other boy, Farah, stood up next to him. Their faces were guilty, and he wanted to laugh aloud.

"What are they worried about, AIDS?" Musse chuckled.

"What is it?" Amin demanded, his face angry.

"Nothing."

He continued to stare and then turned to Farah. "You want something to eat?"

Just like a boy to his girlfriend.

"No, I'm not hungry."

Amin nodded and walked to the bathroom. He emerged five minutes later.

"We need to leave, and take up our positions. There could be crowds. We have to be at the front."

"Very well, we walk in pairs. I will finish up here and follow you, as we are now an odd number."

The other boy nodded and looked guilty. If he hadn't killed Rageh, there would have been eight of them, four each side of the Presidential limo. They got to their feet, awkward in the heavy bomb vests, their eyes dilated and wide with terror; the foreknowledge of what was to come. Amin put out his hand.

"I guess this is goodbye."

The plan was they wouldn't communicate with each other while they waited for the target to arrive. Musse took the hand.

"Good luck, Amin. See you in Paradise."

"Yes."

The rest of them shook hands. The first two youths hesitated only a moment, and then they left. Two more went out five minutes later. Amin and Farah were the last pair.

"Musse, last night..."

"Go! Last night does not exist. There is only now, our sacred duty."

"Thank you, Musse."

They left the hotel room, and he was on his own. It occurred to him he could go on the run, get away from the nightmare that faced him. He laughed. It was too late. But he reached for his holdall and took out the cellphone. As soon as he started walking, he could switch it on. It would be difficult to triangulate a moving cellphone. And then, he could call his mother if she had her cellphone near to her.

Yes, she will, today of all days.

He buttoned up his coat and left the hotel room. There was no need to hide any evidence of their presence. As soon as the job was done, a message would go out on the internet with their names and photos. The street was bustling, crowded with Americans going about their business.

None of them seemed to notice the Somali in their midst.

That will soon change, he thought to himself grimly.

He reached the UN building at 12.30 exactly and picked out the rest of the martyrs. Each stood alone, so as not to attract any attention. But inside their coats, they would already have their fingers on the detonator buttons, the buttons that were dummies. The only way to destroy the armored limo was with a simultaneous detonation, and that would only come from his detonator.

He looked up at the sky. The day was cold, not like it was at home, but the sky was blue. How wonderful to be able to take a last glimpse at it before he departed his life for eternity. He dreamed about his homeland, his girlfriend, and his mother. Then he returned to the present. Ten minutes had passed, ten minutes lost. He'd have to be careful. He saw another young black man about the same age as himself. He was talking to an older woman, doubtless his mother.

Mother!

He turned away, switched on the cellphone, and waited. The message icon flashed. It could be from Sheikh Barre. He pressed the button to listen, and his mouth dropped open as he heard his mother's voice. He listened to her pleas for him to stop, and her statement that Sheikh Barre

was dead. Then he recovered his wits.
It cannot be. It's a trick.

* * *

They were trapped. Will twisted and turned the truck through squalid lanes and alleys, barely wide enough for a family car. They'd circled all around Mogadishu, struggling to find a way through as the hours rolled past. Soon it would be dark, and the boats would be waiting to pick them up off the beach, if they ever got the wreck of a truck that far. He'd torn off the trims over the rear wheels, and both mirrors were a kilometer back, hanging from an electrical distribution pole. The front fender had finally parted company after he tore through a ramshackle roadblock, and when the steel tugged and caught in a burned out car, he kept his foot down and dragged the wreck several meters before it dropped away, taking half the fender with it.

Ayub Ahmed was doing his best to navigate through the noisome streets, slippery with garbage and sewage, but the opposition was hot on their tail. They knew what had happened. The Somalis in the mosque, when they were released, would have delivered the startling news. American Special Forces loose in Mogadishu. Again! This time, none of them would leave.

"Vehicle on our tail," Vince called over the commo. He was propped against the tailgate, clutching his long rifle, "Could be a cop, could be militia."

"Take him," Nolan snapped back. There was no time to consider collateral casualties. These Somalis pursued Navy Seals at their peril.

Vince fired three shots that killed the driver and sent the vehicle spinning into a concrete wall. They hurtled on, but there were more behind, many more. He shouted at Eisner, "Get the machine gun in front in case we run into any roadblocks."

As the operator climbed through into the cab, Boswell fired a long burst into an armed group that had appeared outside an apartment building. Several of them went down, dropping their AKs. One man dropped something more lethal, an RPG7.

Nolan saw a long, cylindrical object poke out over a balcony on the fourth floor of the building next door. He sighted and fired, and when another man ran out to pick up the launcher, fired again. A burst of shots sounded from the front where Eisner had targeted a potential ambush.

Lucas appeared alongside and squeezed off a burst at a youth who ran out into the street and started to fire, John Wayne style from the hip. No one told him they did it different in the movies. His bullets chipped stone off a building a hundred meters ahead. Grant's burst tore into his guts, and his dreams of glory evaporated in a spurt of blood and the agonizing shock of a mortal wound.

Amelia was trying to keep the women safe, Fatimah, Emily, the baby, and Commissioner Ahmed, who was bleeding from the mouth. It seemed they'd hurt him worse than they realized, and something was broken up inside. He groaned when the truck reared up on one side, as Will narrowly negotiated a hairpin bend. Then he whooped for joy.

"Shit, that's more like it," Will shouted, "We've got a clear stretch of road."

He jammed his foot down on the gas, and the heavy

vehicle picked up speed. Nolan called him.

"Will, ask Ayub how far to go until we're clear of the city."

The answer came a few seconds later. "Two klicks, Chief. We're...Shit!"

The truck reared up again on it's side as he left the main highway and drove into yet another narrow lane.

"That was a roadblock. It looks clear this way."

It was also narrow. Too narrow, and at one point the metal bodywork screamed on both sides, as Will did the impossible and drove a three-meter wide truck through a two-meters and a half roadway. The tortured metal was like a flock of banshees bearing in to seize their souls, but he kept going, leaving yet more body panels lying in the road. And then they were clear again.

"Bunch of dudes on motorcycles," Vince shouted, "I'd guess Al Shabaab. You know, the check scarves, the AKs. Let's see, one, two, three cycles..."

At each cycle, he fired a double tap, and a rider parted company with his bike as his strength left him. The heavy Lapua Magnum rounds didn't take too many prisoners.

"We're clear," he announced, after seven riders bit the dust.

"Good shooting," Boswell grinned. He seemed to be enjoying himself in the heat of the action, the reckless pursuit, and the threat of a terrible fate if they were forced to stop.

"Yeah, thanks, we're...no we've got company, people. A tank, it's coming right at us."

Nolan had already spotted it, a T54, a strange sight painted in the usual drab green of Soviet era vehicles, apart for the turret. Someone had painted it in the garish, intricate lacework design common in the Islamic world. Something about it worried him even more than just the sight of the armored monster. Whoever did that wasn't regular army. He was someone with an ego, with an attitude. He keyed his mic.

"Will, we've got armor behind us, a T54. Painted turret, Arabic design, like a shithouse door in a brothel."

A pause, while he asked Ayub. When he replied, his voice was grim.

"It belongs to an Omar Islam. He's third in line of the Al Shabaab pecking order, after Barre and Magan. A hardass, Ayub tells me."

"So he's the number one guy, now we've popped the other two."

Will let out a mirthless chuckle. "I guess so. That's his personal transport, and wherever he goes, there'll be scores of others ready to die for him. Only good thing is those old Soviet era machines didn't have much in the way of radios. He won't be able to report sighting us. And he won't be able to use a cellphone. You know what the noise levels are like in those things."

"Roger that. Any chance you can put your foot down?"

Another chuckle. "I'm working on it."

They fought through the streets, and after a few minutes, Will managed to lose the tank. He slowed. They were in an area unfamiliar to Ayub, and he had to pick his way through carefully.

Nolan checked the time, 20.30, which meant 12.30 back in New York City. He wondered if anything had happened, a terrorist explosion that would take thousands of lives and cause billions of dollars in property damage. Or an attempt on the life of a prominent citizen, like the

President. He picked off another shooter, a man armed with a hunting rifle high on an apartment block roof. Vince was covering the other side, and he brought two more hostile snipers down. Then Will jammed on the air brakes, and they were tossed forward along the truck bed.

"Roadblock three hundred meters ahead. I have to stop. There're no side turnings, and no way through. Dave, get out of sight. If they see your pretty white face, the game's up."

Eisner came hurtling back into the rear, as Will slowed the truck to try and look innocent as they arrived at the roadblock.

* * *

He checked his wristwatch, 12.35, not long now, but he was looking at the youth who was smiling at his mother as they chatted together.

No, I'm not going to my death, not without saying goodbye. And if it was a trick, I will have the pleasure of telling them it didn't work.

He switched on the phone and called the number back. As it was connecting, he could see Amin staring at him, frowning.

Too bad, what is he going to do, kill me?

* * *

They were still one hundred and fifty meters away when the satphone rang. He looked at the incoming call details.

Musse!

He tossed the phone to Fatimah.

"Answer it. Make him stop whatever he's doing."

She began talking in Somali. The language was incomprehensible, but the meaning was clear. Son, don't do it."

She listened and then poured another torrent of Somali into the handset.

Nolan heard Vince say, "Chief, our friend is back."

Nolan glanced a few hundred meters back. The T54 had reappeared. He heard a noise and sensed movement. Lucas had gathered up the Carl Gustav. He put a hand on his unwounded shoulder.

"Hey, don't even think about it. You'll open up the wounds and start the bleeding."

The Seal vet shook his head. "This one's mine. Didn't Ayub say this guy is running things around here? That means if I can pop the tank, they'll be thrown in a total mess. You know what these ragtag armies are like. Their priority will be taking over the top spot, not worrying about fighting the war."

"You're not fit enough, Lucas. I can do it. I'm uninjured, and I can target that thing a lot quicker than you can."

"I can handle it."

He propped the missile launcher on the tailgate and watched the T54 close the distance. Nolan gave in and went to deal with the crisis ahead of them. The truck had stopped, and the shouts from the men guarding the roadblock carried into the rear.

"They want the codeword," Amelia translated.

"The what?"

"Al Shabaab has a different codeword to identify their different groups and affiliates." She listened for a moment. "They say if we're not Al Shabaab, we may be the enemy, and they want to check us out."

Fatimah crawled over to him. "It is the President of the United States. He is the target."

"How long?"

"Four minutes."

It would take that long to patch a call through the chain of command in the US, too late to divert him.

"Can you persuade him to stop?"

"I don't know. He is...strange."

Shit!

Nolan had an idea. "Offer him the funds to build a hospital in Kismayo. We'll name it after you, the Fatimah Barre Medical Center."

"Fatimah Daud. Not Barre, not any more."

"Okay. Tell him! And one thing more, ask if he knows the password."

She shouted into the phone, almost weeping with passion. He could hear Ayub shouting and pleading with the Somalis.

* * *

A hospital! Named after my mother, after all the pain, the suffering she's endured. It's an incredible offer. Yet, the others are staring at me. What should I do?

He listened again.

"The codeword?" He stopped.

He could see the cavalcade approaching in the distance. The crowd cheered and roared a welcome. Three limos, the President would be in the center. Secret Service men ran alongside the cars. Farah was staring at him, his face a mask of hate and determination. Musse shook his head and turned to walk away. He stopped, as he walked straight into Amin.

"Where are you going?"

He stared into the man's mad, fanatic eyes. No, it wasn't madness. It was desperation. He put his hand on the youth's arm.

"You don't have to do this, Amin. You don't have to die, not because of some stupid sexual orientation. You have a life in front of you. You can do anything you want, be anything want."

He sneered. "You think so? What will they say back in Kismayo? The queer who was too frightened to keep his promises to Allah? You're wrong. I do have to do this."

He was shouting, and people around were starting to stare. Musse noticed a Secret Service man staring at him, or he seemed to be staring through mirrored sunglasses. The cellphone in his hand was making a noise, and he realized his mother was still trying to talk to him. He put it to his ear.

* * *

Will's voice came on the commo, a whisper. "They're getting ornery, Chief. What do you want me to do?"

"We're still trying. Stall them."

"We'll have to start shooting soon. And there's a lot of them."

"Roger that."

He looked at Fatimah. "We have to have that codeword. Now!"

She nodded and continued pleading with her son.

"The tank is getting close, about two hundred meters

and closing fast," Vince shouted.

He went to the rear where Lucas had steadied the Carl Gustav on the approaching behemoth.

"You okay, Lucas?"

"Yeah. Hey, they got more fighters coming in, some of 'em carrying RPG7s."

A surge of Somalis in ragged clothes, but their weapons looked mighty businesslike.

"We need to stop them shooting up the truck," Lucas shouted, "One hit and we're done for. I'll take the shot from outside."

"Lucas, no!"

He grinned. "Tell my folks, this one's for my sister."

Before they could stop him, he vaulted over the tailgate, still clutching the heavy missile. He cradled it in his arms, protecting it with his body as he dropped onto the hard road surface. Then he rolled over and disappeared into a squalid, abandoned building. Dave Eisner stared after him.

"You want me to go after him?"

"No, we've enough trouble of our own. We'll pick him up when we've cleared a way through the roadblock."

A burst of gunfire chipped masonry from the building that Lucas sheltered in. They saw him duck down, pulling the missile launcher behind cover."

"He can't do it," Eisner persisted, "He'll be taking fire from all sides."

"I'll cover him." They watched, astonished as Lieutenant William Boswell jumped over the tailgate, landed nimbly, and ran to join Grant. Seconds later, he started shooting, and the body of a Somali still clutching his AK-47 plummeted to the ground from the building opposite.

"Well, I'll be damned." Eisner shook his head.

"Yeah, that took guts." He looked at Fatimah. "We have to have that code."

She stopped speaking into the phone. "I'm doing my best. It's...difficult."

"Chief, if I don't get that code in the next few seconds, there's going to be a bloodbath. And some of the blood will be ours."

"I'm doing my best, Will. We all are."

He saw Ashe Ahmed, the UN Commissioner pull himself up. He was weak; the ill treatment had hit him hard.

"I can talk to them," he said to Nolan, "They may listen to a UN Commissioner. I can always promise to..."

"Shut the fuck up!" Nolan snapped at him.

He looked astonished.

"They'll kill you. Sorry, Sir, I'm kinda busy. Fatimah, it's now or never."

* * *

He stared down at the gun pressed into his stomach, just below the bomb vest.

"I'm going to kill you, Musse."

"I told you, there's no need."

He still had the phone pressed to his ear, and his mother was screaming at him, something about a codeword. His mind didn't register. He was poised on the cusp, between life and death. Not the death he'd come here for, the blinding, instantaneous explosion and oblivion, but if Amin pulled the trigger, it would be just as certain.

Perhaps I deserve it.

Everything went blurred, a sensory overload, his

mother's pleas, the Presidential cavalcade nearing, the crowd shouting, Amin's threats to kill him. He felt tired, immensely tired. No matter what happened here today, he knew he'd let everyone down. The shaheeds, his mother, and his Al Shabaab comrades back in Somalia, all of them.

What is my mother saying? Oh yes, the codeword. The hospital in Kismayo, named after her.

What was the point? He wanted to lie down on the sidewalk, and go to sleep and never wake up. He stared at the other youth.

"Shoot me, Amin. I just don't care anymore."

The gunshots were loud, a total of six bullets. The crowd screamed and started to run.

Strange, it doesn't hurt, not at all.

He saw Amin falling, to sprawl in a bloody heap on the ground. A bunch of Secret Service men stood over him, and one of them wrested the gun from Amin's lifeless hand. Then they pulled open his coat.

"Christ, a fucking bomb! A suicide bomber, get the President out of here! Move, move, move!"

The limos had been turning in toward the crowd, but the lead car jerked away and took off at high speed. In seconds, they were out of sight. He felt a surge of energy tingle through his body.

I'm still alive!

Alone on the sidewalk, the other shaheeds had seen the disaster and melted away. There was only the shattered body of Amin.

As if in a dream, he heard his mother's voice in his ear.

"The code, Musse. Tell me quickly. We're going to die."

To die! His mind came back into focus. "The code is..."

* * *

"Shahid Awwa," she shouted.

Nolan called Will, who gave it to Ahmed, sitting next to him trying to stall the militia. They heard him say, 'Shahid Awwa', although he pronounced it a bit different to Will. They waited, tense, and then Will's triumphant voice.

"We're okay. They're letting us through."

The truck started to move. A burst of gunfire sounded close to the rear, and Nolan looked out the back. He could see Boswell dueling with a bunch of fighters bunched up around the tank, like World War II Panzer Grenadiers, protecting their leader and his valuable armored vehicle from ground attack. Nolan keyed his mic.

"Lt, Lucas, get out of there. We're moving."

He saw Boswell shake his head. "No time. We'll catch up later." Grant gave a small wave.

Catch up later! Are they mad? This is Mogadishu.

He'd said it like they were a short cab ride from Central Park.

"No! Quick, get out of there."

They ignored him, and as he watched, a missile shooter knelt down at the side of the T54, readying his weapon to fire.

At our truck or at the two irritating Seals inside the building?

It made no difference. The T54 had come to a decision, and the turret moved slightly as the main gun lowered, ready to take a shot. Lucas saw the danger, and as Boswell covered him, he stood up with the M3 clearly visible on his shoulder. The turret moved a fraction, and the secondary armament opened up, sending a storm of bullets at the two men.

It was impossible to say who fired first, or which projectile hit first. The 100mm explosive shell detonated on the Seals' position, but the Carl Gustav was already on the way. As the building in which they sheltered disappeared in a hurricane of debris, mixed with the flesh of the two men who'd given their lives, the tank stopped dead. The missile struck beneath the driver's position and exploded. A sheet of flame rose in the air, smoke poured out of the hatches, then a massive secondary explosion as the tank was blown into oblivion; destroyed by the missile and its own exploding ordnance.

Nolan and Vince looked on, numb. Will's voice came back to them

"What happened back there? It looked like the end of the world."

"Almost. Step on it, Will. All the way to the beach."

"What about Boswell and Grant?"

"No. They didn't make it."

A pause. "Roger that."

* * *

The control center of the Southampton was crowded. Nolan's depleted unit, together with Admiral Jacks, squeezed into a corner, away from the crew who were running the boat. They were heroes. The word had gone out about the attempted bombing of the President of the United States outside the United Nations building. As well as the shaheed shot and killed in the street, they'd picked up two more, and after talking to them, were hunting for the others.

Musse Daud wasn't amongst those in custody. As they

were driving away from Mogadishu, Nolan had overheard his mother talking to him on the satphone. It sounded like she was giving him instructions. When the call ended, she'd looked at him defiantly.

"Nabil had accounts set up in offshore accounts. I told him how to get access to some money."

"He's a wanted felon, Ma'am, armed and dangerous. He should be handed over."

"No. He is no longer armed or dangerous. He tossed the explosive vest into the Hudson River, and he has turned his back on Al Shabaab."

"So what's he going to do? Try and stay in the States? They'll be looking for him."

"He wants to be a doctor," she said with some pride, "Eventually, he wishes to work in the new hospital in Kismayo. You haven't forgotten your promise?"

"We'll fix it up. You can be sure of that."

We owe him something. Without him giving us the code, we'd all be dead. Maybe he'll do some good. Healing people, instead of killing them.

"He will make a fine doctor," she added.

"I'm sure he will."

Jacks interrupted his reverie. "A tough one, Chief, but you succeeded beyond belief. You stopped a plot to kill the President and brought back the Commissioner, as well as an American hostage. And of course, the command structure of Al Shabaab is decimated. It'll take 'em years to recover from this."

"It was Lieutenant Boswell, Sir. He deserves a medal. Grant too. What those guys did saved everything."

"A medal? I'll arrange something to go in their records, posthumously. So Boswell came through?"

"Yeah, a brave man, no question."

"I'm glad it worked out. It was just a heavy price to pay. Very heavy."

"Too heavy, Sir. We have to learn lessons from this. If there's a next time, I'd like to bring my unit back intact, not leave them behind in little pieces."

Jacks shuddered. "If there's a next time? You jest, surely. As long as the Islamic crazies are roaming around killing people, there'll be plenty of next times. Chief, you mentioned bringing your unit back in one piece. I'd like it to be your unit."

"Sir?"

"I want you to take over from Boswell. A commission, you could jump the ensign rate, and go straight in as a lieutenant. I'm sure I can swing it. I'm sorry if this sounds like undue haste so soon after the deaths of your men, but the bad guys don't give us any choice in the matter."

"I like it where I am, Admiral."

He nodded. "Think it over. Let me know when we get home."

* * *

A nuclear attack submarine is not a place that allows for any privacy, except when the Exec has handed over his cabin to a female FBI Agent. She'd invited Nolan to join her.

"I feel guilty, having a cabin to myself when you guys all have to share."

"I'm sure they'd appreciate you joining them, if you feel that way."

She smiled. "Right. Maybe I'll give that a miss. Kyle,

I'm sorry about your guys. It must be hard for you."

"It's hard, yes. But when we take this job on, we know what we're up against. Casualties in most Special Forces are pretty high."

"I'm sure that's true. Listen, about what happened between us."

"Yes?" He was wary.

"I don't want it to be the last I see of you. Can we, sort of, take some time together? Spend a few days getting to know each other."

"A vacation, you mean?"

"Something like that."

"I have to go visit my kids. I'm all they have. Their mother was killed. And I need to make sure their grandparents got back okay."

"I know." She waited.

"But afterward, yeah, that'd be nice. Did you have anywhere in mind?"

"My apartment?"

He didn't need to think it over. "It's a date."